To everyone who still believes in fated love.

BOOKS BY M.R. POLISH

Fantasy Romance
Sandman Saga

Shadow Moon
Day Break
Total Eclipse

Paranormal Romance
The Wolf Series

Wolf Love
Wolf Spell
Wolf Dream
Wolf Fate

Fantasy Romance
Ageless Sea Series

Ageless Sea
Endless Shores
Timeless Tides

Paranormal Romance
Saddles and Spells Series

Saddles and Spells
Chaps and Cauldrons
Boots and Broomsticks
Pistols and Potions
Hats and Hexes
Ropes and Runes

Romantic Suspense Stand Alone

Change of Possession

Paranormal Romance Stand Alone

Shared World

Savage Vengeance

Science Fiction – Dragon

Mysts of Santerrian Series

Mark of the Dragon
Orb of Incendia
Title coming soon

Urban Fantasy/Paranormal Romance Stand Alone
(Shared World)

Ash and Scale

DAY BREAK

M.R. POLISH

The Sandman Saga book two

Day Break

Edited by Colleen Nye and Cassie Wilcox

Cover Design by Misty Polish

ISBN: 9798750086283

www.mrpolishauthor.com

My little sun,

Come to dinner as my queen. I can't wait to see you light up the room.

Sander

ONE ~ BEFORE GRADUATION

Sander

DARKNESS SLIPPED ITS WELCOMING embrace around me like a second skin. The Night Kingdom was home, but not right now. Home was wherever Emberlynn was. Even now, the bond between us stretched painfully thin, threatening to break us both. I wasn't sure how I was still standing... functioning. Though I wouldn't be for long. I needed to hurry. Time was against me. Against Emberlynn.

I couldn't fail her.

My soul scorched my bones as I slipped from the mortal realm, leaving her behind. Soulmates weren't designed to be separated–especially by worlds. But we weren't just any mates. We were created by the Gods. Each of us held onto an ancient bloodline and magic far beyond that of other immortals. It was the only reason neither of us had succumbed to the death waiting to bless us caused by our separation. As long as I could still feel her, as long as I knew she was still alive, I would fight it.

Hang on. I whispered down our connection, hoping it would reach her.

Each step down the cold stairwell bit into my soul, jarring me into the reality that neither of us would live if

I failed. My death I could handle... but the thought of Emberlynn's life ending had me pushing through the pain. It was much worse than before we touched. No other pain could compare.

I could hear guards now. Their thoughts carried up through the stone passage filling my head with mundane chatter. Taking a deep breath, I straightened and held my head high. As their king, it was unsuitable for me to show such weakness. It would bring questions and worries. Doubt was not something I wanted in my court.

Here, the shadows swirled around me, not needing an invitation. Night and all its myths ran through my blood. It was something I had mostly concealed from Emberlynn, afraid of her reaction. If she knew how far my power went, how dark the shadows got... I shuddered to think of her fear. The light ruled her. Darkness should be her enemy, and yet her soul chose mine.

The mortal realm concealed a significant amount of my power, and that was the only reason I couldn't tear that invisible wall down, separating me from my soulmate. The only reason Helios opted to play with Emberlynn in that world. If she or I had been here... or the Solis Kingdom? There would be no stopping me. I hadn't seen her full power yet, but I could feel it. It ran through me in taunting waves, teasing me with her pure bloodline. Certainly, she held enough to scare Helios into capturing her in the mortal realm.

But I wasn't ready to share her with the kingdoms yet. I knew as soon as she entered the Immortal Kingdoms, abilities she didn't even know she had would emerge. She would need to train, learn how to harness her powers, and there wasn't a soul in any kingdom who wouldn't want a fraction of her time. Every royal would invite her to their kingdoms, other immortals clamoring for her attention. I hated that I was so selfish. But I wanted a few more months with her. Just her. I knew how badly the kingdoms needed the Solis Queen, but I couldn't bring myself to sacrifice this precious time with the two of us. I had barely found her. Our bond was still so new. I would find a way to save her, and then never would I be separated from her again.

The moment she slipped through the glamoured wall replayed in my mind over and over. In my memory, I'd reached out for her, trying to grasp her in time, but each time I failed. The invisible barrier blocked me from getting to her.

I brushed off the guilt and rounded the last turn in the stairwell. I opted for forgoing my crown as I descended into the dungeon. The depths of such darkness knew me. Anyone who guarded the ancient tomb wouldn't stand in my way. There was only one I sought out. The man behind the magic ensnaring Emberlynn, keeping her within Helios's grasp.

The shadows shifted around the guards, giving me a look at who hid behind the creatures. There wasn't a soul in the Kingdom who could hide from the Night King. The shadows bowed to no one else but me.

As I crested the bottom step, the guards respectfully lowered their heads. One of them had a glamour of claws that shifted around the hilt of the blade he carried. A poisoned tip no doubt hid in the sheath. His eyes were completely black. "My king."

The other man looked more human with only a tiny glimmer of magic. "We're glad to have you home. It's been far too long."

"And it will have to be a while longer. I still have some things that need my attention and will require me to be in the mortal realm for a time." I tried not to breathe now. Invisible fiery talons gripped my insides. "I need to see the prisoner Gabriel brought in."

The clawed one hesitated, looking at the other guard. "My king, Gabriel sealed the door. We can't help you."

The twisting and pulling on my bond with Emberlynn ripped through me in painful waves. I roared. Shadows emerged from the walls consuming half of the sconces, dimming the light in the hall. I didn't dare look them in the eyes, for I knew my pain would be evident. "I didn't say open the door. I can do that. Do you think a mere spell will keep me out? Show me where he is."

The clawed one straightened but didn't cast his gaze on me. Wise choice. Not only was I his king, but I wasn't in the mood to be challenged. And to be honest, I wasn't confident I could hide the pain from my soulmate much longer.

Both guards scrambled to accommodate my wish, leading me down the damp hall. Flames flickered from the torches lining the walls. The shadows danced along, trying to keep up as I passed.

At the end of the hall, the guards stopped at a darkened doorway. But it wasn't the cell I looked for. I quirked a brow at the entrance. Gabriel really was the best for a reason, but to put this particular prisoner in the belly of the dungeon had me grinning.

"This is as far as we can go, my king. Gabriel sealed off the entire lower level." The clawed guard bowed and backed away from the aged and withered entrance.

The iron was so black it looked void of magic, but it was the opposite. It held on tight and was great at keeping unwanted powers from penetrating it. Already I could feel the hum of Gabriel's energy teeming through the metal. Icy tendrils of magic reached out, looking for who invaded the space.

I looked over my shoulder to the guards who just stood there. "If you can't join me, then is there a reason you haven't returned to your post?"

The second man cringed. "I'm sorry, my king, but you seem... off. Is everything okay?"

Even then, every inch of my body felt as if it were being shredded as my soul tried to escape, clawing its way back to Emberlynn. It took all I had to stand straight and not grab the wall for support. "I'm fine."

Bowing, they both retreated into the hall, rounding the corner, leaving me to descend into the depths of the dungeon. Waiting, I listened to their footsteps, ensuring they were well away before letting my body relax. I nearly dropped to the floor. Resting my forehead against the cold iron door, feeling its magical heartbeat, I took in a shaky breath looking for the strength I would need to continue.

I let the door speak to me, hearing Gabriel's magic whisper a warning to any who dared to cross it. I had no doubts that any other man or creature who tried to pass would be killed instantly. Hovering my palm about an inch from the door, I ran my hand down the metal, releasing my own power. With every charm he cast, there was a loophole made for me–for only me.

The loud click of the iron lock disengaging resounded through the hall. Gabriel's magic still hung in a thick layer, creating a warded boundary, but it now sang my name, letting me pass. Pushing the door open, I descended another stairwell. This one was much colder, and the damp air clung to my skin.

No sconces were lit. Darkness consumed the lower level swallowing everything in its void.

"I know you're here. I may not be able to see you, but I can feel you." Kade's voice echoed, bouncing off the walls.

I glared through the shadows. "I'm surprised you are still coherent in this place."

"I'm stronger than you think."

Noticeably. In the mortal realm, I hadn't been able to feel his full potential, underestimating him. But not again. Here I could feel it all. A slight zing ran over my skin as his energy touched mine. There was more to Kade than I thought.

Emberlynn's terror ripped through our connection as her scream pierced my thoughts. Grabbing my head, I doubled over.

Kade cried out. "Damn it! What did you do?" Fire roared to life on each sconce down the wall, illuminating the room with a small cell in the middle. Kade's eyes anchored on mine, venom laced his words. "You left her."

Trying to hide my surprise over his magic in the dungeon, I straightened and fought to control myself with Emberlynn's plea. It killed me to know she was scared, alone, and hurting.

Kade gripped the iron gate that trapped him behind bars. His white-blonde hair reminded me of Emberlynn's, and they both shared the Solis golden eyes passed down from the gods. "Get me out of here!"

"It's your magic that imprisons her." I rushed the cell, letting the shadows swarm around him. "You did this to her."

"I would never hurt her," he sneered. The whites of his eyes were red, but his countenance fell. "I don't remember doing it. It wasn't me."

Whatever energy I had was nearly depleted. I was out of time. "I need you to help Emberlynn. Release her from your magic."

"You put me in your dungeon!" For the first time since seeing him, his face looked sullen, and his shoulders drooped. "I can't do that from here."

"Then I'll release you."

Kade looked up. "Just like that?"

Even exhausted, I couldn't contain the smirk. "I think we both know this won't be the last time we see each other."

He shook his head.

"What are you to her?" I had to know. "You made her life hell. You hurt her. And yet, you protected her. Why?"

"It wasn't me. You have to believe me! I don't remember any of it." He gripped the bars. "Please. Let me out. She needs me."

"Why?" Emberlynn tugged on my soul, I knew I had to hurry, but I needed to understand. I yelled again, "Why!"

"There is more than one soul she can be bound to."

I shook my head. "No. You touched her. I saw for myself. It's my mark she carries, not yours." My stomach flipped in revulsion. The thought of him being fated with my soulmate made me sick.

"We don't have time to argue this. She needs me. Don't let her die because you're jealous." Kade's jaw clenched, his fists tightly coiled. "You're wasting time."

Yanking on the cell door, I threw it open. "Don't make me regret this."

I pushed the spell open wide enough for Kade to slip through using the last of my strength. "Go. I'll be right behind you."

His shadow slipped past me, merging with the dancing darkness from the fires on the wall. Lifting one foot in front of the other, I made my way up the stairs. At the top, the two guards held Kade at the base of the next stairwell.

"My king, we caught him trying to escape."

I waved them off. "He is with me, and you will let him pass."

"But," the one with claws started but stopped.

Kade shifted his weight to look back at me. "Your demons need a bit more training. Had they been Solis guards, I would have been dead for escaping."

"Be grateful they let you live. I may not once we are through."

The second guard stepped forward with his dagger still drawn toward Kade. "My king, are you certain you want to let him go?"

I could feel Emberlynn slipping away. "Yes."

Each man took my word and moved from Kade's path, bowing as I passed, following Kade into the stairwell.

Kade's steps were fast and unwavering, though I stumbled on the last stair. "We must hurry."

He pushed open the door, and the salty night breeze greeted us. The dungeon was deep inside the rocky mountain island, surrounded by an ocean of water crashing into the base. The only way on or off was either a Fores or a ship. A Fores was a portal, bridging the worlds together. Only a few remained in the mortal realm. Thankfully the closest one to Emberlynn was in the building where she disappeared. An old church of sorts for the mortals.

The Fores here on the island looked like a tattered wooden arch, worn by the salt air and waves.

Kade looked over his shoulder at me. "This is where we part."

He stepped forward, but I grabbed his arm. "Bring her to me."

A silent moment of truce passed between us. Kade gave a curt nod and then slipped from my grasp, stepping through the portal.

Emberlynn called out to me once more, and I fell to my knees. I would get back to her. I had to. Crawling to the portal, I let it take me back to my soulmate. The shadows swirled around me, clinging to me as I slipped from the Night Kingdom. They carried me through to the old church, where they laid me on the floor.

"Sander!" Perseus ran to my side. Emberlynn's loyal guard had stayed behind to watch for her while I was away. His appearance did nothing to calm my frayed nerves. If he was here, then she was still trapped.

"Emberlynn." My voice was barely audible as it cracked. I tried to pick myself up.

Perseus lifted me and braced me against the wall. A golden tattoo of the sun marked his forearm and glistened under the stream of light flooding in from the tall stained-glass windows. "She is not back." His own fears laced through each word. No one knew what she faced beyond that wall.

It had been Perseus who discovered it was Kade's magic and not Helios's that kept her trapped. Without him, I wouldn't have let Kade go free. A bargain I'd gladly pay again if he could help Emberlynn.

"Kade?" My apprehension about letting him go built like a fire raging out of control.

Perseus shook his head. "He went in, but..."

I tried to swallow. To breathe. Had I sent Emberlynn to her death by Kade's hands? I should have interrogated him more. I shouldn't have left him unattended and forced him to take me with him through the barrier. But all I could think of was Emberlynn and how she needed help, and I was too slow. Sending him ahead of me was the quickest way to save her.

Rage filled every particle of my body. I pushed Perseus off and summoned every shadow in the mortal realm, compelling them to force their way through the wall. If I couldn't be there, I would use every ounce of power I had available in this realm to save her. A part of me would be with her.

Darkness filled the room as the night answered my demands. I would send her my shadows, my magic, and with it, my love. I would give her the last of me.

As shadows covered the sun, the light disappeared from the realm. Much like it would in my world without her. She was the light in my darkness, and she was not here. I wanted the worlds to know how I felt. The shadows trembled as they slipped from the room to carry her home.

"Sander." Perseus eyed me as if I were a wild animal, his arms out as if to coax me down from the unstable ledge I perched. "You're going to consume the world. You have to stop."

"Without her, there is no world." A weak tug on my soul anchored me to my soulmate. I'm sorry, Sander. Emberlynn's strained words shattered my heart. Power surged from me as the dark seized us.

The building shook as the world rattled. But it wasn't me. Hope flared in my chest. One last yank on our connection from Emberlynn, and I gave everything I had left to her, hoping it was enough. My body shook and I drooped against Perseus. There was nothing left of me without her.

A crackling sensation rippled through the air as electricity tickled my skin. A boom loud enough to echo across the valley rent the air. Light seared through the darkness, and the sunlight illuminated the realm in steady rays.

Kade walked through the barrier, Emberlynn's limp form hung in his arms. She was like a magnet, pulling me to her. There was nothing in any world I could use to deny the call of her soul. Her need to be with me, for my touch, consumed me. I rushed to her, taking her from him.

She was pale and unmoving. I placed a hand on her chest, feeling it barely rise. Keeping her tucked in my arms, I lowered us both to the floor. "Emberlynn," I whispered against her cheek, pressing kisses over her face. I wept openly, not caring who saw. "Please, come back to me."

My mark on her wrist shimmered under the tears in my eyes. I raised her hand to kiss her there. Nothing. No movement.

"I think she's exhausted herself. When I got there, she was..." Kade kneeled next to us, his hand resting on her shoulder.

It was too soon for anyone else to be so close to my mate. His touch was like a branding iron on my soul. "Do not touch her."

Kade looked at me but didn't remove his hand. "You're going to have to understand that her soul is bound to more than one of us. Just not the way you think."

Perseus drew his dagger and pressed it to Kade's throat. "The Night King gave you an order. Do not touch my queen."

"You of all people should know how deeply tied I am to her." Kade removed his hand and glared at me. "Her bloodline is a direct descendant from Adhaya Cyrus."

"I already know where her bloodline descends from." Shadows flickered around my mate and me. "Do not forget where mine comes from." I cradled Emberlynn against my chest and rose. The shadows followed, holding me and my mate up. We needed to get her to Lara.

Kade grabbed my arm. "Then you know Adhaya had a royal guard linked to her."

I sneered at his hand and then anchored my eyes on his. "Let go of me."

His fingers dug harder into my flesh, pleading with me to listen. "The Trejan."

The shadows gripped his hand, pulling him off me. "A myth." I pushed past him.

He stepped in front of us and ripped his shirt open, revealing the Solis mark over his left breast. The gold glittered like Perseus's tattoo, but it leeched out with his veins, a part of him like a birthmark. "I am not the only one." He glared at Perseus. "He has the mark too."

Perseus stiffened. "You betrayed the Trejan when you sided with Helios."

"I did what I had to in order to protect our queen!" Kade roared. "I didn't see any of you stepping up to sacrifice yourselves to save her."

"How dare you assume I wouldn't sacrifice myself for her," Perseus countered. His dagger was still drawn and held tightly in his grip.

Emberlynn's chest rose with a shaky breath, drawing my attention back to the emergent situation in my arms. "Enough! You both will follow me back to the Knight's, and we will finish this there. Right now, I need to get Emberlynn to Lara."

Kade glared at Perseus once more before nodding. "You're right. She comes first. We can talk about this after she's been taken care of."

My only concern at the moment was making sure my mate was okay. Nothing else mattered. But then... Kade had a lot of explaining to do.

TWO

Sander

I COULDN'T STOP MYSELF from reaching through our connection to make sure Emberlynn was still with me. Her faint heartbeat thumped next to mine. The fear of losing her clung to me. There was nothing I wouldn't do for her, to keep her with me. She was everything to me. I had gone so long without her in my life that I knew I wouldn't survive without her.

Perseus drove while I cradled Emberlynn in my lap in the backseat, not trusting anyone else with her wellbeing. Kade sat in the front but kept looking back. I wanted to hate him, but the apparent concern for her health did not go unnoticed.

"How is she?"

I sneered a warning, not ready to let go of the anger. "She is not yours to worry about."

He scoffed and shook his head. "You know nothing. It's too bad, really. She is more mine than you will ever know."

"She is my soulmate." I didn't contain the hatred from seeping out of me in dark shadows. "She is also your queen. I don't expect you to live long with the insolence slipping off your tongue so easily."

"That's enough, Kade," Perseus spoke as he turned up the Knight's driveway. "We all need to talk. That much is certain, but right now isn't the time."

I hardly had the door open before Jamie ran outside. "Ember?"

With Emberlynn cradled tightly against me, I lifted her from the car and strode to the house. "She needs Lara."

Jamie wasted no time flinging the front doors open. "Lara!" He led the way down the hall to the makeshift room Lara used as an infirmary. "Lara! Hurry, it's Emberlynn."

Lara came so fast it was almost as if she emerged from the air. "Ember?" She touched Emberlynn's forehead. "Bring her to the bed. Quickly."

I did as she said, gently placing Emberlynn on the white sheets.

The woman moved swiftly, gathering bottles and supplies from the shelving. She was a skilled healer from the Verum Kingdom, but I worried if she would be enough right now. The black streak in her hair fell from the tawny braid as she swung around to Emberlynn.

"What happened to her?"

I still wasn't sure. Not being the one with her through her demise would haunt me. Sending Kade in my place nearly killed me.

"Helios drained her. He wanted to see how strong she was here. He kept her away from the sun so her powers couldn't revive." Kade stepped into the room, his eyes on Emberlynn. "For the record, she is much stronger than anyone I've ever seen in the mortal realm, including Helios."

"What is he doing here?" Lara picked up a pair of scissors like a dagger and aimed them at Kade.

I wanted her to use them on him, but I couldn't let her yet. He still had information I needed. "I had to release him. He was the only way to get Emberlynn."

Jamie's large frame filled the doorway. "Somebody better tell us what happened."

"Not now." Lara's face paled as she leaned over Emberlynn. "I need you all to leave. I can't do this with an audience. There are too many of you, and I feel everything. I need to be certain with what I feel from her."

If anyone could have punched me and took my breath away, it was with those words. I didn't think I had enough strength to leave. My hand wrapped around Emberlynn's. She wasn't strong enough for me to leave. "I can't."

Lara touched my arm. "Not you, you stay. You are the only reason she's still with us, I'm sure."

Kade folded his arms and leaned against the doorframe. "Yeah, I'm sure. It's not like I didn't just walk into her own personal hell to save her. But naturally, it's because Sander saved her."

I may not have my full power in the mortal realm, but right then, there wasn't a shadow not willing to bend to my will. Icy cold, ebony fingers swirled around Kade's form like smoke, threatening to suffocate him. His piercing glare held me as the shadows wrapped around his throat, but he never moved, not even when the air grew stale in his lungs.

"You will remember to whom you are speaking." The shadows released him as I beckoned them back. "It is because of me that you are not dead."

He had no clue what kind of hell it was for me to send him after Emberlynn. How hard I fought with myself about releasing him from my dungeons. But it was her safety that mattered most.

Kade coughed as the air returned to him. "You will have to learn that I'm in her life. And that kills you."

Perseus grabbed Kade's arm. "You are no one to our queen unless she says you are. You are lucky the Night King has freed you and let you live."

Jamie roared, "Enough!" He pushed both Perseus and Kade out of the room as if they were mere children being reprimanded. "Out, both of you. My daughter needs help, and I refuse to let you two idiots continue this quarreling, preventing her mother from healing her." His voice trailed as they moved from the room.

Lara's shoulders relaxed slightly. "That's much better." Her face softened as she hovered her hand over Emberlynn's unconscious body. Lara sighed in relief after she finished assessing her. "She will be okay. Kade is right. Helios drained her. I think he was looking to see if he could extinguish her powers. It's possible in this realm but rare." She looked up, her hand still over Emberlynn. "She still feels strong. If anything," she stopped.

"What?" I waited, afraid of what she might have felt.

"If anything, Helios might have made her stronger. I'd have to be back in the kingdoms to know for sure. I can't feel enough here to be certain."

I gripped Emberlynn's hand tighter and leaned over, placing a kiss on her forehead. "I don't care if she has power or none at all as long as she lives."

Lara touched my back. "She will live. She has you fighting for her." She gathered a few more items. "I'll give you a few minutes while I get a few things to help her and check on Jen."

The mention of Jen's name rolled my stomach. I'd forgotten it wasn't long before Emberlynn was caught by Helios that she had been stabbed. "How is Jen? Is she okay?"

I couldn't imagine what Gabriel was going through right now.

"She is fine. She is resting in the guest room. I expect her to be up in the next day or so."

"That's good. I'll go see her soon." I just couldn't leave my soulmate yet.

Lara nodded. "I'll let Gabriel know what's going on. I'm sure he'll want to be in on whatever is going on with Kade being here."

I had to hand it to Lara; she was exceptionally perceptive. "Thank you."

With Lara gone, the room was quiet. Too quiet.

Emberlynn's steady but slow breath comforted me. The soft sound soothed my soul. It was oddly terrifying that such a small woman could hold my entire existence within her very breath.

Her fingers were relaxed and limp while I traced small circles with the pad of my thumb over her knuckles. "Don't leave me. Please." I hung my head in defeat. I could bring an entire kingdom to its knees, but I couldn't save my soulmate.

The shattering of my heart echoed in my ears. The silence gave me too much time to think about what happened and what could have happened. The adrenaline that rushed through me earlier was now gone, replaced by grief that threatened to consume me.

I promised Emberlynn I would protect her.

I failed.

"Sander." Lara winced as she closed the door behind her. Her presence in the room made me feel dwarfed as I wiped a tear from my eye. "I know this is hard for you, but you're going to make me sick with that much despair pouring off you. You did not do this to Ember. Helios did this. Direct your emotions justly."

Anger replaced the hollowness. She was right, I did not do this to her, but I would never fail at protecting her again. I couldn't. Helios would soon know the wrath of the Night King.

Lara huffed. "Well, I guess I did say to direct your emotions."

I picked up Emberlynn's hand and gently flipped it so her wrist was up. Bringing it to my lips, I kissed my mark on her skin. "I'll be right back." It was a promise not just to her but to me. I couldn't bear the thought of leaving her.

Lara touched Emberlynn's shoulder. "Don't worry. I'll take care of her."

There were no words I could say to make this easier. Letting Emberlynn's hand slip from mine as I left was harder than seeing her in Kade's arms. The memory of him carrying her riled me like an inferno.

Kade.

He still had a lot of explaining to do before I sent him back to the dungeon.

It was easy to follow Gabriel's stern voice as he expressed his thoughts to the rogue prisoner. If I wasn't in such a sour mood, I would have chuckled at the scolding Kade was receiving.

Entering Jamie's study, I found them waiting. Jamie paced by his desk, looking up when I entered. "Is she okay?"

"You'd know it if she wasn't." I made my way to the desk and took the chair. "Kade, I am not in the mood for your stories. Whatever you have to say, make it quick." Already the strain from Emberlynn pulled tight. She was too drained for me to be gone long. We had already endured the separation of worlds when I went to the Night Kingdom. It was too much now to be apart.

Kade's form flickered, something only I saw. A gift from my bond with Emberlynn. "I told you, I'm bound to her. I'm a blood descendant from the Trejans. I was literally born to protect her."

Perseus casually leaned against the wall, flipping his knife, catching it by the blade. "Is that why you left? To protect her?" He stopped flipping the blade. "Why didn't I do that?" He stormed over to Kade. "That's right... because I stayed to fight for her. How dare you even use the title of Trejan after you betrayed our queen and became a traitor to the Solis Kingdom."

"So, the Trejan is real?" Jamie asked.

Gabriel kept his place near the desk, ever the present guard. His duty was exhausted tonight by the strain from his injured soulmate only a room away. "I am afraid so."

Every muscle in my body tensed. "And Kade, you believe you are part of this ancient line of guards?"

Kade's jaw clenched as he ripped his shirt open once more. The golden sun was a mark of status in the Solis Kingdom. It was the mark of a royal guard. For the ink to bleed in the skin like a birthmark meant it was a birthright. The Trejan.

I waved him off as if it were a meaningless tattoo. "If you were Trejan, then tell me, why would you hurt her? A Trejan guard, from what I was told, could never hurt those they are assigned to."

Jamie tensed, probably remembering when Kade grabbed Emberlynn's wrists so hard he left a bruise. I knew I would never forget the moment she showed me the marks. "Or what about the words you said to her, creating emotional pain?"

Kade glared at me first. "I don't expect you to understand, or you," he glanced at Perseus, "but I don't know why. I don't even remember hurting her."

"Explain." I was growing short on patience, but he still had a lot to tell us.

"Eighteen years ago, I was a guard for Emberlynn's parents. I hadn't ever felt the call or bond of the Trejan with them but knew I was meant to be a royal protector. I knew I was Trejan, but you don't get to decide which royal you are attached to. When Solomon and Selene were murdered and Emberlynn disappeared, many guards sided with Helios. He ordered them to find her at all costs. I worried about her." Kade slipped to the couch and leaned forward, his elbows on his knees. "Every part of me broke not knowing where my queen was. It was the first time I'd realized I was bound to her. I'm tethered to her as one of her protectors."

He stared off, lost in thought, while we waited. He shook his head and continued, "I made my way to the fountain, wanting to find a way to ease my grief. I thought maybe if I was close to the blood, I would be close to her. I had some strange idea that maybe I could find her if I went there. Once I was there, I remember watching the blood run over the sides. Her blood. I knew she was alive. But then, my mind ran rampant with what Helios would do to her once he found her, and I knew right then I could never let that happen. I went to Helios and deceived him into believing I was another guard willing to betray the queen.

"Years went by, and I earned his trust. I got close enough to hear hints of Emberlynn's whereabouts. I traveled each world looking for her. Using scouts to get me information on anything I could use. About a year ago, I stumbled across her here in the mortal realm. Well, not her, but for the first time in forever, I felt her. Here, in this small town. So, I stayed, hoping to find her. I joined the high school, knowing that if she was here among the mortals, it was most likely where she would be. Some days I could feel her strongly, and then others nothing at all. Helios picked up on my hesitation to leave the area and decided to scout it himself.

"Then, she was there at school. I knew it was her, but I couldn't just grab her and leave. I wanted to be everything she needed, a friend, a protector, but Helios showed up and was sniffing around. I couldn't let him know I'd found her. This is when everything is fuzzy for me. I don't remember." His voice cracked. "I remember meeting her, but then, the memory is distorted. It's all jumbled in my head, and I can't make out what is real or..."

"What about Moonstone?" Jamie asked, pressing for the same answers. "You called her out in front of everyone. If you were so concerned with keeping her a secret from Helios, why would you do that?"

Kade groaned. "I told you. I don't remember. I know that sounds like utter crap, but I'm serious. I know whatever I'd done had ruined any chance of her trusting me by that point, but I kept coming back, giving you every chance to get her out of here. She wouldn't have been so vulnerable in the Solis Kingdom."

"So now it's my fault?" I rose from the chair and rounded the desk. "You blame me?"

He looked at me. His eyes not wavering. "Yes."

I folded my arms, trying to contain the shadows from killing him. "Of course, you do."

"You should have taken her from here. Even in the Night Kingdom she would have stood a better chance!" He stood and met me face on. "I did what I had to do to protect her here. Every chance I got, everything I can remember, it was for her. I'm sorry I hurt her. I don't remember any of it. But I tried to protect her. I did my job. Why didn't you do yours?"

"I would never do anything to hurt her." Lies. I had already done that. Kade was right. I should have taken her to the kingdoms. But I was selfish and didn't want to share her yet. But at what cost?

Kade looked as if he could see through to my thoughts. "You keep telling yourself that."

Gabriel grabbed my arm as I stepped forward. He must have known I wanted to strangle Kade.

I shrugged off his grip. "One more accusation that I don't have Emberlynn, my soulmate's, best interest in mind, and it will be the last thing you say."

Jamie ran his hand down his face. "As much as I want to watch Sander box your ears, I still have questions before you die."

Kade's entire frame shifted, and he smirked as he returned to the couch, stretching his arm out over the back. "He won't kill me. He's going to need me."

Perseus growled. "We won't need you, traitor."

I watched him as he glared at Emberlynn's guard. Something was off.

"I already told you, I'm not a traitor." Kade leaned forward and clasped his hands together, then looked at me. "But you will need me. I know what Helios is planning, and being one of her Trejan, I am not about to let any of it happen."

Now we were getting somewhere. Though his words didn't match the conviction in his tone, I decided to press. "What is he planning?"

"To take over. He wants to end the Cyrus line and claim the Solis Kingdom. He has been dabbling in the darker side of his energy. I wasn't privy to all that information, but I do know many guards have disappeared since the last battle."

"That doesn't tell me too much. We already know he wants the Solis Kingdom." My parents had fought with Emberlynn's. They tried to protect the Solis Kingdom and, in turn, protect the Night Kingdom.

Others had done their best to defend their kingdoms as well. Every realm was under attack. I thought back to the last battle I fought in, the day Emberlynn vanished and I became King. It was the last day I spent in the Solis Kingdom. I never returned.

There was a flicker of sadness in Kade's face quickly replaced by a sadistic grin. "No, but he has more than one reason to kill Emberlynn."

Perseus stiffened. "What more could he possibly want?"

Kade's eyes narrowed on me. "He knows she's your soulmate now. If she dies..."

"I die." And that would leave the Night Kingdom vulnerable. "He won't succeed."

"Look," Kade sat forward, "the only reason I didn't kill Helios myself is that he's stronger than me. His bloodline is a direct descendant from the gods. He's not Cyrus blood, thank the sun for that, but one of those who failed at succeeding when the worlds split."

"I know. This is not new information." Why was Kade drawing this out? He babbled on with useless facts, keeping me from Emberlynn. A twinge in my chest shot a sharp pain up through my neck and shoulders. Emberlynn was slipping. She needed me, and I needed her.

"I want to go back to Helios. He doesn't know I'm a Trejan." Kade looked hopeful. But it was fake. It was as if he was pleading with me in a silent secret dialect.

"Why would you want to go back to Helios?" Jamie quirked his brow.

"Because he can keep tabs on the enemy," Gabriel offered. "He can help keep us updated on his plans, and in turn, we can keep Emberlynn safe."

I immediately opened my connection to Gabriel. "Are you sure that's a good idea? Letting him go?"

"Keep your spies close to stay ahead of your enemies." His voice filled my head like he spoke through a tube. I could almost hear his grin in my mind. "If Kade returns to Helios, he might be able to lead us right to him."

"Helios trusts me." Kade stood. "We need to know what his next move is. If tonight has proved anything, it's that you can't be blindsided by him again. It almost cost Emberlynn her life."

Jamie stopped pacing, blocking the door. "Yeah, about that. What I don't understand is why was it your magic that held her? It's almost as if you wanted her to die."

Kade released a strangulated groan. "I already told them." He gestured to Perseus and then me. "I didn't know he was going to throw me in the dungeon. I was supposed to be there, to save her."

Jamie let out a harrumph of denial. "I still don't trust you."

"I'm here, aren't I? I could have escaped several times by now, but I have told you everything. Why would I risk the life of my queen?"

The room darkened as the shadows swarmed, my anger settling back in. "Your queen is my soulmate, and you have been less than forthcoming in the past. Her life was endangered because of you and your secrets." I lifted my hands to guide the shadows toward him. "You could have told us who you were, but you didn't. You could have warned us... her! You didn't warn her!"

Kade stupidly stepped toward me. "I tried!"

Shadows wrapped around his mouth. Already my power faded. I hadn't recovered from being apart from Emberlynn, and she was using whatever I had through our connection. I used what I had to make the shadows squeeze around him, but I had to let go or fall over. And I refused to show him how weak I truly was at that moment. "You failed. Gabriel, take him back to the prison. He committed treason against both the Solis and Night Kingdoms. It was his magic that held the Solis Queen. He didn't disclose information about himself or his intentions that could have prevented her demise." My legs shook, but I held firmly in my place, my eyes boring into Kade's. "He is a traitor, and traitors lie. Don't believe anything he's said. No Trejan would harm their royal."

A dark form slipped from Kade just slightly. Enough for me to see it walk out behind him. I watched intently, knowing no one else could see it. It stopped and smiled at me. Another gold shadow slipped from his proper form and faced me. A wide, hollow expression formed on its face as he tried to yell at me to help

Emberlynn. The gold shadow ran from the room, leaving the smirking darkling and Kade behind.

I rushed after the gold shadow. "Take Kade, now!" I yelled behind me. Gold wispy trails left a path to follow. Its form faded the farther it got from Kade. It was clear that it headed for Emberlynn.

Barging through the door to the room where I left her, she was alone with Lara. Her still form on the bed stopped me.

"Sander? Is everything okay?" Lara looked around me, her brow drawn in confusion.

"Sander!" Gabriel yelled as he ran to the room. "He is gone. He vanished into the air before I could grab him."

I ran a hand through my hair and dropped to the floor next to Emberlynn in exhaustion. Slowly, I reached up and took her hand in mine, leaning my head on the mattress. Kade was gone, and now I had more questions than I started with.

THREE ~ AFTER GRADUATION

Emberlynn

STARDUST SPARKLED UNDER THE SUN'S RAYS as I rolled my hand, inspecting the ring for the millionth time.

The balcony off my bedroom offered peace and calmed my senses. Closing my eyes, I leaned my head back and soaked in the sun's energy, feeling it ripple through me. The heart of summer thrummed in the air. If I focused hard enough, I could feel the vibration flowing through the blood of the squirrel scurrying up the tree or the bumblebee as he worked on the dandelions near the front stoop.

Jen would be proud. I grinned even wider as I thought about how Sander's pride would trump hers.

My soul reached for his. The ease at which I could detect and follow our connection now was beyond fast. It was an instinct given to me by the gods. Soulmates are fated. Our souls were tied together long before we were born. Perhaps Adhaya and Eeshan knew what they were doing, pairing us together.

Sander was close. Keeping my eyes closed, I gripped the railing of the balcony and waited anxiously.

Breathing deeply, I took in his dark chamomile and bergamot scent. His energy crackled like he was the creator of the sun. My heart sped up. He might not control the sun, but he ruled the moon. My soul connected with his, twirling and blending in a euphoric dance. My soulmate.

Butterflies in my stomach raced my heart. He was so close the anticipation of his touch lit a fire across my skin. I needed to connect with him, to touch him. His breath tickled my neck as he wrapped his arms around my middle and pulled me in. "I figured I'd find you out here." The slight lilt in his deep voice caused shivers to run the entire course of my body.

Mmm. Leaning back, I peered up at him. His eyes were focused on me. His square jaw had a rough stubble over it but nothing to distract from his sharp chiseled features. One could compare him to a god. I smirked. But inarguably, they wouldn't be wrong.

A shimmer of silver coloring escaped his sculpted frame for only a second, giving me a glimpse of the soul deliciously entangled with mine. The way I connected to those of the four Immortal Kingdoms, seeing their souls, their pasts, their true selves, was still a bit of a challenge for me, but I was learning how to control it with Jen's help. At least I wasn't surprised anymore when a spirit or ghost popped out from another person. Being a Seer meant I could see the truth within the soul of a person. Sometimes that meant I saw their past reenact as well, but they couldn't hide from me–not even a Shifter could hide behind his illusion.

"I needed the sun," I answered.

He twirled me around, so I faced him, pressing against me. I was caught between the railing and his hard body. But nothing about it was wrong. Soon, he would be my husband, and we would travel to the kingdoms. My stomach somersaulted as I imagined being introduced as his queen–his wife.

You're already my queen. His voice whispered in my head.

"When can we go?" I asked, wrapping my arms over his shoulders.

His chest rumbled as he laughed. He swept his hand over the side of my face, brushing away my hair. "Well, we had to wait for your graduation. Your stipulation if I recall. And now you are ready to go? Just like that?"

I couldn't contain the groan. "Why does it feel like you are trying to keep me away?"

The Solis Kingdom was mine. While I couldn't remember being only an infant the last time I was there, I felt it call to me. My blood hummed with a demand to go–to be there.

"You know it's my job to protect you. I need to make sure it's safe before we go."

I regretfully pushed out of his arms and walked inside. My fingers brushed over the pendant dangling under my throat. It was the only thing I had left from my parents. Aside from a kingdom. "What about the note left for me at graduation?"

He followed me through the bedroom. "Emberlynn, there is so much going on in the Solis Kingdom. We need to make sure it's safe before we go parading through the worlds. I'm not entirely sure who is working for Helios and who is still loyal to the Cyrus line."

He didn't have to say Kade's name to know his strange disappearance after I was rescued from Helios bothered him.

I sighed. "But they need me." The note left for me at graduation worried me. *You were our greatest sacrifice, but now we need you. Come home, my queen.*

I needed to get back.

Sander spun me around, stopping my escape. "Look at me." His voice strained.

I could feel our connection tighten.

His thumb caressed my chin before tipping my head up. The way he looked at me frightened me. Not of him, as I didn't think I could ever fear him, but of the unknown. The future. The kingdoms. He knew so much more than me about what awaited us in the Solis Kingdom.

"Emberlynn, I should have told you more about the Immortal Kingdoms. I blame myself. But there is so much you don't know. It's not like here in the mortal realm. There are other dangers besides Helios. And since you were so young when you left, we don't know what kind of power you will have once you cross over or how strong it is." He bowed his head, not meeting my eyes but taking my hands in his, rubbing small circles over my skin. "I'm guessing you will be very strong since you're powerful here."

"Sander, what are you talking about?" I pulled my hands from him, hating the strain between us. "What could be so different that you're scared to take me there? I was born there. Why can't I return?"

I took a step back, and his shoulders fell in defeat. "You can. You will." He carved a hand through his blond hair. The blue in his eyes rivaled a storm over the Mediterranean Sea. "I've been around for a long time. I need you to trust me."

I smirked, folding my arms over my chest. "I trust you. I do. I know you would protect me. I just feel this..." I couldn't put it into words. I reached out and grabbed his hand, pulling it, so it rested over my heart. "This. I feel this." I poured every emotion I felt coming from my kingdom into our connection. The tugging, pulling, urgent demand that screamed at me to return home.

His head dipped, and he raised my hand to kiss the mark on my wrist. His mark. His lips in gold marked my delicate skin on the underside of my wrist. As he did, the gold shimmer of my mark on his lips reminded me that he was mine. No matter what we would face in the kingdoms, he was mine. We would get through it together.

"We will leave for the Night Kingdom tonight. We can then decide how and when to go to Solis."

An actual squeal escaped my throat. "Really?"

He chuckled. "Yes, really. You're right. We are needed there and have been away too long."

Doing a little jump, I wrapped my arms around his neck and kissed him quickly.

I went to pull away, but he held me firmly to him. "That was not a kiss, little sun."

His lips lowered to mine. We were like magnets, and each time we touched, it was harder to break apart. A deep flutter filled my stomach, and I arched into him.

His fingers gripped my shirt. Moving his mouth over mine in soft touches leaving me wanting more.

More. I felt the word but couldn't speak. The connection between us sparked as the word escaped my mind.

The phantom beat of his heart thundered beside mine, and his lips pressed harder.

Need. His husky whisper filled my head, and nothing else mattered. I understood the want for more. The need. He consumed me in every way, and I delighted in it. But there was more. We both knew it. I could feel it. The need to completely be one.

With each kiss, it was becoming harder to resist the urge to seal our bond as soulmates. Touching wasn't enough. There was a primal instinct pushing us together, making it almost impossible to breathe without wanting the other.

Breathless, he pulled back. "Soon, little sun. Soon." It was a promise, not just for me. I knew that.

No matter how modern I was, he was old-fashioned and wanted me to have every human experience, including a maiden wedding night. The very notion made my cheeks warm and darken in a blush.

"We should tell Jamie and Lara we are leaving." It was the first time I worried about leaving them. It had only been ten months, but they had become my parents, and I loved them. Leaving was inevitable, but I never thought I'd be worlds away. Literally.

"I know I'm immortal, but maybe you should tell them so Jamie doesn't kill me." He chuckled and slid his knuckles down my cheek to my chin. "Not that death would keep me from you." He winked and stepped back.

I feigned a dramatic sigh. "So, you send me to the wolves. I see how it is."

A silver and wispy black tendril escaped him, but it left as quickly as it started. "You are the queen of wolves. No one would dare harm you."

"Not with you behind me." I wondered if I'd ever fully see his shadows and what kind of power he kept from me. At times I felt it grow inside of me like a blanket of darkness, but I could never grasp it.

I had a feeling that I was about to learn a lot about my soulmate. As the Night King, he had to be powerful, strong, even scary. But to me, he was just Sander. He had taken our binding slow and steady, letting me accept everything in my own time regardless of how it affected him. I couldn't imagine him any other way.

Downstairs, Jen and Gabriel were with Jamie and Lara in the kitchen. Of course, they were in the kitchen. It was the best place to gather in the house.

Lara picked a grape from the fruit bowl, but Jamie leaned over her shoulder, stealing her grape. She playfully swatted at him and laughed as she grabbed more from the bowl. "You are rotten. I don't know why the gods put me with a fruit stealing soulmate. I would have been better off alone."

"You don't mean that." He took another grape and plopped it in his mouth.

Gabriel guarded his own plate of meats and cheeses like a dragon hoarding treasure. "I think she does."

I stalled in the kitchen entrance. My heart sank. While I wanted desperately to go to the kingdoms, I was going to miss this. I had finally gotten comfortable with life, and now it was going to be upheaved once again.

Sander's hand warmed the small of my back. "Are you okay?"

I forced myself to nod.

"Oh, honey, I didn't see you come in. Can I get you something?" Lara scowled at Jamie, who stole the last grape. "But unfortunately, if you wanted grapes, you're too late. Your father ate them all without consideration of anyone else living in this house."

A small nervous laugh escaped my lips. I didn't want to sound so quiet but telling them I was leaving was more complicated than I thought.

Lara's face sobered. "Ember, what's wrong?"

I knew I couldn't keep anything from her. "Well, um..."

Jen sat down in her mate's lap. "I'm gonna miss this."

"Miss what?" Jamie looked at her, then me. "Ember, what's going on?"

Looking over my shoulder at Sander, I needed his support. Through our connection, he held me up. A subtle nod reassured me that I needed to do this. It needed to come from me. Looking back to the Knights, I couldn't stop twisting my fingers together. "Sander and I are leaving for the Night Kingdom." I swallowed, trying to keep the anxiousness down. "Tonight."

"What? No." Jamie grabbed the counter and leaned over. "We haven't talked about this."

"But we have," I reassured him. "We knew after graduation I'd be leaving for the kingdoms. It's been a week, and well, it's time. We both feel it. We're needed back home."

Home. It felt strange to call a foreign world home. I knew nothing of the Solis Kingdom, let alone how to be its queen, but I couldn't deny the connection I felt to it.

"Ember," Lara started.

"No." Jamie stood and shook his head. "This family isn't separating yet."

I offered him a smile, but it was sad even to me. "Dad, this is something I have to do." It was the first time I'd called him dad. It felt so natural, and I knew I meant it.

He looked at Lara, who nodded. His gaze fell back to me. "Alright, kiddo. Then we're going with you."

"What? Are you sure?" I wanted that, yes, but I worried they'd be leaving their life here just for me. It was a life that made them so happy.

"The kingdoms are our home too." Lara came to me and took my hands. "And I couldn't imagine you going without us."

Jen gave a content sigh. "It's just like I'd imagined. We'll all be together."

I looked around Lara to Jen. "You imagined this?"

She shrugged and stole a piece of cheese from Gabriel's plate. "I wasn't worried. I don't think the gods could tear this family apart."

"Hey, do not be tempting the gods, my mate." Gabriel gave her a stern look. I wasn't sure if it was over the food theft or her statement.

"Oh, I'm not tempting anyone." She leaned in to whisper. "Except for you."

Jamie tapped his fingers on the counter. "It's been a while since we've been to the kingdoms. I suppose since we're traveling with the Night King, we won't need permission to stay in the Night Kingdom?"

Sander stood tall and sure. "Family never needs permission. You will always be welcome in our home."

He wrapped an arm around my waist and pulled me close.

I could feel the excitement and pure joy radiating off him. He was ready to return to the Night Kingdom. A small part of me felt guilty for keeping him in the mortal realm for so long.

He leaned in so close that only I heard his whisper. "Little sun, I would never be happy without you. It is knowing you will be there that makes me so delighted. Do not let fake remorse hold you. There is only room for my arms around you."

The slight lilt in his deep voice caused a sensual shiver to run through me. He had that kind of impact on me. Just a simple phrase, and my toes would curl.

"Well, school is over for the year, so we can leave at any time." Jamie looked around the kitchen. "We won't have to sell the house. We can use it for when we come back to visit."

I hadn't thought about the fact that we could come back. It was a relief that allowed some of the pressure to lift from my chest. I wanted to have both realms in my life. I couldn't imagine not ever being in the mortal world again.

Sander rubbed small circles on my back. "My little sun, you are about to see how powerful you are. As a queen, there will be many things you'll have to learn, and I'm sure there won't be an immortal in any kingdom who won't want to meet you, but I'll be there every step of the way."

My heart sped up. "I guess I was naive about the whole queen thing. Like it would go away. What if I fail?"

Now that the time had come to finally announce my presence in the kingdoms, I felt sick. My biological parents were the last rulers of the Solis Kingdom, and I had no idea how to follow their lead. I knew they died for the kingdom, but what else had they done for the people? What would be expected of me? It was like I already had predetermined expectations bestowed on me by a title. A title I wasn't sure how to carry.

"Emberlynn, look at me." Sander's request was commanding but gentle.

Looking up, I saw only love in his eyes. A calm settled over me.

"You are worthy of so much more than I can give you. Your title has been passed down through your ancestors. Only Cyrus' blood has ruled over Solis. You will learn what is expected of you, but until then, you must remember that failing is not in your blood." Sometimes it was still creepy how he could feel what I was feeling or thinking. But right now, I was glad he knew my fears. He had a way of comforting me that only he could accomplish.

I only wished I could have met some of my ancestors. A small chat with them might do wonders for my worries. Letting anyone down–dead or alive–bothered me. Sander said failing wasn't in my blood, but how could he be so sure?

Jen gasped, breaking the moment. Her wide eyes landed on Sander. "I saw Kade. He's coming."

Sander stiffened but continued to rub my back. "Did you see anything else?"

It wasn't hard to guess what he was asking. Helios has been hiding since the incident at the old church.

Jen shook her head. "No." Her eyes shifted as she watched time unfold. "But we only have a few minutes before Kade arrives. He's..." Her mouth dropped. "He's hurt."

Lara stood and rushed to her pantry. It was her go-to place for easy and accessible remedies.

Jamie went to her, grabbing her hands. "He may not need your help."

Her eyes watered. "I can't sit back and not help someone, Jamie. You know that."

It had to be extremely hard to feel everyone around you. I worried about Lara returning to the kingdoms. She once told me her gift was much stronger there.

Jamie kissed her forehead. "I know, love."

"Do you know why he is coming here?" Gabriel went to the windows and began checking the locks. The guard in him was never off duty.

Jen sat on the barstool closest to me. "No. But he isn't coming through the windows. He's a traitor, not a burglar."

"Traitor?" I asked. The last we saw of him was after he saved me from Helios.

Three knocks on the back door made me jump. But it wasn't Kade. The only one who used that entrance was Perseus. It was some sort of guard code. Back doors seemed sneaky, I suppose.

Jamie unlocked the door and ushered Perseus in, clicking the lock back in place.

"My queen," Perseus said, dipping his head. "We've spotted Kade. He isn't far from the house."

My brow scrunched. "We?"

Perseus nodded. "I have been putting out a call to the other Trejan. Last night Brayson showed up. It's slow because we can't tell anyone about the Trejan or where you are without your full guard. But I think over the next week we should see more."

"How many Trejan are there?" I had no idea how many more to expect.

Perseus stood stiff. He was a more serious bodyguard than Gabriel. Though, I was sure Gabriel had more than just experience on him. "The numbers are unclear. Many have been lost, and we need to be sure they are your true Trejan."

"Meaning what exactly?"

His eyes shifted around the room, watching Gabriel before settling back on me. "We need to know they are bound to you. That they are loyal to their birthright and title of Trejan... loyal to you."

"Maybe that's why Kade is coming?" Jen asked, reaching for the fruit bowl. She picked through the leftover pieces and chose an orange. "He's Trejan. Maybe he couldn't deny the call?"

"Wait, what? Kade is not Trejan." I spun to face Sander. "That man is not guarding me."

Sander frowned at Jen. Obviously, I was the last to know this new secret. "Sander, what have you not told me?"

He took my hands in his. "Emberlynn, when Kade was here last time, he revealed his birthright as a bound Trejan."

"That's stupid. There is no way he will ever be bound to me. Nope. I refuse." I shook off his hands, though the separation created new anxiety inside of me. "Is my life one big chess piece that you can all move around and decide where I go, what I do, and who can bond with me without my approval? I am sick of not having a say in anything."

"Emberlynn," Sander said softly, coaxing me to calm down.

But it was too late. I was beyond frustrated with them all. They had kept yet another secret from me. "No." I shook my head and left the room.

I knew Sander wouldn't be far behind me, but hopefully, he'd wait a minute to give me some space. At that moment, I realized I'd never have freedom again. Not truly. I was mated with Sander, the Night King. I was a queen over a world I didn't know. I had a line of Trejan bound to me. It was the last part that creeped me out the most. I didn't like having a group of men who could feel me.

A revolted shiver rolled through me. Bile rose into my throat. I couldn't stand that so many people had access to me. ME. The idea that Kade, of all people, could be one of them pushed me over the edge.

I stopped in the foyer. I was done running. The slight tingle of electricity warmed my fingertips. Every time I felt overwhelmed, I ran, I left, I hid. But I was done.

Flinging open the door, I marched outside. Kade was on the sidewalk. His eyes locked on me. But it was how he held his side that caught me off guard. I shouldn't be worried about him, but I was.

"You!" I yelled as I held my head high, walking right up to him. "You are not my Trejan. You will never be bound to me."

The hollow look that glazed over his face made me almost regret my words. He looked gutted... sad. "Emberlynn..."

"Why are you here?"

He winced and grabbed his side harder. "To warn you."

His breathy words stalled my heart.

"Emberlynn!" Sander called from the front porch. He ran to me, pushing me back, so he stood between Kade and me. "I'm surprised you showed your face after you left last time."

"Sander, please..." Kade doubled over. "She's in danger."

A black ghost leisurely strolled up behind him. It stopped to look at me and grinned. It took one step toward me, but a gold shadow emerged from Kade, blocking it.

I'd never seen two distinct colors form from one person. Kade always had a wisp of black threaded through his gold, but this was new. I couldn't tear my eyes from them. The black one never took its ebony eyes off me.

"Emberlynn, get back. Go!" Kade's desperate plea cut through the air.

Sander pushed me back and watched with me as the two colors got closer. The gold one blocked the darker one, almost as if preventing it from getting to me.

Kade fell to the ground. Blood pooled around his hand that covered a wound. I rushed to him and rolled him over. "Lara!"

The gold aura flickered as Kade's eyes closed. A faint whisper of my name on his lips. Even the gold ghost seemed weak as it staggered back to Kade.

The black form continued to walk toward me, but darkness covered me like a blanket. Swirls of shadows blocked me from the second aura. "Sander!"

What was happening? I was wholly consumed by the thick, inky clouds of shadows.

Stay there. I've got you. Sander's voice was clear in my mind, but my heart raced not seeing him.

The wispy fingers of the shadows touched my skin. The touch was cool and familiar. I looked around in awe. These were Sander's shadows. I had never seen this part of him.

Kade went limp, his hand falling from his side. "Kade, you jerk, I don't want to save you." I hated him for many reasons, but I owed him. He came to my rescue once. I couldn't let him die. I pressed my hands to his wound to try and help stop the flow.

His hard muscles contracted under my touch, but his face remained motionless. The hot sticky fluid continued to pour from him despite the pressure. "Lara!" I needed her to tell me what to do.

I couldn't see past Sander's army of shadows to know what was happening beyond. Maybe Lara couldn't hear me or even get to me through the darkness.

"Sander, help. I don't know what to do." I pressed harder.

Thrumming energy tingled in my fingertips. Hot light burned from my hands through his shirt, singeing his skin. The smell assaulted my nose, making me cringe, but I kept my hands pressed against him. Blood stopped flowing from his side, and I worried he died.

With shaky hands, I lifted them to see my handprint seared into his flesh. My stomach rolled with the stench of charred skin and my mark on him. But his wound was closed.

I sat back on my heels and stared at my bloodied hands. I wasn't sure what I'd done or how I did it. I couldn't stop shaking.

The shadows vanished as if they'd never been there. The sun shone down on me, filling me with a renewed strength.

"Emberlynn!" Sander wrapped his arms around me and pulled me up to him. He cradled my face in his hands. "Look at me. Are you okay? Are you hurt?" I reached up to touch his hands, but he grabbed them. "You're bleeding."

I shook my head. "No, it's Kade's blood."

He pulled me to him, wrapping me in his arms. His heart thundered against mine.

I held on to him, afraid of letting go. "What happened?"

"I'm not sure. I have a theory, but I have to wait until Kade is awake and talking before I can confirm it." He looked down at Kade. "Is that your handprint?"

"Yeah. And before you ask, I don't know how I did it."

Sander's brow arched. "I'm not sure I like him having your mark on him."

I pushed back and knelt next to Kade, inspecting his wound. "What was I supposed to do, let him die? Besides, I didn't do it on purpose."

"I'm not upset with you, little sun. I just think it will feed his ego." He crouched beside me. "But I suppose any man who carried your mark would feel like a king. I know I do."

"Ember, Sander, what happened?" Lara rushed across the drive to Kade's unconscious form.

It was then that I noticed Gabriel, Perseus, and someone I didn't recognize standing guard. I wasn't sure when they got there. Everything happened so fast.

Lara touched the wound on Kade's side. "Dagger. Someone wanted him dead."

"It wasn't a royal dagger, or he wouldn't have made it this far." Jamie picked Kade up and carried him to the house. "We don't need the neighbors calling the cops. Let's get inside."

I pulled on Sander's hand, making him hang back with me while they went inside. "We need to talk."

He waited until the door closed. "Are you not alright?"

"It's about before. And during. You lied to me, Sander. You didn't tell me a vital piece of information that pertained to me. That's not how this," I pointed to him, then me, "works."

"I know. I'm sorry. Truly I am. It's just... I didn't think it was important for you to know then."

"And now?" I flung my arms up. "Now I was caught off guard and nearly attacked by a shadow!"

His jaw clenched, and he stared at the house. "Yes. It was a mistake on my part. I won't let it happen again."

I wanted to believe he meant the secrets, but I felt it was more about being attacked. He took it so personally to see to my every moment's safety that if I got a papercut, he overreacted.

I touched his arm. "Your shadows protected me. I'd never seen that side of you."

He tilted his head back and closed his eyes. "I think maybe that's part of why I have delayed returning to the kingdoms."

"I don't understand."

"Here, in this realm, I am as close to a mortal man as I'll ever be. You have been raised as such, and I worry you will regret being bound to someone like me once you see me in a different light." He sighed. "I have tried to contain the shadows, to control them while around you so I wouldn't scare you. But today..." His jaw clenched. "The dark one came for you, and there was no stopping them. They are a part of me, and they knew you were in danger."

"Sander." I took a step closer, leaning my head on his chest. "Nothing about you scares me. I would never regret being your soulmate."

His arms wrapped around me, and he took in a shaky breath. "I couldn't live if anything happened to you. I would do anything to protect you. I'm sorry I've been so secretive." He kissed the top of my head. "I have had years of hiding from others, keeping things to myself to protect my kingdom. I'm not used to sharing details, but I can see how it is important, if not prudent, to include you as well."

I tipped my head back to look up at him. "Is it really that different? The kingdoms? That you would willingly hide from me?"

"Yes."

I wasn't sure what to expect now. "We should get back inside before Perseus comes looking for me." I left him standing in the drive. I needed to wash Kade's blood off and find answers.

FOUR

Kade

I WAS SCREAMING. I was sure of it, but no sound came from my lips. Emberlynn's hand was burning me. The intense heat seared through to the very depth of my soul. For the love of the sun, why didn't she stop? Why was she torturing me?

My mind went fuzzy, and I couldn't remember why I was here. I tried to think, to focus, to recall anything from the past day. Nothing. Darkness clouded my memories like so many others before this. It had been years since I'd been able to remember simple day-to-day actions or conversations. I was a prisoner in my body. When I was allowed to move on my own, I could never remember what I did.

Save her.

It was the only clear words I could make out, so I clung to them. I was afraid if I let them go, I would lose the last of myself to the darkness.

More words came to me, and I repeated them until they were engraved in my brain.

I am Trejan. I will not fail.

I am Trejan. I will not fail.

I am Trejan. I will not fail.

Save her.

I tried to open my eyes, but I had nothing left. No fight, no energy.

If only I could remember...

FIVE

Sander

IT WAS NEVER MY INTENTION to show Emberlynn my power that way. But I saw the darkling coming for her, and I reacted. The shadows had come without hesitation, willing to protect their queen.

Jamie touched my arm as we entered the house, stopping me. He nodded to the study, and I followed.

He closed the door and locked it. "What happened out there?"

"I'm not sure. There was a dark ghost that seemed to want Emberlynn. Kade's aura took shape and blocked him until he went unconscious. I'd never seen anything like it before. I used the shadows to protect Emberlynn while it challenged me. But I couldn't touch it. My hands went right through its body." I combed a hand through my hair. "The shadows, though, they could. They went after the darkling, but it vanished before they could detain it.

"Where do you think the darkling comes from?"

I folded my arms and stared at the door. "I'm worried that Helios has found a way to control his guards. Remember when Kade said Helios had been dabbling in the darker side of his energy? What if he found a way to use that on others?"

"So, you think Kade has been controlled by Helios this entire time? If what you're saying is true, then none of our kingdoms are safe. If Helios can control a Trejan to hurt Emberlynn…"

"I know," I stopped him. "I think it's time to leave. I will need my full powers to protect her, and I can't do that here."

Jamie nodded. "I agree. What about Kade?"

"We take him with us." Already, I relayed orders to Gabriel to not let Kade out of his sight.

Jamie unlocked the door and pushed it open. "Sander, if Helios can control a Trejan, could he control a soulmate?"

The thought made my stomach roll. "Let's hope not."

Outside Lara's infirmary, Brayson, the new Trejan, guarded the door.

I gestured to the position he was in. "Gabriel's orders?"

He nodded and pushed the door open for me.

Kade was still unconscious. Emberlynn's handprint was deeply seared into his flesh. There was no way that wouldn't scar. Perhaps a memory he would remember.

Lara was cleaning up his wound. She never looked up at me, but I knew she could feel my unease.

"We're leaving. Take whatever you will need with you. I'll send others back with Gabriel to collect what you can't carry."

She stopped and rolled her head, working out kinks. "What about Kade?"

"He will be coming with us." There was no way I was letting him go again. The dungeon was a fitting place for him until we could figure out what was going on and if Helios was, in fact, controlling him.

"Sander." Emberlynn's voice was quiet as she entered the room.

I turned to her, taking her outstretched hand. Just having her close ebbed the mounting concerns I carried. "Little sun, are you ready?"

She curled up next to my chest and looked at Kade. "I'm worried. What if there are others like him? What if..." She buried her face in my shoulder. "What if the other Trejan are dark like that?"

I kissed the top of her head. "Don't worry. I won't let anything happen to you."

"I'm not sure I want anyone else to guard me right now. Not until we know for sure."

I had also wondered if maybe Brayson should stay behind and watch over the Knight's home in case Helios returned. This was possibly what would need to happen until we could determine his clearance. "Let me talk with Gabriel. I trust him. We can make a decision about your guard when we get to Astraios."

She nodded and turned to Lara. "Mom, would you like help packing anything before we leave?"

"I think I have a good bag packed. The rest will have to be brought later." Lara covered Kade's side with a piece of gauze and tossed the medical tape in a leather duffel bag. "That's all I can do for him right now. Ember, you did most of it for me. If you hadn't cauterized the wound, I'm not sure I could have saved him."

"Great, so I saved the enemy. Somehow, it doesn't help my mood."

Lara offered a lopsided grin before giving Emberlynn a quick hug. "Healing isn't always about what we feel is best for us, but what we can give to be the best for others."

My chest constricted as a flood of shame poured from Emberlynn. I could feel the shadows dance under my skin, wanting to comfort my mate. Keeping her snug against my side, I leaned in to whisper, "There is no dishonor in feeling regret. Not many are willing to help an enemy. It is a quality of a true queen."

She rolled her eyes and scoffed. "A true queen wouldn't be disappointed that she saved him." She huffed a heavy breath and looked up at me. "But, deep down, I think I'd be upset if he'd died. I couldn't just let him...." She turned her eyes back to Kade. "I couldn't let him die. It's stupid."

"It's not stupid, Emberlynn." I hated that I couldn't take away her grief. She would have many more opportunities to contemplate her actions but saving a life shouldn't be one of them–no matter who it was. That was the woman I loved. She wasn't an executioner. Her light was life, not death. I wondered then how I would be able to help take that burden off her in the future. "We should go."

Guiding her from the room, I felt her stiffen as she passed Brayson. Her safety was my biggest concern. If she was uncomfortable around her Trejan, then I would entrust Gabriel with her new security detail.

My link with him was still open, as it usually was after an incident. "Gabriel, I need you to oversee a new team of guards for Emberlynn. She is worried Helios might be able to influence them as well and does not feel safe with her Trejan, and I concur."

"I had already put together a guard for the queen with the same assumptions. I have just been waiting for you to give me permission to lead her new protectors."

Of course, Gabriel would already have a security team in place for Emberlynn. He was the head of my guard for a reason. "We are ready to leave. I assume you have enough men here to watch over her while we use the Fores?"

"Certainly."

"You seem lost in thought." Emberlynn's voice echoed in my head as if down a long tunnel while I focused on my surroundings.

Inside her room, I pulled her to a stop. "Gabriel has a new guard in place for your protection. We will leave your Trejan here and find a way to vet them before allowing them near you."

She nodded slowly while nipping at her bottom lip. Her brow furrowed as she thought. "What about Perseus?"

Perseus might be the only Trejan we could trust, but I still had reservations. The idea that Helios could control anyone was a game-changer. What if Perseus was already being manipulated? "We take him with us, watch him, decide if he is under Helios."

"Okay," she said, grabbing her bag from the end of the bed. She stopped and made no effort to move. "I can feel your shadows. That's how I knew it was you in the driveway."

I smiled. I'd be lying if I told myself that didn't affect me. My skin flushed as I thought about the shadows caressing her skin. "Little sun, there is almost nothing I don't feel of you. It will be even more when we complete our bond." Already the pull of her soul tugged on mine. I took a step toward her. I had to touch her. Her skin was soft under my fingertips as I ran them down her cheeks to the hollow of her neck. "The intimacy between two souls is something unexplainable. It is something I cannot wait to experience with you. To fully fall into you and feel your soul inside mine will be an honor." Every part of me was on fire with the need to take her. A desire so profoundly enflamed in my soul to make her mine roared to life. Suddenly, the air burned my lungs, and I knew she was the cooling antidote.

My lips found hers as I sought to find the relief I desperately needed. Her body trembled under my touch, and a soft whimper escaped her throat. That sound caressed my ears and made it harder to leave her, to remember we were waiting. Kissing her was like kissing the sun. The heat from her lips burned through to my soul.

The need to be with her grew. The ache in my soul pleaded with me to be with her. The shadows swirled around us, blocking us from the world. I wasn't afraid to share them with her any longer. Giving myself to her meant giving everything. I had never wanted anything more than that.

Her fingers slid up under my shirt. Her touch sent a zing of power through me. Everything. I wanted everything. Life wouldn't be fulfilled without completing the bond between us. Preventing it was like going against a natural urge, a gift from the gods that we were neglecting. Each second was harder to deny the intensity through our connection. But this was my soulmate. She deserved the moon and stars, everything I could give her. She deserved to experience our first night as husband and wife with a promise from me to love her until the end of the kingdoms. The coupling that would take place between us would tie us together for eternity. It was an unbreakable bond between soulmates, and I wanted to give that to her on our wedding night.

It was only that thought that pulled me back to the present. Out of breath, I clung to her as I rested my forehead against hers.

She swallowed hard. "If you don't stop kissing me like that, we won't make it to our wedding."

She was right. The feeling I had warming my body was nearly impossible to ignore—to reject. I backed up and took her bag from her shaky hand. "I have waited over three hundred years to have you. I will not rush you into anything."

"It seems I am the one trying to rush you." Her mumbling didn't go unnoticed, but I just grinned at her.

If only she knew how much I wanted her. "Come on, little sun. We need to get going before I kiss you again."

"You say that like it's a bad thing." Her hips swung more than usual as she sashayed toward me. "I happen to like being kissed by you."

I let loose a deep growl from my chest. I could feel my blood rushing through my veins, pulsing and pushing against my skin, urging me to take her challenge. "You are a tempting creature, my mate. However, the first time I take you will not be while there is anyone around. Now, let's go before Gabriel comes looking for us."

Her cheeks tinged with a deep red. "Gabriel is always ruining everything."

I laughed with her. "You'll get used to it."

Leading her downstairs did not douse the flames of desire. Whatever we started upstairs, I feared could not be stopped.

Searching through our connection, I felt the longing pool inside of her as well. The tension was so tight either of us could snap and give in to the urges. We would have to be careful.

"What took you two so long?" Gabriel held his hand up. "Never mind. I do not want to know. I have already sent Perseus ahead of us, along with Kade and his guard. Jamie and Lara are outside waiting with Jen. I have an entire guard ready for our departure."

"Emberlynn and I can follow Jamie's car. I assume you will be with us?"

"You assume correctly. Until we figure out what is going on, you are stuck with me." He looked at Emberlynn. "You both are stuck with me."

Emberlynn shrugged. "That's fine, but I'm confused. I thought the portals were all out of commission here in this realm. How will we leave?"

I handed Gabriel Emberlynn's bag and led her outside. "After that run-in with Helios, we have begun checking all the Fores here. The Knights have been reporting back with their findings. It seems we were misled into believing they were shut down. Many are still operational but unguarded. Something we are rectifying as quickly as we find them."

I opened the door for her to get in the back seat of the SUV. She slid in and waited for me to sit next to her. "Wait, Jamie and Lara are reporting to you?"

"No, Hanis and Gerivee Knight. They are the king and queen of the Somnium Kingdom, Jamie's parents."

Jen got in the front passenger seat and turned to Emberlynn. "I have been waiting for this day forever. I can't wait to show you around the kingdom."

I leaned toward Emberlynn. "We'll talk more about this later." Giving her a wink, I sat up straight and let them have their girl talk. I was glad Emberlynn and Jen became such good friends. She would need someone like Jen. I had a feeling the coming months weren't going to be easy for her.

Driving into the city, I watched Emberlynn for any sign of fear. The last time she was here, Helios had tricked her, trapping her while he drained her. Jen kept her occupied as she rattled on about all the places Emberlynn needed to see.

"We are here." Gabriel pulled the car up next to the sidewalk.

Thick branches on the tall trees covered in dark green leaves shadowed the ground. The last time we were here, they were barren and dry. I hoped the subtle differences made it easier for Emberlynn.

The timeworn, red-brick cathedral building remained untouched since we last saw it. I had made sure it was boarded up and kept vacated by the mortals. Not an easy task, but I had a council ready to make it happen.

The kingdoms needed to assign permanent guardians to each Fores. But until then, I knew a member of each royal guard was tasked with overseeing each portal.

Jamie and Lara were at the doors waiting for us.

Jen squealed and grabbed Gabriel's hand. "Let's go home."

I hated knowing it was me who kept them from returning for so long. Still, I was eternally grateful for their friendship and loyalty through this entire time. If anything, these months helped me reflect on the kind of king I wished to be. A restart of purpose.

"Home," Emberlynn whispered.

I took her hand as well, bringing it to my lips to kiss my mark on her wrist. "Home."

Jamie pushed open the doors and stepped inside first.

The cool air from inside greeted us. Emberlynn hesitated, stalling at the door as if approaching a bad memory. I wanted to help her battle the thoughts rushing through her mind. "I'm sorry we have to use this portal. It's the closest one without traveling out of the state."

The one at Moonstone would have been preferred, but we didn't have the time it would take to arrange that option.

She touched my forearm. "It's okay."

She followed Lara and Jen through, meeting Gabriel and Perseus in the large open room. I gestured to Jen and mouthed, "Are you okay?"

She smiled and nodded. The last time here was painful for her as well. Only a few feet from where she stood, she had fallen with a deep slash to her abdomen.

Perseus watched the entrance and windows. "My queen, I have scoured the entire building. There is no trace of Helios."

Emberlynn held her head high. "Thank you."

Gabriel nodded to six men lined against the far wall. Each of them wore head to toe black and had a silver moon pinned over their breast. "Emberlynn, this will be your guard until we can verify your Trejan."

Perseus grabbed the handle of his dagger. "I will be making those decisions for my queen. I am the head of her Trejan."

"I am not debating that," I stepped in. "However, I believe a member of the Trejan was controlled by Helios. I need to make sure Emberlynn is safe. Until further notice, Gabriel will be overseeing her guard details. When I am assured that each member of the Trejan is not corrupted, I will hand it back over to you."

Perseus stiffened. "I have proven myself. I would die for my queen."

"I am not willing to risk my soulmate." Each word echoed off the walls as I made my stance known.

Lara winced. I worried about her entering the Night Kingdom with her ability.

I lowered my voice. "Now, you may come with us and help us figure out how to inspect the Trejan, or you may stay here. Either way, you will be under the same scrutiny until I know for certain Helios has no control over you."

His eyes fell on Emberlynn. "It is you that I serve. What is it you wish, my queen?"

"I would like for you to come with us. But after... after what I saw with Kade earlier, I want to make sure the Trejan is unattached to Helios. It was my idea."

Jamie stepped forward, placing a hand on her shoulder. "And no one would fault you for that. It is a very respectable decision that I'm sure didn't come easy. We all know how much you have trusted Perseus. I think it shows what a great leader you will be some day."

Jamie always had a way of smoothing over the situation, deescalating moods and tension. I'm sure it was for his wife's benefit, but he had become so adept to it that it was a natural response for him. It wasn't hard to imagine him being raised in the Somnium royal home. He had a decorum of nobility that exuded off him.

Perseus nodded. "I can see the concern behind the decision."

Gabriel clicked his tongue and gave a subtle shake of his head. "I have to ask you to remove your weapon. Just until we figure all this out. You understand, right?"

Perseus shifted his weight, staring off down the hall. "I understand." He unbuckled his sheath and held the swathed dagger out for Emberlynn. "Though I trust no one more than you to retain this for me."

Emberlynn gripped the handle and pulled out the blade. "I'm sure it will be returned soon." She turned it over, inspecting the details. "It's exquisite."

He watched her closely. "It is made from sundust and engraved with your symbol. It was forged in the blood of the fountain in Sarcatan."

"Sarcatan?" She slipped the dagger back to the sheath.

"The capital city of Solis. It is where the Cyrus fountain resides in a cave of the Floures Mountains." Perseus's eyes softened as he spoke.

I doubted Helios was strong enough to take Perseus. His love for their kingdom was evident. He would be a good guard for Emberlynn. But I wouldn't take the chance. I needed to find a way to make sure.

"We'll wait for you on the other side, give you some space," Jaimie said. He took Lara by the hand and led her from the main room.

Perseus nodded in agreement and went with Gabriel and Jen. "I suppose you are going to keep me in the prison?"

Gabriel laughed. "It was my first idea, but your queen saved you. There is a room prepared for you in the castle." He winked at Emberlynn and then guided the small group out of the room.

Emberlynn gripped my hands and looked up at me. "I can't believe I finally get to see the Night Kingdom. For so long, it's been nothing more than a myth."

I locked my eyes with hers. "No myth, little sun. I will show you the worlds. There won't be a shadow who doesn't know your name, a tendril of magic that you won't touch. Everyone will bow to you."

She softly chewed on her inner cheek. Her mind was lost in thought. "What if I don't want them to bow."

"They will bow." I knew it would take time for her to realize her role in the kingdoms and understand her bloodline... but until then, I would make sure she received the respect owed to her. "Come on, let's go home."

Taking her to the next room, I did my best to block her from the left side. The wall still had the markings in the stone, reminding us both that it wasn't a dream. She had been taken, and we were separated. My stomach rolled at the idea of that happening again.

No.

I would not let it happen.

The stone stairwell leading to the upstairs Fores spiraled up. The narrow passageway was only big enough for one person at a time to ascend. The old wood creaked under our weight as we crossed the upstairs room to the end of the hall. A guard watched as we approached.

His blue sash had a goldcrest imprint with a half-sun and half-moon. The Somnium royal family mark. The Knights, to be exact.

He bowed his head slightly as we approached. "King Lux."

Emberlynn nearly tripped over her own feet. I tightened my grip on her arm to keep her from falling, pushing through our connection to determine if there was an immediate threat I was unaware of. "Are you okay?"

She kept her head high but gave me a subtle nod.

Flutters of anxious nerves stirred through our bond. I knew this was all new to her, but there was nothing on the other side of the portal that would hurt her. At least not in my kingdom. I would keep her safe.

"I just wasn't expecting him to say that." Her soft whisper was only loud enough for me. "I guess I'm a little more nervous than I thought about this. Like, it's a whole new world, not here. What if they hate me?"

I pulled her to a stop, not caring who could see us. It was my duty to comfort her, to ease her suffering. "Little sun, there is not a soul, mortal or immortal, who will hate you."

She raised her brows. "Helios."

A low chuckle rumbled in my chest. "Okay, besides him. Though, it is not you that he hates. It is his desire for power that drives him to do hateful things. Besides, would his opinion of you be so high that you are willing to doubt your own self-worth?"

"Well, no. It's just..." She dipped her head and twisted her fingers together. "I barely made it as a mortal. How am I supposed to be a queen over an entire world?"

"With help." I slipped my hand under her chin and lifted her head. "I will be there. As well as others who will teach you. No one will expect you to know everything immediately. Give yourself some grace. You will be amazing."

She sucked in a long breath and nodded. "Okay, let's do this."

Leading her the rest of the way to the Fores, I smiled. I was finally going home. And this time, I wasn't alone.

The portal was behind the old wooden door. Grasping the bronze handle, I twisted and pulled the heavy entryway open. An iridescent layer stood between us and the other worlds. When I touched it, my fingers slipped through the silky cool seam of magic. "When walking through a Fores, you must know where you are going. If it is to a place you have never been, you will need a guide." I held my hand out to her. "Let me take you home."

Her hand fit perfectly in mine. "Don't let me go."

"Never."

Quickly, I pulled her to me and stepped through the portal to the Night Kingdom. I knew where to go, picturing everything clearly in my mind. Torches illuminated the dark room surrounded by green trees and ivy hiding the obsidian walls. Moss covered the ceiling. A dais of black stone held the Fores. Blue mist hovered under the marbled arch, barely grazing the onyx floor. The underground room was highly guarded and used only by a select few. It was my personal portal under the castle grounds.

My heart raced as everything returned to me fully. My powers, my heightened senses... the love for my soulmate. Everything I'd felt for her before was now magnified. I couldn't think without her. Our bodies acted like magnets. It was as if the world disappeared as I pulled her to me, my mouth crashing down upon hers. Even with her lips under mine, Emberlynn wasn't close enough to me.

Shadows swirled around us, and the flames from the torches roared. A slight sizzle of warmth ran over my skin. Emberlynn melted into my arms. A slight groan escaped her throat.

Her lips eagerly pressed against my mouth as her hands made their way to my waist, where she gripped my shirt. Her brazen new action had me fighting reality. I wanted to scoop her up and take her to my room where we could hide for days savoring each other, but I promised I would wait. Although I hadn't realized how much harder this would be once here.

Somehow, I heard someone clearing their throat. It sounded far off and muffled behind a layer of fog. I needed to focus and remember where we were. My soul screamed at me as I pulled back. Breaking the touch with her had me shaking.

Focus. Where were we?

The Fores room under the castle. We were in the kingdom.

The temptation to kiss her again grew. My arms wound around her, keeping her pressed against me, but didn't kiss her. I wouldn't stop if I had. She was everything to me and she deserved a man who took her first time slow. Not in front of a portal with everyone watching.

I nuzzled her neck and whispered low enough for her to hear. "As much as I would love to explore every inch of you right now, we have an audience, and I don't think I'd like to share that part of you with them. Nor do I assume they would appreciate the show."

Emberlynn sucked in a sharp breath and peered over my shoulder. Her grip on my waist tightened. "That's embarrassing."

"Nothing about the affection of a soulmate is embarrassing. It is natural. Once we are together, our need to consume each other should calm down." I grinned and winked. "But I wouldn't count on it."

The red in her cheeks darkened. She cleared her throat and tried to take a step back. "It is so much harder to leave you."

I nodded. "It is harder for me too."

"Not as hard as it is to watch you two," Gabriel said. "It is not hard to spot young mates."

"You hush," Jen teased. "We're still that way when no one's looking."

Everyone chuckled, and I forced myself to let go of my mate but took her hand to help appease my soul.

"Well, we certainly don't hide it," Lara said, getting up on her tiptoes to kiss Jamie quickly.

"Love, we only dance in front of the kids." Jamie winked and then twirled her around.

Perseus groaned. "Had I known I'd be surrounded by love-struck mates, I'd have asked for the dungeon."

Emberlynn's laugh filled the cavern. It made my heart soar hearing her happiness in my world. Her infectious melody soon had everyone laughing.

"Come on, little sun, let me show you my home."

SIX

Emberlynn

STEPPING THROUGH THE PORTAL, a surge of emotions and strength thrummed under my skin like a tsunami. Everything was a hundred times magnified. A thousand. A million. I couldn't breathe.

Sander.

All I wanted was him. I needed him in ways I would never comprehend.

Every nerve in my body flared in excitement when he pulled me in. His touch heated my skin until I was warm all over. But we weren't close enough. I needed to feel him. I needed...

Gripping his shirt, I ached to feel his bare skin under my fingertips. His kiss deepened, and I nearly exploded. My body spoke to him with a slight whimper.

A primal urge to claim him in my soul raced to the surface. Mine. Sander was mine. The king of night was my soulmate. I hadn't thought much of what that meant to me before, but right then, pieces of my history, our history, fell into place. Tingling magic welcomed me to the kingdom as I fought to keep control of my body while Sander's lips were on mine.

It was all too much, too fast. But I couldn't stop it. I needed more.

He pulled back slightly, resting against my neck. His hot whisper close to my ear made the room sweltering. How was I supposed to live while burning to death under desire? His words made no sense. I couldn't focus.

He said something about an audience. But I was certain we were alone. We were the only people in existence. There was only him.

Except... I was wrong. My flushed skin was probably a crimson red in my cheeks as Jamie and Lara came into view. Looking over Sander's shoulder, I could see that Gabriel, Jen, and even Perseus were there too.

Oh no. There was no way under the sun I could meet their entertained stares now. I'd been practically ready to tear Sander's clothes off in front of them. "That's embarrassing."

Sander said something about consuming me. But it was the way he grinned and winked at me that had me heating up all over again. "But I wouldn't count on it."

I could feel my blush darken. Clearing my throat, I tried to take a step back, but I couldn't. He was like the magnet to my iron heart. "It is so much harder to leave you." I physically was unable to tear myself from him.

Sander rubbed a small circle on my hand. "It is hard for me too."

Everyone tried to make light of our situation. I was sure it was to ease my embarrassment. Still, I knew

Lara, of all people, knew exactly what was going through me right then, and honestly, shame was not at the top. Sander consumed all top places of emotions right then. But knowing she could feel what I felt, maybe embarrassment should be at the top. I clutched my pendant and tried to center myself.

Sander tucked me into his side and guided me off the dais. The room we were in was more like a cave or cavern. Green foliage covered the ceiling and dark walls. The Fores was carved from obsidian. The floor was marble. Wherever we were, it wasn't for the lower class. Torches lined the walls, leading us out through a tunnel.

Sander was calm and confident as we strolled through the black walls into the night air. A surge of energy filled me as we left the tunnel. I gasped. A wisp of white light swirled around my fingers. Sparks of energy flickered like embers of the sun.

I shook my hands, trying to get it off me. "Sander!"

"It's okay," he said, taking my hands in his. He winced slightly. "It's a bit hotter than I expected, but it's okay. Look at me."

I couldn't. All I could do was see the light grow, along with the sparks. "Let go of me. I'll hurt you."

"Emberlynn, you won't hurt me." He smiled this time, though I could feel a slight twinge of pain through our connection. "You have to control it, not let it control you."

"We should have trained more," Jen said. "If you don't want to hurt him, you need to pull it in. Using it up can drain you, and trust me, you don't want that."

"Well, I'm not trying to do anything. It's doing it on its own!" I shook my hands free of Sander and stepped away from him. Tiny sparks flickered to the ground. Black shadows engulfed them as soon as they bounced off the stone path.

"Emberlynn, look at me." Sander's voice was calm but commanding.

My eyes caught his gaze, and I stared right through to his soul. He wasn't scared of me or whatever was happening. If anything, the amusement and pride flowing from our bond overrode any concern he had for me.

I got lost in his gaze. The blue in his eyes rippled like waves. Any breath I tried to draw in was strangled. But I didn't need air. I needed him. My skin flushed as a new heat rolled over me.

Sander's smile widened. "You are incredible, little sun."

His words broke my moment, reeling me back to the present. I wasn't sure why I kept slipping away. I needed to keep focused.

"Ember," Lara cautioned. She gingerly stepped toward me. "Take a slow breath and try to relax. I don't want you to be scared, but I think you're so overwhelmed that the sun is trying to protect you."

"What?" Bringing my hands up, a trail of flame followed. I freaked. They were on fire. I was on fire! White flames were dancing on my skin. "Make it stop! What's happening?"

"Emberlynn, it's okay," Jamie spoke softly. He tried to approach me, but the flames danced higher.

"Stay back." I didn't want to hurt any of them. What was happening? I took another step back inside the tunnel, watching as my flames illuminated the entrance. Panic set in, and I wanted to scream. Everyone moved toward me, but the heat kept them from advancing much farther.

"I didn't think she'd be this strong this fast." Jen's voice sounded far off, but it was the worry lacing her tone that scared me.

"Someone, please tell me what's going on," I pleaded. I wrung my hands, but it did nothing.

The tingle of energy raced across my skin like a thousand ants.

"Ember, you have to calm down. Breathe." Jen stepped into the tunnel with Sander. "I never felt this before. Sander, I don't think she can do this yet. We need someone to train her. I don't know this power."

"It's the sun." He gave me a lopsided grin. "She is the sun."

Her hands went to her hips as she shifted her weight. "Yeah, well, how does the moon teach the sun? Because none of us are from Solis. Her power exceeds almost all of ours."

"Not mine." He stepped closer. His outstretched hand reached for me. "Trust me."

I shook my head. "I don't want to hurt you."

"Trust me," he repeated. His eyes locked with mine, and once again, I was swept off to a reality where it was just him and me.

He grasped my hand. A slight pull on our bond warned me of the pain I caused. I tried to pull back, but his hand tightened around mine. "I said trust me."

"Sander..."

As soon as his name left my lips, we were enveloped by his shadows. The cold tendrils caressed my skin, dousing the flames. A silver image of Sander slipped through the ebony wisps. His ethereal fingers trailed down my face while Sander's tangible arms pulled me in close. It was the first honest look I'd had at his colors, his true self. It was only a glimpse, and then it was gone, but I'd seen him.

"Emberlynn, you are mine. You are the Solis Queen. You rule the night alongside me." The shadows were now so thick they covered us like a second skin. Sander kept whispering in my ear, "There is nothing we cannot do together. Now let the energy pool inside you, hold it. You control it. Harness the sun and let it know you rule over it."

I buried my face in the crook of his neck and squeezed my eyes shut. I could do this. Starting with my fingertips, I pushed the power deep inside, collecting it. It formed under my skin, warming my body. The tingling I now recognized as the flames, or the sun, tried to burst through, but I held it down.

I ruled the sun. I controlled the flames.

Sander's deep voice rumbled in his chest. "That's it. You're doing great." The shadows rolled away, slipping back into the night.

I wasn't sure how long I could wield the sun's energy. How Sander kept the shadows and the moon controlled so effortlessly confounded me. What if I could never do that?

Sander used his thumb under my chin to lift my face. "You will do that. Do not doubt yourself, little sun."

"But you've all had years of experience. I'll never catch up. What if it's too late? What if I've been gone too long?"

"Yes, we have had years. You've had five minutes. It takes time. You'll see. And then I can't wait to see what you can do." He smiled and gave me a quick kiss. "Until then, let's get you settled in the castle before you burn down the gardens. We can begin training tomorrow."

I gasped. "Tomorrow? We just got here." I had hoped to see the kingdom. Maybe take a tour or something.

He nodded. "And knowing how much stronger you are than we thought means you need to learn how to control it. Just like a guard, if you are untrained with a weapon, it is useless to you in war."

"But I'm not a guard. And we aren't at war." Are we? I knew Helios wanted to take the Solis Kingdom, but war?

"Emberlynn, you may not see war the same way we do. The mortals have declared battles as wars, but there is so much more to it. No, we are not going into battle, and if we were, I would not allow you to set foot on the battlegrounds. Not yet. Not untrained. But there has been a war raging for years, and the gods are unhappy. I think they are pushing for unity."

"Is that why we are soulmates? Is this just to appease the gods and their unity?" I swallowed. Not sure I wanted the answer.

"No. We are soulmates because we were created for each other. You are in every way my equal, my other half, my queen. I refuse to let you believe we are only pawns in a war because what I feel for you is something that not even a god could create." He took my hand and placed it over his chest. "My heart only beats for you."

"The sun only shines for you." We needed to move before the world slipped away again. The need to be with him grew each second we stood there declaring our love.

Jen loudly cleared her throat. "Now that you're all calm and not burning, I think I'm gonna help Jamie and Lara settle in."

Sander nodded but kept his eyes on me. "Yes, please do. I will see Emberlynn home. We will see everyone at dinner tonight."

His words created a warmth under my skin. My fingers tingled and stomach tightened.

Sander held out his arm for me to take. I linked mine with his and let him lead me out into the night.

I gasped and stopped. I had been too preoccupied with my self-induced inferno earlier to see the beauty of the Night Kingdom. A massive moon filled the inky black sky. It had to be an illusion. I'd never seen the moon take up such an extensive amount of space. Millions of stars twinkled like diamonds for as far as I could see. Silver dust glistened in the air as it fell from the sky.

"What's that?" I held my hand out to catch the glitter.

"Moondust. It is near the end of the Griatto Season. There are two seasons in this kingdom. Each new moon is celebrated, but not like a season. The moon sheds at the end of the Griatto and Perinian seasons, sending moondust to the kingdom. It keeps this world with magic." He tugged on my arm. "Come, let me show you."

He led me to the edge of the garden that overlooked a city. Lights warmed the windows of almost every home and building. Small cottages dotted the horizon in fairytale fashion.

"Over there," he said, pointing to a group of men and women. They were catching the moondust in glass jars. They each were laughing and smiling, their world utterly unphased by my arrival. Thank goodness. "They take the moondust and use it for baking or to make strong drinks."

"So basically, you all are moon-aholics. Got to get your moon fix in somehow, might as well be in a stiff drink." I tsked but couldn't contain the short giggle.

He grinned. "Wait until you taste it. It is not like anything you've had in the mortal world. And when you consume it, you are filled with a sort of renewed energy."

I shivered. I wasn't sure I wanted any more energy than I already had. I'd probably burst out like a mini sun and spread daylight over his kingdom.

He pulled me with him away from the ledge. "There are many drinks made with the moondust, but my favorite is Slava. Eclipse berries mixed with moondust gives it a bit of a kick."

"Oh, I remember the eclipse berries. They are in that silver drink, right?"

His laughter echoed through the garden. "No, that was moonsliver, and that's made from the moonberries. Eclipse berries are a liquor-filled berry found only here in the Night Kingdom."

We rounded the edge of the garden and fell under a shadow covering the grounds. Looking up, I froze. "Sander."

"What?" He tensed and scanned the area.

"That." I pointed to the castle looming over us. How I hadn't paid it any attention was beyond me. He had said castle before, but I hadn't expected there to be an actual castle with turrets and guards. It was so tall I had to crane my head back to see the top. The black rock looked like dragon scales shielding the massive fortress.

He searched the castle with a fury of concern. "Yes, what's wrong?"

"It's a castle."

His brow furrowed together as he returned his gaze to me. "Yes..."

"An actual castle."

His bright smile lit up his face, giving his eyes a wave of happiness. "I told you I was king, right?"

I stopped gawking at the palace long enough to stick my tongue out at him. "Yes. I know that."

He released a long playful sigh. "Good, because that would be awkward to explain now."

I frowned and rolled my eyes. "I just didn't think it was real. Hearing about it is one thing, but seeing it is another."

What kind of a life was this? Girls didn't just wake up with supernatural powers, a sexy soulmate, and a kingdom to run. They didn't get to live in castles guarded by dragons. Okay, well, there weren't any dragons that I knew of, but... it was still a castle.

Marble stairs gently sloped up, leading us to the massive front doors. The heavy iron doors reached high above our heads, arching into points crowned with black glass. Two guards moved to open the doors, bowing their heads as we approached. As we neared them, a slight shift rippled over each of them. Colors so dark they were practically invisible projected from them. But they weren't entirely men.

I watched, intrigued by the new nature of the colors. Claws, fangs, and solid eyes stood before me, but even the colors bowed.

Sander led me inside, but I turned to look over my shoulder as the guards closed the doors behind us. They were men. But they weren't. "What are they?"

Sander glanced over his shoulder. "The guards?"

I stopped to peer at the door suspiciously, almost hoping one of their ghosts would come through so I could see them again. "Yeah. Their colors were... well, they were different. They weren't exactly men."

Sander grunted in agreement. "They are guards. Many are formed after the night. Immortals aren't human."

"But you don't look different." I had only seen his colors in a fleeting moment, but he was most definitely a man. I didn't need a ghost to tell me that much.

I felt him tug playfully on our bond. "Ah, but we are from the gods. We were created in their image."

"And they weren't?" I was beginning to feel more inadequate about being in the kingdoms. There was so much I didn't know–or understand. This was a whole new world, and I was nothing more than a stranger.

"There are some who are made from the kingdom in which they serve. They are born just like you and me, a creation of two soulmates, but they are bound to the kingdom in a way that... alters them. They chose this life, knowing they will never have a soulmate." Sander picked up my wrist and kissed my mark. His lips were soft on my skin.

Already my mind began to get fuzzy, wanting to fall into the delicious desires, but I wasn't sure I was strong enough to pull out of it again. "Wait, so they have to choose between love and sacrificing their soul to become... whatever they are?"

He rubbed small circles over my palm with his thumb. His eyes glazed over with a longing that matched my own. "It is not a bad thing, little sun."

I had a hard time catching my breath enough to form words. "But you never... you never chose that?"

His mouth curved into a sullen grin. "No. I didn't have to. As a direct descendant of the Lux line, I am already bound to the kingdom. I was forced to wait for you." His thumb moved up to trace my mark. "You see, every immortal soul has to be bound to either a mate or their kingdom. After so long, they are forced to choose. Many are happy to bind their soul to the kingdom."

I tried to swallow, but my throat tightened. "Would you have chosen it? To tie your soul to the kingdom instead of me?"

"Hmm." His face contorted as if the memory he sought was painful. "At one time, I wanted to. It is a lonely existence when your soul is missing its other half. I thought I was being tortured by the gods. But you were worth the wait." He looked up. "I'd wait a thousand years for you."

The way he stared at me had the sun's energy rushing back to the surface, but I shoved it back down before I burst into flames again. Tucking my hair behind my ear, I turned from him. The entry was massive. Two statues faced each other on either side of the hall. They were almost angelic, with strong black wings made of iron. Their stern stone faces held a sense of confidence, almost daring us to pass them. Just like the guards' ghosts outside, they had sharp claws. I went to them, drawn to their dark beauty. "What are these supposed to be? Angels?"

"No." His slight chuckle filled the room as he swept over to me. "They are my personal guardians." He touched the shoulder of one of them. It was about half a foot taller than Sander, but honestly, they looked equally menacing. I had seen Sander fight already and knew he wasn't weak.

"Personal guardians?"

"Each ruler has a set of guardians to look over them. It is probably more of a myth than anything, but anything you give energy to is bound to carry some truth. These have been with my family since the beginning of the kingdom."

"Family heirlooms, got it." I ran a finger down the stiff, long, bird-like feather of one. "Do I have any hand-me-down guardians?"

He nodded. "If they haven't been removed, they would be in your castle, watching over your kingdom."

I sighed. "And you believe that?" It was hard to think anything, or anyone would be watching over anything that was mine. Let alone a castle or kingdom.

He closed the space between us. His hand gently caressed my cheek. "You are still here. You aren't dead. You have been saved for a purpose, Emberlynn. I think I am beginning to trust the gods know more than I want to credit them for. Even if it was a slight possibility that your guardians had anything to do with you surviving, I would build altars."

I coughed and sputtered through a mocking laugh. "If they helped me survive, they were not very good."

"Ah, but you are alive, so I disagree." He held his arm out for me. "Come on, let me show you your room."

I was surprised to see people walking around the castle as if this were an everyday thing. The one thing I noticed was their clothing. Everyone wore black or red. Though no one mentioned anything, I felt out of place walking past them in my jeans and a short-sleeved shirt.

Even Sander had on his regular black pants and a matching button-down shirt. I had always thought he just liked black, but now I saw it was more than that.

Just like the guards, everyone we passed bowed. A few women giggled and whispered as we walked away, but I didn't know a woman who wouldn't be infatuated with Sander.

Each hall put us deeper into the heart of the castle. I lost count of the turns we took and almost tripped when I saw the staircase. The wide stairs wound up in a circle to the upper floor. But it was the light from the moon filling in through the strange glass dome-like ceiling that captured my attention. We were truly in the middle of the massive palace. I leaned back to look up at least five floors.

"This is incredible." The moonlight spilled down through the center of the staircase. I walked under it, letting it fill me with peace. Tipping my head back, I closed my eyes and soaked it up.

Sander took my hand and wrapped his arm around my middle, pulling me to him. Slowly, he began to move us in a circle. It took me a moment to understand he wanted to dance with me. My feet stumbled as I tried to move with him. He shook his head. "Trust me."

"I trust you, but I can't dance."

He tucked my hand over his chest. "Feel me. Go through our bond and find me."

Closing my eyes once again, I let myself fall into Sander's embrace. His steady breathing and small movements relaxed me. It wasn't hard to feel his soul intertwined with mine. It seemed we were already dancing. Taking a ragged breath, I took a step with him. It was fluid, and I felt him.

Under the moonlight, he twirled me around. My body moved with his just like that first day we met. Like magnets, I moved where he moved. The push and pull between us created tickling energy that ran barely under my skin, causing me to shiver. I laughed and fell out of step, only for Sander to catch me.

Dipping me low, he whispered in my ear, "I love hearing you laugh."

Then, all too soon, he swung me up and had me standing once again, but his arms held me steady, not letting me falter or fall.

"Well, after that, I'm not sure any room in this place can compete. I think this is my favorite spot."

"We'll see about that." Pulling me by the hand, he rushed to the staircase.

Laughing, we ran up the steps. More people stopped what they were doing to watch us down the hall before bowing their heads as we passed. Sander ignored them all and kept dashing through the halls to the end of the second main passage. The corridor was dark, lit by three black glass chandeliers. Two sets of doors were framed in iron next to each other. He stopped at the first set.

"This is your room. At least until we are married." He pushed open the doors and stepped aside for me.

"Are you serious?" The room was almost as big as the entire second floor of the Knight's house. Maybe bigger.

Unlike the rest of the castle, this room was white with intricate gold accents painted along the molding. The brightness sent a thrill of excitement through me. Sheer curtains floated in the breeze behind open drapes. A private balcony looked over the city of Astraios.

Fresh flowers filled a vase on the vanity. A plush stool welcomed me to sit in front of it. The light from the crystal chandelier reflected off the dressing mirror.

An enormous platform bed with a cushioned headboard sat upon a raised dais. Suspended from the ceiling with an elaborate dentil molding, white drapes with gold suns embroidered along the edges hung over the head of the bed like a crown. Tasseled tiebacks held the long material together. One tug from the ties would have the bed hiding from view—and the people in it. I touched the soft fabric, letting it glide between my fingers. "You did this for me?"

He leaned casually against the door frame, watching me. "The Solis Queen deserves to have her kingdom represented while in the Night Kingdom."

"How? When?"

He crossed his arms and smiled. "Right after we touched."

"What's behind those doors?" I pointed to the double doors across the room from the bed.

He coolly walked to them, flinging them open. "It is my room."

I tried, but I couldn't keep the blush from creeping up my neck and face. We'd slept in the same room many nights, the same bed even, but this felt... more intimate.

His room was equally dark and beautiful. Exactly how I imagined the Night King's bedroom to look. Charcoal-colored walls with gold trim complemented the dark marbled flooring. The four-poster bed had sheer black material encasing it, with each section tied off to a post. It wasn't hard to imagine Sander stretched out on the down bedding. I could see his shadows curling up next to him, watching over him while he slept.

My heart rate picked up as I ventured closer to the bed. He snuck up behind me, reaching his hand around on the flat of my stomach. He nuzzled my neck and pulled me back to him. "Perhaps showing you my room was a mistake."

"Oh?" I tried to play coy, but I wasn't fooling either of us. I pressed my back harder into him, knowing I couldn't get close enough to satisfy the craving I had for him. Being in the Night Kingdom only intensified it.

"I'm tempted to lock the door and christen every inch of this room with you."

"Then why don't you?" I wouldn't stop him. I probably wanted it more than him.

"Because you deserve to have everything, including a wedding night." He twirled me around to face him. "But then, little sun, there will be no leaving this room." His lips crashed down on mine in the same heated passion that consumed me.

My legs shook and began to buckle under me. I was so weak all I could do was hold on to Sander and hope for him to change his mind.

SEVEN

Emberlynn

SANDER WAS SUMMONED to Night duties, leaving me alone in my room. It felt strange to be so isolated from everyone. At least back home, I could roam the house freely. But here, I would get lost. And I wasn't sure I was even allowed to leave. I wasn't a prisoner, but I'd grown up changing homes, always trying to predict the rules. Never assume. That had gotten me in trouble a few times.

I could only pace so long before I grew tired of waiting. The balcony beckoned me. Flinging open the glass doors, a rush of fresh air greeted me. I inhaled long and slow. A sweet citrus scent drifted on the breeze. It was still dark out. The moon hardly moved across the sky since we'd arrived.

My soul pinged for a moment missing the sun. How long would it be before I could bask in its warmth again?

Closing my eyes, I let the moon's energy fill me. I could almost feel Sander's touch. The Night Kingdom truly was his. I felt him everywhere.

A soft knock on the door had me turning back inside. A petite woman entered, carrying a stack of packages. She gave a small curtsey and smiled broadly. "My king has finally found his mate. It is a good day for our kingdom. I am Clearie, and I will be your court lady while you are here."

"Um, thank you?" I wasn't sure what I was supposed to say. However, I was sure thank you wasn't correct. Ugh. Where was Jen or Lara to help me?

She held out the wrapped parcels. "These are from our king."

"Thank you," I said again, taking the boxes. "I'm Emberlynn."

"I know who you are." She smiled. "The rightful Solis Queen. However, some might argue your title. You've been gone a long time, and some have worked to gain your kingdom for their own."

I couldn't decipher if she was warning me or threatening me. "And where do you stand?"

"With my king, who stands with you." She bowed her head and backed out of the room. "Dinner will be in thirty minutes. If you need help washing or dressing, let me know."

I wasn't sure what a court lady was, but I didn't need her to dress me like a child. That was just strange. I set the packages on the foot of the bed. "I think I can manage, but thanks."

"As you wish."

I waited for her to close the door and listened to make sure she was gone before opening the first box.

Lifting the lid, I let it fall to the ground. My jaw dropped as I pulled out a sequined black dress. "Wow."

Did she say dinner was in thirty minutes? Was I supposed to wear this dress?

Quickly I opened the next box. A pair of strappy heels were carefully placed under the tissue. I could hardly open the last box. The ribbon was tied almost too tightly. A note was under the lid.

My little sun,

Come to dinner as my queen. I can't wait to see you light up the room.

Sander

I placed the note on the side table to keep and then finished unwrapping the contents of the package. A diamond crown sat nestled on black satin.

I gasped.

A crown.

It wasn't like the one in my bedroom covered in blood back in the mortal realm. This one was gold set with ash diamonds. Tiny stones lined the base that mirrored my engagement ring.

The box suddenly weighed a thousand pounds. The reality that Sander is a king was real. He'd always simply been Sander. Relaxed, calm, confident, secure...

The energy around me shifted as I forced myself to sit on the bed. If I didn't, I was afraid I'd pass out and fall to the floor.

Each breath came short and fast as I stared at the crown.

A tiny spark flew from my hand, and I quickly pushed the energy back down.

I was in the Night Kingdom. I wasn't in the earthly realm anymore. My soulmate was a king. I was expected to be a queen.

Bending over, I dropped the box and tried to focus on my breathing.

"Are you okay? What's wrong?" Sander's voice came to me stronger than I'd ever heard before. It was as if he was in the same room.

I shook my head even though he couldn't see me. "You're a king."

I could almost hear his slight chuckle. "I thought we established this. What's wrong? Are you hurt?"

"No, I just... I can't breathe." It was too much. For months he talked about this, but now that it was here, I didn't know what to do. I should've paid more attention, asked more questions, trained more. I think I somehow didn't believe everyone fully. It was a fairytale that was now a reality.

"I'm on my way."

"No," I said aloud, shaking my head again and picking up the box. "I'm fine." It was a lie. We both knew it. But I had to do this. If I was to be a queen, I needed to be able to at least get dressed for dinner without help.

He didn't say anything more, but I could feel him tugging on our bond. He left himself open for me, alert and attentive.

Making sure my door was locked, I stripped off all my clothes and tossed them in a pile near the bed.

I rushed to the shared bathroom between Sander's and my room to do my best to freshen up. I didn't have time for a shower. I stopped at the counter and looked at the faucet. How did I turn it on? The basin was deep with a bronze spout but no knobs.

Using my connection with Sander, I whispered, hoping I wasn't interrupting anything important. "How do I turn the water on?"

His lighthearted chuckle echoed in my head. "Use your foot to press the pedals."

Pedals? At my feet, there were three bronze levers barely under the cabinet. It didn't take much pressure to open the floodwaters into the basin. Left was instantly scalding hot, the middle was pleasantly warm, and on the right, it was frigid.

Now that was something the mortals were missing out on.

A massive clawfoot tub beckoned me from the corner, but I didn't have time to enjoy it yet. But maybe tonight... Yeah, tonight I would make time for a long bath.

The water felt good as I washed up, cleaning the mortal realm off my skin. Everything felt new. Including me.

Darting from the room, I slipped on the dress. It had spaghetti straps and zipped up the side discreetly with a low v-cut in the front bodice, accentuating my breast and showing off my pendant. The dress billowed out around me, touching the floor with a slit on the right side all the way to my thigh.

Taking up the bench at the vanity, I slid on the heels and then stared at my reflection. I was a bit flushed, but oddly I had a soft glow. Inspecting the drawers, I found several hair accessories and pulled out a brush. Running it through my hair, I decided to leave it down.

"Before I forget," Sander's voice filled my head once again. A playful lilt laced his words. "I have selected a guard to escort you to dinner. I will meet you there."

"I guess it's the guard's lucky night. Getting to be the first person to see me in this dress should be a privilege," I teased back.

"You are correct. Perhaps I should order him to cut out his eyes first?"

It was a challenge. I felt his frisky banter through the bond. "Hum, just have him lower his eyes. No need to torture the poor man."

"I am unsure how I feel about you worrying about another man."

I laughed. "Don't you have work to do? I have to finish getting ready."

His laugh flowed through our connection, and I smiled.

Turning, I looked over at the package still on the bed. With a long breath, I crossed the room and took the crown from its box.

"I guess this is it." Placing the crown on my head, I twirled around to the mirror.

The woman I saw was not the same girl I knew yesterday. Nor was it the girl who grew up in foster care. But was I enough to be with Sander?

A knock on the door startled me, interrupting my thoughts. I guess it was time.

Opening the door, a young man bowed to me. Well, I suppose he could have been hundreds of years old, but he didn't look older than me. At least his colors weren't jumping out at me.

"My Favored." He stood upright, and his mouth fell agape for a moment before he recovered and gestured for me to come out into the hall with him. "I am here to escort you to dinner."

I was a bit disappointed Sander wasn't the one to walk with me, but I supposed he had to get back to taking care of his kingdom. I wondered how long he would be. I nodded and stepped out into the hall.

My escort shut the door to my room and stood to my right. "Shall we?"

"We shall." It felt weird pretending to be so formal. The only etiquette I'd been taught was when I was little and watched The Princess Diaries. Oh, how I understood that character more than ever now.

My escort didn't say anything more as we walked. He kept about two feet between us and let me lead by a step–which wasn't smart. I had no clue where we were going. We passed about two hallways before I slowed down.

"My Favored, are you alright?"

I stopped entirely and scrunched my face as I turned to him. "What?"

His look of concern was a bit comical. "Are you alright?"

I waved him off. "Yeah, I got that. What did you call me? You called me that before. What does it mean?"

His head cocked slightly as he processed my request. "My Favored. It is a respectful title for my king's soulmate."

I dropped my shoulders. "Well, I haven't heard that one before. Where I come from, Her Majesty is set aside for a queen."

His head flinched back slightly. "Would you prefer Her Majesty? I meant no disrespect."

"Oh, no! I don't want that at all." I wrinkled my nose over the idea of being called Her Majesty. The thought left a bitter taste in my mouth. I felt more like an imposter with every second we debated my title. "I was only commenting. Everything here will take some time for me to get used to. I should have expected titles and words to be different too."

"I suppose it would be different." He looked around nervously. "We should continue on. My king's orders were to escort you safely to dinner and not converse with you in the hallways." He leaned forward slightly. "It could be seen as improper."

"Then lead the way." I lifted my hands to show him I was ready to follow. "Seriously, lead the way. I have no idea where I'm going."

His smile widened. "I will take you."

Following close behind him, we wound our way through the castle. Downstairs he stopped at a set of floor-to-ceiling double doors. He gripped the iron handles and pulled them open.

I froze in my spot. I was not prepared for this. I couldn't do this. I wanted to run back to the safety and seclusion of my room, but I knew I would never find it alone.

A long table filled the room. There had to be at least fifty people around the table, all standing to get a look at me. Gasps and whispers followed their stares. Colors started to spring out from each guest. I forgot how to swallow, and the lump in my throat grew.

"I can't," I whispered to no one.

Sander's mental touch caressed my thoughts. Excited pride flowed through our bond.

I backed up a few steps.

More whispers slipped through the air while everyone watched me. A few auras braved getting closer to the door, but none left the room.

"Emberlynn." Sander's voice grabbed me. He rounded the corner and slid his hand to the small of my back. "You look exquisite."

There was no denying the heat radiating between us. I had seen Sander in a sort of business casual for months but was not prepared to see him like this. The magnetic pull I had to him clicked into place, and all I wanted was to touch him.

Head to toe black, with a long jacket. Small, black intricate phases of the moon were embroidered along the collar. His top shirt under the coat had silver latches acting as buttons.

An obsidian crown encircled his head. A single dark diamond, like the ones on mine, was set in the front. A swirl of shadows danced inside of it.

The darkness of his attire made the blue of his eyes stand out even more. His approving stare as he openly admired me locked me in place.

I could feel the heat in my cheeks as I blushed. He cocked a lopsided grin. "Little sun, I do believe you approve."

"Very much." I took a step to the side, barely letting the slit in the dress reveal my leg. "And you? Do you approve?"

"More than you could ever know." He held his arm out for me to take. "Let me show you off."

I gulped and remembered where we were. Everyone was still standing, waiting for us to enter.

"Sander..." The colors were still mingling throughout the room, but even they stopped to stare.

He tucked me in close to his side. "I'm right here with you."

I looked up at him, trusting him to keep me standing and not falling on my face in front of everyone. "Don't let me go."

"Never."

He led me into the room, and everyone bowed their heads. All too soon, the buzz and energy in the room grew, and with it, voices muddled together as everyone began talking at once. A plump man with an oddly trimmed mustache and beard eyed me eagerly before bravely walking up to us. I found it hard not to study the sharp points to his beard. He wore completely black attire that was better suited in the eighteenth century.

"My king." He bowed. His mouth pursed as if he bit his tongue to keep from speaking more.

"Alred, it is good to see you. I hope you've been fairing well during my absence." Sander's arm tightened around me. "I am pleased to introduce my soulmate tonight. Emberlynn Cyrus."

Alred kept his eyes focused on Sander. "It is an honor to have been introduced to my king's soulmate."

The pride and love rushing through our bond made the room spin. It was all too much for me. Heat surged under my skin, seeking a way out. I worried I wouldn't be able to contain the flames and I'd make a spectacle of myself as a flaming inferno.

"Just breathe. I've got you." Sander's voice calmed my mind.

Before I could fake a smile at Alred, Sander had me whisked off to meet other guests. Though I wasn't sure meeting them was the correct term. It was frustrating to be sought after but ignored. No one actually spoke to me.

He stopped at a woman who reminded me of Jen with nearly white hair. But her eyes were not like diamonds. They were dark brown. She grinned at me but quickly averted to Sander and bowed her head. "My king."

Sander greeted her. "Hali, it is good to see you."

A man with equally white hair emerged from the crowd. "My king." He bowed. His green aura popped out from his body to mimic the gesture. "Hali and I were thrilled you found your soulmate. This is a big night for the kingdom."

I was right here and yet... nothing.

Sander managed a quick side smile for me. "Remember, it is out of respect they don't speak to you unless permitted. I'm allowing them a great honor to be introduced to you but to remember their place. Our crowns aren't just for show, little sun."

I tried to contain the plastered-on grin for Hali and who I assumed was her mate. Being royal was something I had to learn; it obviously wasn't common sense. Rules, etiquette, speech… it all was so foreign.

Sander held his head high, his shoulders squared. "Thank you, Jepp. This night has been a long time coming. Seeing the kingdom rejoice with me is uplifting."

Jepp had a wandering eye that kept rolling toward the table. I wondered if he was born that way or was injured in some previous battle. I tried to picture Jepp, scrawny, lanky, and freckled in a fight. Try as I might, I had to think of something else for fear of laughing out loud. He was nothing like the warrior-king standing at my side. But then, I was certain no one could ever measure up to my soulmate.

Jepp scratched his bare chin. "Have you heard from Sal?" His spirit sidestepped to get closer to me but watched Sander cautiously.

A slight twitch in Sander's jaw ticked. "Now is not the time to talk about Sal or Ingrim. But rest assured I am being kept well informed."

Jepp lowered his gaze. "Forgive me, my king." His aura fell back and hid behind him.

Sander clapped a hand on the man's shoulder. "Enjoy the evening, Jepp." Leading me away, he released a long breath. "I worried someone would want to talk about Sal tonight."

"Who is Sal?"

He kept walking around the table. "He's a council member that went missing about a week ago. Ingrim went searching for him, but nothing yet, and now there's been no communication with him either."

After what felt like an hour, we'd met almost everyone in the room. My feet ached and begged for me to sit down. Court members and other essential kingdom citizens were introduced to me, though not a single permission to speak to me was granted. It was a long evening, but I had to admit not having to speak pretending I had a dignified air about me was lovely. Sander finally bypassed the last few lingering guests and went straight to the head of the table, where two empty chairs remained.

Jamie and Lara were there, and Jen and Gabriel. I almost ran to them. I was glad they were there. At least not everyone was a stranger.

Sander pulled out the chair on the left for me. I was the first to sit, which felt weird. But Sander quickly filled the chair next to me. Once he was seated, everyone around the table took their seats.

Lara was closest to me. She reached over and gave my hand a gentle squeeze. "You're doing great."

I leaned in to whisper back, "I feel like fainting."

She gave me a sad smile. "I know. Just keep breathing. It's a lot, but after tonight it should be easier."

"You don't have a room full of people and ghosts staring at you."

"No, but they are staring because you are beautiful. When you walked into the room, I almost didn't recognize you. You wear that crown well." She gave my hand a pat. "I'm proud of you."

Sitting back up, I noticed Jen giving me two thumbs up. She mouthed, "Oh, yeah."

I couldn't contain the smirk as I stifled a laugh. She looked stunning in her red dress. Her long, almost white hair hung in curls tonight. She'd applied a shade of lipstick to match her dress and a thick coat of mascara to lengthen her lashes. She didn't need a crown to look like a queen. I pointed back at her and mouthed, "Hot."

She grinned and elbowed Gabriel. "See? She thinks I'm hot."

Gabriel shrugged. "Am I supposed to be jealous? Because I am not. I am proud that my mate draws the attention of anyone, including a queen."

Jen rolled her eyes. "You might change your mind."

I smiled and let my gaze leave my friends to venture down the table. I had met most of them, but I wasn't sure I'd remember their names. I leaned toward Sander so I could speak to only him. "Who are all these people?"

"They make up some of my court. They are who have been helping take care of the kingdom while I was away." He picked up his glass and took a sip. "This dinner is to show off my soulmate, their future queen, the Solis Queen. But it is also to say thank you. I owe them a great deal of gratitude for stepping up for so long."

A ping of regret settled in my stomach. It was because of me he was away so long. I had selfish desires to stay in the mortal realm and graduate high school. And he stayed. He left an entire kingdom just so I could achieve one small, measly, human dream. It didn't mean as much to me now that I knew how much he put off letting me accomplish it. And not once did he act resentful to me for it.

Sander took my hand and held it tight under the table. "Little sun, remember that our world is not the same as the mortal world. There is not a person here who despises caring for the kingdom. It was an honor. And I would have stayed away longer had it been safe to do so. I wanted you to adjust to the kingdoms before throwing you in, but the decision to come was made for us. I refuse to let Helios have you. I can protect you better here."

I nodded but honestly felt worse. Looking at all the people, I realized I wasn't one of them. I might not ever be. I felt like a peasant in a costume, trying to trick everyone into believing I belonged there.

Sander dropped my hand to slide his up through the slit in my dress, coming to rest on my bare thigh, right above my knee. It was the most intimate gesture he'd ever done. My heart sped up. His thumb traced tiny circles on my skin, making me hot all over.

"I think I like this dress," he teased through our connection.

With his hand so close to the very place that ached for him, I couldn't focus or form words. It took all I had to keep the sun's energy from blowing up the entire castle.

Lara took a drink and sputtered. A tinge of pink flushed her cheeks.

Great. She probably felt everything right now.

Sander's hand never moved higher, but the heat from his hand burned all the way to my soul.

All too soon, he stopped and stood. "Thank you all for coming tonight. It has been too long since we've all gathered for dinner."

There wasn't a soul there who didn't give Sander their utmost attention.

He looked down at me and smiled. "As you know, after many years, I have found my soulmate. She is everything I had ever hoped for in a mate. The fact that she is the rightful Solis Queen should not go unnoticed. For eighteen years, we thought she was lost to us. We will reunite her with her kingdom and then unite our kingdoms for the first time since the divide."

A resounding excitement was muttered all around the table. Many nodded their heads, while some lifted their glass to bear their congratulations.

"Emberlynn Dawn Cyrus is the Solis Queen and my soulmate. She is the future Night Queen." He gestured for me to stand, so I did, hating the attention. Everyone else stood too. With fists held tightly closed, they each pressed them to their foreheads and bowed.

Even the ghosts had fists pressed against their heads.

Gabriel gave me a subtle nod before doing the same.

I turned to Jamie and Lara, who stood with their fists and tears in their eyes.

I gripped Sander's hand. "What is going on?"

"It is an ancient form of respect, one rarely given." He cast a loving gaze down at me before joining them.

"Sander, don't." I turned to the table, wanting to scream at them to stop. "Then why waste it on me? They don't even know me."

He lowered his fist, and then like dominos, all down the table, hands dropped back down to their sides. "You are a symbol of hope. For too long, we have been divided."

"But why me?" I took a step back, shaking my head. My gaze flickered between Jamie and Lara, then back to Sander. "You should have told me. It's been six months. Not once has this been brought up."

"Ember," Jamie said quietly. "We weren't sure how the people would react. It wasn't until this afternoon we understood how strongly your arrival to the kingdom affected them."

Smiling faces looked my way. A few had hopeful expressions I hadn't understood before. I still didn't.

Sander took his seat and tugged on my hand to sit too. "Almost nineteen years ago, we all lost so much. Many of us lost family, friends... some lost their homes, their kingdoms. There are some here tonight who sought refuge in the Night Kingdom after Helios began killing his opposers. They have been separated from their families. They haven't returned home for fear they will reveal a loved one's true support. Afraid they will die upon seeing their kingdom."

Tears welled in my eyes. "You told me it might not be safe to go to Solis. You said we had to find out who still supported the Cyrus line or who followed Helios. I just didn't think it was that bad."

He twisted to look at me, resting an arm on the table. "I wanted to wait for the right time to divulge more. I didn't want to put too much on you too fast."

Since arriving here, everything has been too much, too fast. Why would this be anything different? "But you should have. If that's my rightful place, my kingdom, my people, then I should have known. We wasted months."

His fingers teased the stem of his glass. "Emberlynn, answer honestly. Would you have been ready to lead an army to war and go marching into a foreign kingdom even three months ago?"

"No." I removed my hand from his and folded them in my lap. "But I still can't help but feel you set me up tonight. Don't do that again."

A flood of regret poured through our bond. I focused the energy bubbling under the surface to block it. To block him.

Then, like nothing happened, a swarm of men and women filled the room, serving dinner plates to every guest. My stomach rumbled in anticipation. I hadn't thought about how hungry I was since arriving this morning.

A soft murmur of conversation hummed down the table, but those closest to me were quiet.

I picked up my crystal glass that looked like a medieval goblet. Moonsliver. Taking a sip, I decided that I would indulge in the Night drink. I wasn't sure if I should be celebrating with them, but they were happy, and they were Sander's people.

The bubbly liquid felt cool down my throat. I sputtered only a little before setting the glass down. "You said it was near the end of the Griatto Season. Aside from collecting moondust, is there anything else people do to celebrate?"

A slow smile lifted Sander's lip. "Yes, at the end of each season on the new moon, there is a festival. The end of Griatto and the beginning of the Perinian season is called Night Fall. There is a ceremony and then a masquerade."

"It is so much fun." Jen practically bounced in her seat. "I'm so glad we are back in time to celebrate."

Sander leaned in. "Jen is the one in charge of the ball."

"Somehow, that doesn't surprise me." I flashed her a smile.

"You can help me!" She clapped her hands together.

"Oh, I don't think so. That is not my area of expertise. The last grand ball I threw flopped terribly." I tried to take another drink, but watching her confused expression made it nearly impossible to swallow without spitting it all over the table. "I'm just teasing, Jen. I haven't planned any dances."

She stuck her tongue out at me. "Being raised mortal was equally terrible and fascinating. I can't imagine not ever attending a Night Fall or Morning Court."

"What is Morning Court?" I asked. The food on my plate resembled that weird bird-fish thing at Moonstone. I really hoped that wasn't what it was.

Jamie picked up a roll and slathered it in butter. "Morning Court is when the Perinian season ends. It's about a week after Scurradiem."

I followed suit, deciding that bread was probably safer than the meat at this point. "So, basically, it's your New Year's celebration, but with a new moon and season?"

He shrugged. "Kind of, yeah."

I tore a piece of the roll off but paused halfway to my mouth. "When is Night Fall?"

"One more week," Jen said, scooping up a forkful of food.

One week? The wheels in my head started rolling faster, spitting the words out before I could stop them. "What if... What if we got married during Night Fall? I mean, is that allowed?"

Jamie spat out his bite and coughed, grabbing his glass to chug the silvery drink.

"Oh!" Jen's eyes widened.

The phantom beat of Sander's heart raced beside mine. "Little sun, anything is possible if it is what you want." He took my hands in his. "Are you sure?"

"Wait," Jamie coughed. He thumped his chest. "Wait. That's so soon."

Lara rubbed his back. "It's okay."

"But..." Jamie's shoulders drooped. "It's just fast."

Sander's hand slipped back to my leg and gave me a gentle squeeze. "You know Emberlynn and I cannot wait much longer. Being here has intensified everything, including our bond. Honestly, I'm not sure how to survive a week without giving in to my soul. Had we stayed in the mortal world a few more months, maybe. But not here."

Especially if he kept touching me like that.

Jamie stared down at his unfinished roll. "I know."

I glanced at Lara, worried I might have hurt Jamie or her. She gave me a subtle shake of her head and a quick smile. "Dear, you are like a sad little puppy. If I recall, we only made it a...."

His head shot up, and he placed a finger to her lips. "Okay, I get it. No need to tell everyone how impatient I was."

Jamie's translucent rainbow-colored ghost came out to meet Lara's. It swept hers up and twirled her around. Their souls were dancing again. Seeing that gave me a sense of comfort.

He looked at me and smiled. "Alright, kiddo. It looks like tonight we have one more thing to celebrate."

I released a long breath and turned to my soulmate. "So, Night Fall?"

He picked up my wrist and kissed it. "Night Fall."

EIGHT

Sander

LAST NIGHT DIDN'T GO exactly as I'd planned. In some ways, it was even better, but the part where I caught Emberlynn off guard went so wrong. I didn't know they were going to salute her, especially like that. It had been years since I'd seen that kind of unity.

All morning I tried to focus on issues in the kingdom and how to assess the Solis Trejan, but my mind was with my mate. I kept checking our link to make sure she hadn't blocked me again. I worried I'd upset her too much and didn't know what to do to fix it.

I gave her space last night, even though it killed me. Even though she set a date for our union, I knew she was still mad at me. Honestly, I would have ordered everyone to pull off a wedding last night had she wanted it.

Leaving my study, I went in search of Emberlynn. I wanted to see how her training was going and take her out to see the city afterward. Following our bond wasn't hard. She was wide open and using a lot of energy. I knew she was with Gabriel and Jen.

Lights flickered down the halls. I passed Clearie barely leaving the laundry hall. She did a quick curtsy as she fussed and frowned at the lights. "They've been doing it all morning. Everything on this side of the castle is on the fritz. Blasted sun and all, I can't even get all my chores done since the electricity keeps going off."

I chuckled and touched her shoulder. The woman was probably the oldest in the castle. She was around when my grandmother was born. "I'll take care of it."

She let out a harumph and continued down the hall.

"Again," Jen demanded, her voice floating loud and clear from the weapons room.

"You know, this is borderline abuse." Emberlynn's irritation rippled out to me.

Calling the shadows to me, I let them consume me, keeping me hidden near the open doorway. Emberlynn was mesmerizing. I would have to thank Clearie for getting her the very form-fitting training outfit later.

I watched as my soulmate created a white flame in her palm and then closed her hand, extinguishing it. She opened her other hand, and the fire jumped to life. She tossed them up and caught them in her other hand before they disappeared.

The surge of pride filling my chest swelled to the rest of my body. Mine. She was mine. The woman could wield the sun and hold the moon.

She stopped and looked right where I stood. "If you're going to spy on me, at least attempt to keep your thoughts to yourself."

I let the shadows fall from me and walked toward her. "I wasn't spying. I was admiring."

She grinned and reached out for me. Her fingers were still hot, but it was worth it to feel her touch. A tendril of black wrapped around our hands, caressing her with cold shadows.

Her eyes closed, and she tipped her head back. "That feels so good."

The tender hollow of her neck pleaded with me to kiss it. My lips grazed her flesh until I felt her tremble under me. My soul screamed her name.

Jen snapped her fingers next to us. "One week. You can manage one week, can't you? But right now, it's my turn with her. She has to train."

I held my hands up and took a step back. "My apologies." I winked at Emberlynn. "I'll simply have to admire you from over there."

I left her with Jen to stand with Gabriel. "What's with the water?"

He picked up the metal bucket next to him. "This?"

I raised a brow.

He laughed. "For your soulmate." He pointed at a few burn marks along the room. "She is worried she will not be able to stop the flames."

Folding my arms, I leaned against the back wall. "Has she been able to control them all?"

"So far. She is determined." He elbowed me. "But with you in here, she might be distracted."

Jen placed her hands on her hips and groaned. "Ember, you have to control it before it even leaves you. There can't be a moment it doesn't know who commands it."

Emberlynn flung her hand, trying to rid herself of another flame. "I'm trying. This is a lot different here than back home. I only felt the tingle of magic, I didn't have fire shooting from my hands there." The flame danced up her arm. She groaned and then yelled. "Stupid fire magic."

I pursed my lips together to keep from chuckling. I shouldn't find it so amusing.

The flame disappeared, and she stomped back to the middle of the room. "It's starting to hurt."

That made my stomach twist. Instinctively, I tensed. The need to protect her at all costs, even from herself, gripped me from deep inside. "That's enough for today."

She shook her head. "No, I just need to cool off. Jen's right. I have to learn how to control it."

"Not if it's hurting you."

"No pain, no gain, right?" She flung her hands out in front of her. "I can't stop. I've wasted enough time on myself."

I knew this stemmed from last night but had to get her to realize it wasn't worth risking her life. "Emberlynn, the people know you aren't going to be ready overnight. It takes time."

Her eyes snapped to me. "We don't have time, Sander. You, of all people, know that. You're the one who kept that from me."

A sizzle of her energy spread through our link. I felt it hum under my skin. She watched me as she pushed harder. When I called the shadows and used the moon's powers, it felt dark and cold. But this... this was hot and bright. She raised a brow and cocked her head. "How about we train together."

Her challenge wasn't voiced, but I heard it. She needed a release, and I was the only one who could take it. I summoned the shadows to stand by in case we needed to cool her off. "Together."

A white flame danced in her cupped hand. She pulled her arm back and threw the fire my way. It was faster than I anticipated, but I caught it without taking my eyes off her. Seizing the flame, it flickered and singed my skin. I wouldn't throw it back. I would take them from her. I would take everything she threw at me if it helped her.

Shadows swirled up from the floor and doused the flame, cooling my hand.

Again, she threw another flame at me. I didn't look at anything but her. Catching the fire was easy. She turned and threw another and then another right after.

She didn't stop but began throwing them around the room. She was fast, but I was faster. Dodging the fire while catching each one before it could touch anything became a game between us.

The more she threw, the more the protective energy inside of me awakened fully, and I knew this was hurting her. She was letting it out... all of it. I had to stop her. I tried to move closer, but she continued to fling fire from her fingers. Tears wet her cheeks.

"Emberlynn." I held my hands up, showing her I was done.

She slumped to the ground crying. Her skin was red but not blistered. She was only flushed from the heat of the sun's energy.

Rushing to her, the shadows followed and wrapped around us, using their icy fingers to cool her off. I picked her up and placed her in my lap. She buried her face in my chest and sobbed.

"Shhh." I ran my hand through her hair and down her back. "Shhh, little sun. I've got you."

"I'm sorry." Her words were mumbled as she sucked back another sob.

"For what?"

"I just... I just needed to get it out of me." She hiccupped and cried more. "There's just so much."

"I know. So much has been dormant in you for so long I think it's all rushing to the surface at once." I kissed the top of her head. "We'll get through this."

"Together," she added.

I nodded. "Yes. Together."

The red in her skin turned to light pink. She took in a shaky breath and relaxed in my arms.

Gabriel set the bucket of water down next to us, letting it slosh over the top. "When you two are done trying to burn down the castle, we need to talk."

Emberlynn sat up and wiped at her face. "That sounds important. You should go."

"Not until you're okay. You are my first priority, always. In every situation."

"I'll be okay. I feel much better. Lighter. Thank you." She sniffed and looked over at Jen. "Besides, we have wedding stuff to talk about."

"Okay. I won't be long." The promise was more for me than her. I wasn't sure how long I could leave her side right now. The intense need to continue to protect her still raged inside of me. But the way Gabriel spoke did seem crucial.

She stood and tried to smile, but it still wasn't true. I could feel it. She was upset with herself.

Getting up, I brushed off my pants and turned to Gabriel. He watched Emberlynn intently. Something was wrong. I nodded for him to follow me out into the hall. "What's wrong?"

"I had a thought while you two were sparring with the sun's energy. Something I do not recommend you doing, by the way." He frowned. "None of us know how much power she has or what she can do with it."

"That is why she's training in a supervised weapon room by my head of the guard." I folded my arms and fought the urge to run back into the room. "What was your thought?"

He straightened and puffed his chest out. "I am glad you have confidence in me, but I don't have anything more than a bucket of water to stop her powers." He looked over his shoulder at Emberlynn and Jen. "My thought was about Perseus and Kade."

"Was there an incident I should be aware of?"

Gabriel sighed. "No. Kade is still unconscious, and Perseus is still pacing in his room. Their guards have not let anyone in or out. Aside from Lara, who is the only one I have permitted to attend to Kade."

"I'm not sure I'm following." The need to return to Emberlynn mounted. Gabriel better make this quick before I had no control over how quickly I moved to her side again.

"Emberlynn has the sun's energy. But she can also see anyone's true form. I wondered if she was strong enough to burn through metal," he pointed to a suit of armor hung on the far wall of the room, "if she was strong enough to essentially burn through a spirit."

I narrowed my stare on the hole in the armor and released a heavy sigh. "You mean like cut Helios out? That would be like burning Kade's soul. Not only do I think that's impossible, but would anyone even survive that?"

“I do not know.” He paused. “What about Perseus? Emberlynn should be able to see if Helios is attached to him.”

“Not if his spirit doesn’t show itself.” I clenched my fist, letting my nails dig into my flesh to keep from sprinting away. My stomach rolled and fought against me, urging me to move.

“About that...” He rubbed the back of his neck. “I was talking with Jen, and she thinks it is possible Emberlynn could force a spirit out. Perhaps maybe the colors she sees now are only drawn to her like a magnet, but what if she has the power to actually compel them?”

“That would be a fairly strong power to manipulate or coerce a spirit.” But what if...

“But if she could see, she could vet her Trejan and let us know of any who might be supporting Helios, even unintentionally.”

“Have you talked to her about it?” The last time I sprang information on her, she almost burned my weapon room down with me in it.

He shook his head. “No. I wanted to talk to you first, and then maybe you could talk to her about trying.”

Pursing my lips, I nodded. “You truly think she’s capable of this? I mean, compelling a spirit? I still don’t see how she could separate Helios from someone.”

He stepped further away from the doorway. “I do. So does Jen. And if Helios is using dark energies to control others, then maybe Emberlynn’s light will cancel it out. She’s a lot stronger than we thought. And who knows what other powers she might have that are still dormant."

"But we don't know if she can do any of that. And we don't know what it will do to anyone she tries it with or what it will do to her." I wasn't okay with her testing out any theory. If she got hurt, I wouldn't handle it well. I was afraid of the monster I might become to protect her. I didn't have to be in the situation to know I would have no caution when it came to her.

"That is why we start with Perseus. And the only ones in the room besides them would be you, Lara, and me." He had planned this all out, which didn't surprise me. Gabriel was always plotting ahead, figuring out a battle plan.

"I'll talk with her. But if she says no, then we don't push her." I stared at my best friend. I knew he had my best interest at hand, and Emberlynn was my main interest, so he wouldn't do anything to jeopardize her life. I just couldn't seem to let go of that protective urge.

Emberlynn darted through the door. "Oh, I thought you guys left."

I smiled and reached for her. My heart sped up having her so close. "Just waiting for the most beautiful woman in the kingdom."

"Hey, excuse me." Jen slipped through the entry. "I'm right here."

Emberlynn laughed, and I was glad she found some happiness again. I needed to work on making her laugh more. I clamped a hand on Gabriel's shoulder. "Well, my friend, it looks like we both got lucky."

Jen rolled her eyes. "Oh, please. You're clearly trying to cover your tracks." Her eyes hazed over, and I knew she was lost in a vision. She blinked, and her smile widened. "You," she pushed a finger to my chest, "need to get going."

I cocked my head, wondering what she saw. I hadn't told anyone about my plans to tour the city. I wanted to pry into her thoughts but thought better of it. Jen was a mess in her head, and it was best to let her sort out her visions herself. If it was important, she'd tell me. But...

"No," she said, shaking her head. She wagged a finger my way. "I'm not saying anything." She pulled Gabriel with her, leaving down the hall. "We won't even be here to stop you."

"What is she talking about? Sometimes I think she's lost it." Emberlynn leaned on my shoulder. "Do you think her visions are always real, or do you think she daydreams and only says we should do what she says?"

I laughed. "In my experience, it is best not to disregard Jen or her visions."

"Well, then where are we going?"

"Out." It was all I'd give her. I didn't want to ruin the surprise.

Emberlynn looked down. "I guess I should change first."

"No," I said too quickly. "I like it."

Her cheeks reddened. "But everyone will stare at me in this."

"Everyone will stare regardless." I wouldn't blame a single person for looking at her. She was gorgeous.

"You are not helping." She smoothed her hands down the front of her. "This is a bit revealing. I'm not sure it's what a queen would wear out and about in the kingdom."

"You're a queen, but you aren't mortal. I think your ideas of royalty are misconstrued. There isn't anything you can't wear." I was selfish. I knew it, but I wasn't done appreciating her in the training outfit.

Her hands went to her hips. "But look at you. You're not as formal as last night, but you're still in something halfway normal. I look like I belong in the hunger games."

"You could always wear the dress from last night," I teased. Although it wasn't a bad idea either. My body reacted to the memory of my hand on her thigh. "Actually, maybe not that dress. We won't make it to Night Fall if you wear that again."

She laughed. "I'll just go up and see if Clearie has anything else for me. It would help if I knew where we were going."

I kissed her on the forehead. "Go get changed into something comfortable. I'll meet you by the stairs."

NINE

Emberlynn

THE SUN'S ENERGY STILL TINGLED under my skin, but the mounting urge to release it was gone. I wasn't sure what happened back there. But Sander seemed to know what I needed. He always did. One minute I was simmering, barely restraining the energy. The next, my soulmate was dodging firebolts. The safe feeling he gave me to allow me to release it was everything to me. He wasn't afraid of me and helped me through it. Together. Always together.

I worried I had gone too far, worried I'd hurt my mate, but Sander's love rushed through our connection, reassuring me. The way the power emerged scared me. I really needed to get a handle on it and control it. I couldn't afford for it to escape me and hurt someone. This was a dangerous game I was playing with myself.

My head was still reeling as I crested the top of the stairs. Sander wanted to take me out–in public. A split fraction of a minute was spent worrying I'd not be able to control the sun while around other people, but I quickly pushed that thought back. No. I would control it.

Instinctively, I reached for the pendant around my neck. I'd kept it tucked under the tight shirt during training, needing to keep it close to my skin. I traced the familiar sun with my fingertips. I wondered if either of my parents had the same energy flowing through them. How did they control it? I wished they were here now. I could use some help from someone who understood.

When I got to my room, I noticed Clearie had already left a change of clothes on the bed. Black–again. Billowy nearly sheer pants with slits up past the knees and a matching sleeveless blouse that tied at my waist. A pair of strappy black sandals finished the look.

The crown Sander gifted me sat on the vanity, but there was no way I was wearing that outside the castle. It was too precious, and I didn't want anything to happen to it. Besides, he wasn't wearing one today, so I assumed crowns were a formal thing. And after that breakdown I had in the weapon room, I didn't feel very queenly.

Quickly, I slipped out of my training clothes and pulled on the new outfit. Pulling my hair out of its messy bun, I ran the brush through it and left it down. I thought back to the time when I would have cringed at leaving my hair down. It drew too much attention in the mortal realm. Each strand nearly glowed with the sun's energy. I didn't understand why then, but now... Now I had answers. Well, some answers. Mostly I had more questions. Like, how was I supposed to control the sun, what were my responsibilities, where was Helios hiding, and most importantly, when would he attack?

My blood sang with a song I didn't know, calling me home. The Solis Kingdom needed me. I knew that. But what could I do about it? For the people? I wasn't raised with the knowledge of any of this. I didn't even know if they spoke another language!

I wrapped my arms around my middle and sank to the vanity bench. Oh, what if they did? I barely passed high school Spanish. I wasn't sure I could learn a second language.

Sander tugged on our bond, but I didn't have time to push back. The door flung open. "Emberlynn?"

Looking up at him, my eyes teared. He was everything. He was a king, an immortal who knew all about the kingdoms, a warrior who fought in a war I didn't remember. He was my soulmate, and I felt like I was failing him. I was not someone he should be with. The gods were wrong. Maybe fate made a mistake. He should have someone who knew if the Solis Kingdom spoke another language!

In two strides, he was with me, pulling me up into his arms.

"I'm sorry," I blubbered into his shoulder. "All I seem to do is cry today."

He ran a hand over my hair and down my back. "There is no need to be sorry. You've had a lot tossed at you the last few days, and you feel everything so much stronger here. You're not used to it."

There was no way I'd tell him what I honestly thought about being here. I pulled back first, hating myself for leaving his comfort. Sucking in a ragged breath, I wiped the tears from my cheeks. "Maybe, but I hate it."

He chuckled and helped me wipe the tears away. "Your hate will be stronger here too."

I rolled my eyes and stepped back from his reach. "I underestimated how I would feel leaving the other world. It still feels so… strange. Like it's not real. Almost as if we traveled to Alaska where it's night most of the time."

He closed the space between us and tucked my hair behind my ear. "Let me help with that. Let me show you Astraios. Let me show you the Night Kingdom."

I wasn't sure that would help, but I nodded. I felt so out of place. It was like all the world had a secret, and I was the last to know.

Sander led me from the room. His body was like a magnet, and I followed where he moved. Guards stepped to the side, letting us pass through the halls. Each one had a shimmer of color I tried not to notice. Some were still too strange and inhuman for me to comprehend.

"You're awfully quiet, little sun."

Each step closer to the front door had me wondering what more I would see in the city. Was everyone so unusual? "I'm just thinking."

His lopsided smile made my heart flutter. "I'd love to know."

I scoffed, trying to focus on anything but the way he made me feel. "Don't you read minds?"

"Only if you want me to." He pulled the front door open, bringing in a fresh breeze from outside. "Come on, you won't want to miss this."

I cocked my head but took his outstretched hand. The darkness enveloped us as a million stars twinkled overhead. Sander pulled me along. "Hurry."

I laughed as we ran through the gardens. Dark violet flowers bloomed as we sped by, and small insects crawled along the path, their bodies glowing.

We reached the edge of the garden where he brought me yesterday.

He stopped behind me and wrapped his arms around me. His chest heaved from running. "Right here."

"What are we doing?"

"You'll see."

Slowly, the sky began to change. I sucked in a sharp breath as I watched the sun grace us with its presence. Barely, it began rising over the jagged mountains. The slight yellow light shimmered over the city, making it look as if it were on fire. The early sunlight danced along the horizon and over the homes of Astraios.

"It's beautiful." I held my hand out as the light changed to an orange color. The rays didn't just touch my skin, but I felt them go beyond, into my very core. My breathing picked up as I tried to keep calm.

The sun spoke to me. It was happy to see me. It knew me. I slipped from Sander's arms and walked out toward it. It rose higher in the sky. Not slow like how I was used to, but quickly as if it didn't want to overstay its welcome in the Night Kingdom. I begged it to stay longer—to stay with me.

"Emberlynn," Sander said.

Blinking, I turned to him. "Do you feel it?" Its magic thrummed inside of me. It was so intense it was almost tangible. I could feel it, touch it, move it. I controlled it.

"I feel you." He ran a hand up my arm.

I shivered under his touch. It was like ice. I pressed closer to him, wanting to feel him all over. My gaze locked with his. I needed him. There was nothing else that mattered at that moment. The sun was overhead, wrapping us in its heat and light. It was exhilarating. Having Sander pressed against me only excited me more. It was like the sun drugged me. I was intoxicated by love and power. I needed both, but right then, it was only Sander that I craved. I'd go a thousand years without the sun if I could just have him once.

His lips crashed down on mine. There was an urgency that hadn't been there before. I met his kiss with my own need. He gripped my arms and pushed me back until I was against the side of the garden wall. The rough stone didn't give as he pressed into me, trapping me in his arms. And I silently begged for more.

My hands were in his hair, then slipping down his back. Untucking his shirt, I grazed my fingers over his taut skin. His muscles flexed under my touch. and he groaned. "Little sun."

"Don't tell me to stop," I begged. I didn't want to stop. I wanted him.

"Never." He picked me up, and I wrapped my legs around his middle.

My heart came to life and fluttered as my soul left in search of his.

A loud cough echoed in my head. It was so far away, but I tried to focus on it, knowing it wasn't right. Slowing the kiss, I tried to catch my breath. "Sander."

He stopped and rested his forehead on mine while he also fought to control his breathing.

Another cough.

This time I knew it wasn't either of us nor was it only a sound. The world around us came back into focus. The sun had already started to dip across the sky. Its coloring left a pink hue over the city.

Jen rocked back on her heels, trying to act innocent while Gabriel faked yet another cough.

Nonchalantly, Jen looked around the garden. "We thought you might want some company while you toured Astraios."

Sander and I were still wrapped around each other and panting heavily. But that didn't stop the blush from heating my entire body.

"As you can see, company isn't exactly what we wanted." Sander's arms tightened around me, unwilling to let me go.

And I didn't want him to. This last kiss made it clear that we weren't meant to separate. Our souls were tired of waiting. The pained look in his eyes told me he felt it too.

"Well, if I recall, it was you who said a wedding must happen first." Jen shrugged. "King's orders."

Sander's shoulders fell. He set me on the ground. My legs were weak and shaky. I held onto him, fearing I'd fall without him.

"I don't care about a wedding. I don't want to wait." Reaching through our connection, I tried to plead with him.

"I won't take that from you." He grimaced. "So much has been thrust upon you. You deserve one normal thing."

"Normal is overrated." I pouted, crossing my arms over my chest. I didn't want normal. I wanted him. I craved his touch, his soul, his body. I needed it almost more than I needed air.

He tipped up my chin to look into my eyes. "This is not easy for me either."

I nodded. If I said anything more, I was afraid I would cry again. I hated feeling so overwhelmed with emotions here. I refused to cry again today. But I wanted him so badly it hurt.

Sander grumbled at Gabriel. A clip of Gabriel's thoughts slipped through the connection, and I knew Sander could hear his thoughts. Or maybe they were talking through their strange link.

Jen clapped and smiled. "This will be fun. I figured we could get some wedding plans out of the way while we were out too. We still have so much to go over before next week."

For the first time since I mentioned it, I was mad I asked for a Night Fall wedding. A whole week away. "Honestly, I don't care as long as we get married. I'll wear what I'm wearing right now if it means I get to be with Sander."

"Well, you'll be with Sander no matter what. Soulmates are for life. But you can't tell me you aren't a little excited about your wedding?" She looped her arm through Gabriel's and swooned. "It's so romantic." She playfully swatted her mate's arm. "Why didn't we get married at Night Fall?"

Gabriel grinned wide. "You did not have the patience of our king."

Jen gasped. "I don't recall you wanting to wait. Besides, I don't think anyone has as much patience as Sander in the history of the kingdoms. No one has waited this long to complete their joining."

Sander gripped my hand. I knew his need to be with me was as high as mine, if not worse. "Alright, if you're going to come with us, then at least try to keep your thoughts to yourselves. This is already hard enough."

I stepped back, wanting to run from the entire situation. "Sander, maybe we should wait to do this." I had so many emotions running through me that I worried I wouldn't be able to control the sun's energy inside me.

Sander forced a smile. "I think this is the perfect time to do this."

Jen and Gabriel started walking ahead of us, and I couldn't help but wonder their true intentions by meeting us out here. They had impeccable timing. I sighed. Maybe Jen saw something and knew precisely when to show up. Either way, I resolved to forgive them for interrupting me and my soulmate.

Jen called over her shoulder to us. "Come on, the sun is setting. That means the market is opening up for the night."

"The market?" The pink light in the sky faded into violet, and I knew it wouldn't be long before the sun would be gone. An hour a day. It wasn't much, but I wasn't sure I needed more with the amount of adrenaline it gave me.

Sander braced my arm to help me down the steps from the garden leading to the town. "The city is kind of sleepy until the sun blesses us. Then everything opens, and the city comes to life. We are a nighttime kingdom for a reason."

"So basically, everyone got to sleep in but me?" I carefully plotted where to step next. The cobbled stairs were short and neat but also extremely steep.

Sander's laugh rolled over me. I loved the way the deep sound carried through the air. "No. Almost everyone in the castle has been awake. You made sure with your training session with Jen. There wasn't a light that didn't flicker all morning. I know Clearie was fussing about it in the halls."

I stopped and gaped at him. "I didn't wake anyone. Besides, it was Jen's fault the lights flickered."

"Oh?" he asked. "Do tell."

I planted a hand on my hip. "Well, she made me exhaust myself trying to form that stupid fire spear."

"Mmhm. So, it is Jen's fault." He rubbed his chin. "Tell me, how should I punish her?"

I nearly fell off the step. "What? You wouldn't do that."

His mischievous smile widened. "I must. If she is exhausting the queen to a level unhealthy and unstable enough to wake an entire castle, it must be dealt with. I will not have my future wife and mate drained."

"You're incorrigible. Don't tease me like that." I took another step. Only a few more to the bottom.

"Oh, little sun, having you here is more than I'd hoped for." He stepped off the last step onto the grass and helped me down. "Come on. Let's go see Astraios."

TEN

Emberlynn

EVEN THOUGH THE SUN WAS GONE from the sky, its effect on me lingered. Jen talked on and on about the wedding, but I heard none of it. All my senses were focused on Sander. My body ached with more than merely a human need. It was almost like before we touched.

Slowly, other noises besides the fast thumping of his heart echoed around me. Laughter, music, talking... it all mixed in a dizzying effect. It was also the first time I paid attention to the fact that there were no other sounds like cars or sirens. No constant hum of tires on pavement.

The mountains to the west loomed over the city like guardians of Astraios. Gentle lapping waves swelled to the east. Standing on the edge of the city, I could see past the houses and buildings to the ocean of stars. The inky water reflected the twinkling lights. From my balcony, at the castle, the sea couldn't be seen. But Sander's room would have the perfect view of it all.

Gray stone cobbled the roads between the houses. The violet flower I saw in the gardens seemed to be a local favorite as it was everywhere. The homes were simplistic and not what I'd imagined. Too many fantasy movies ruined the idea of what to expect, I guess. They were all concrete, though some were painted, and some were not.

Two guards stopped on the road, bowing their heads. Jen and Gabriel walked by as if they didn't even notice them. The colors that emanated from the two men were unlike the ones in the castle. They looked completely human.

Sander gave them a subtle nod as we walked by. He gave my hand a gentle squeeze.

Ahead, colorful lights danced along a string, inviting people to enter a fenced-off section near the middle of the city. Loud, heavy beats of music vibrated up through my feet all the way up my spine.

The colors faded from one to another, eclipsing the ground and surroundings in brilliant shades. Jen and Gabriel were already wrapped around each other, swaying to the music. Their ghosts intertwined in soft wispy forms encircling them.

Other couples joined the apparent dance floor. Slow dancing turned into soft kisses, moans, and caresses. Most made no effort to hide how they felt, and I couldn't help but blush and look away. The open display of affection was more than what I was used to. This was more than under the bleachers at a high school football game.

Casting my gaze downward, I tried to ignore the heated look Sander held me in. "Are they going to... you know... right here in the open?"

He chuckled. "No. Our soulmates are precious, and our love for them is sacred. Joining is not something we would do with an audience, though we aren't afraid of showing our affection with others around."

Jamie and Lara had undoubtedly proven that one. They were always dancing in the kitchen. I relaxed and covered my face with my hands. Of course. Now it all made sense.

I was still too embarrassed to watch the others make out. "Well, if we did that, I wouldn't want to stop."

"Neither would I, little sun." He skirted me around the edge of the square. "But this is not why we came down here. Perhaps later we can come back." He winked at me, and I knew my blush was redder.

"What about Jen and Gabriel?" I asked, braving a look over my shoulder. They were completely caught up in each other.

"You know how we would not be able to stop?"

I nodded.

"Well..." He stopped for a moment. "I think it's best to let them find us later." He chuckled. "I don't think I've seen you this red."

I playfully swatted his arm. "Stop it. I'm just not used to it. Everyone is so open here. Like, leave something for the bedroom."

"We are not mortal, Emberlynn. Their rules do not pertain to our rules. Our soulmates are everything to us. We put them above all else. To openly show the world how much I love you will be an honor."

The air warmed, and the energy inside of me sizzled in response. "Okay, you need to stop talking like that, or we're gonna have to get married tonight."

He pulled me to his side. "Don't tempt me."

A woman curtsied and smiled widely. "My king." Her eyes landed on me.

"You may speak." Sander's permission reminded me of the night we fled Moonstone. His driver never spoke to me, nor did the guards placed at our door in the hotel until after he granted them approval.

Come to think of it, the only people who have talked to me without him around were Clearie and my escort last night to dinner. I wondered if Sander gave them permission ahead of time. The guests at dinner were greeted but never given clearance.

Her eyes lit up. "Thank you, my king." She curtsied again, this time to me. "You are exquisite. I am honored to meet you. The soulmate to our king must be a woman from the gods. Every blessing of the moon be on you."

"Thank you," I said.

The hopeful expression burst from her with her ghost. "Is it true? Are you the lost daughter of Solomon and Selene Cyrus? Are you the Solis Queen?"

It was hard to ignore the ghost as she reached for me.

Sander growled, and the spirit backed away, bowing to the Night King.

The woman's brow furrowed, completely unaware of what was happening with her aura. "I'm sorry, my king. I didn't mean any disrespect."

I gripped his arm tighter, afraid of how the ghost was reacting. It reminded me too much of Helios. "I am Emberlynn Cyrus."

The woman looked equally perplexed and excited.

Sander gave her a slight nod. "Thank you for the blessing on my mate, but we should get going now."

"Indeed, my king." She bowed her head and stepped to the side.

Once we were out of earshot, I released my breath. "What was that?"

"No one touches you. Not even a spirit."

We continued to walk through the city. "I guess I should rephrase my question. I knew why you scared it away, but why would it try and touch me?" Having him share my gift of sight was sometimes a blessing, but I still wasn't sure if it was constant. His gift of hearing thoughts came and went for me, not always something I could access. And sometimes it scared me because I wasn't prepared to hear them.

"I don't know, but I think it is because you are like a treasure to all the kingdoms. Your presence, your status, your fate, your blood... you are like the fire that attracts the insects."

"It's creepy." I shivered. "I don't like it."

"Neither do I. There was only a portion of a second I had to regain control of myself and not kill the woman for what her ghost was about to do. Being your protector is not something I've had to deal with in our kingdoms before. The feeling is more intense than almost any other, aside from my need to be with you." He forced a smile for me. "I will have to work on keeping my focus when others are around you." He shook his head. "Do you know how many men I wanted to kill last night at dinner for simply looking at you? But then, you stole my breath away and held me captive in your stare. I wanted to carry you upstairs and rip that dress from you and just...." He swallowed hard.

"I wanted you to do that too." This conversation wasn't helping either of us. Damn him and his ridiculous idea that we should be married first.

Our connection pulled tautly, and the air was knocked from me.

He stopped and yanked me with him. "Wait."

"What?"

He pushed me behind him and watched the road. "Gabriel is on his way. There was a sighting of uninvited guards from the Solis Kingdom."

I sucked in a sharp breath and froze. "Helios?"

"I don't know yet. But we should get back to the castle."

I nodded.

Shadows swirled at my ankles. Already Sander had them ready to hide me as he did before with Kade. Tiny sparks flickered at my fingertips, waiting to be molded into something more. I wasn't sure what, as I had only begun training with them that morning, but at least I wasn't completely empty-handed.

A dark, hooded man emerged from the side road. The symbol of the sun—my sun—was on his cloak. He was a Solis guard, but he didn't make me feel safe.

His ghost was like a double of him, but there was something oddly familiar about it. It shook unnaturally as if it fought against itself. The orange coloring quickly shifted to black.

Instantly, shadows wrapped around the man, restraining him. But his ghost continued to walk my way. A sly grin spread over its wispy face as it passed its host.

It was the same smile Helios had while he held me hostage. White flames burst from my palms. "Stay away from me."

The spirit paused and looked at the fire dancing over my skin. But it only seemed to become more excited. It took off again, surging toward me.

Memories of being trapped with Helios flooded me. I could feel the walls closing me in, cutting me off from Sander. The air thickened as I pushed my hands out to stop him.

Sander roared, and shadows consumed the ghost, trapping it before it could get closer. I wasn't trapped, and it wasn't Helios. Tremors of phantom pain trembled through me as the memory faded.

Turning into Sander's arms, I couldn't stop shaking. He was here. We weren't separated.

Gabriel rounded the corner, an entire army of men behind him. His orders were direct; capture the intruder and bring him to the dungeon. Only Sander and I could see the aura and the shadows were the only thing stopping it from getting to me.

"Go with them," Sander ordered the darkness. His strong arms held me to him, protecting me from the guard and his colors.

Gabriel noted the swarm of black tendrils wrapped around the ghost and nodded. He had to know what was inside, even if he couldn't see it.

Six guards surrounded us, each one bowing their heads to Sander.

"Do not leave Emberlynn's side. This was too easy, and I will not have her unguarded." He kissed the top of my head and went to move.

I clung to his shirt. "Wait, where are you going?" Panic struck me, thinking he wouldn't be with me.

"To find out who he is and where the others are. He came for you." Pure rage filled my soulmate's countenance.

"I'm coming with you." There was no way I was going to leave his side now. Honestly, I didn't think it was possible at this moment.

He cringed and looked away. I felt him tug on our bond. An attempt to test our ability at being apart.

Gabriel touched Sander's shoulder. "Maybe now is a good time to let her try?"

"Try what?" I asked.

Sander shook his head. "No."

I ignored him and stared at Gabriel. "What are you talking about? What should I try?"

Gabriel looked pained as he forced himself to stay quiet. Of course. Sander might be his best friend, but he was still the king, and Gabriel was the head of the guard. If Sander said no, then Gabriel couldn't go against that.

But I could.

The sun sizzled inside of me like electricity. I tried to bury the energy, to save it for later. It wasn't as easy as I'd hoped, but at least I was finally getting the hang of it. Carrying my head high, I walked past them both toward the Solis guard.

"Emberlynn, stop," Sander commanded.

But there was no way I would be ordered around while he kept even more secrets from me. Even if leaving his side caused us pain. I was draining, both in energy and mentally. I wasn't sure how much more I could handle before breaking. Every step had to be calculated, thought out, processed. Each breath carried the promise of the sun, fiery explosions waiting to be released as I exhaled. The strain on the bond with Sander made me weak. I felt sick and dizzy. But I couldn't fix any of it. I had to keep my head high and pretend I was okay. No one needed an unstable queen. Especially one with the power of the sun. I still wasn't sure what I was capable of.

The guard watched through the tiny slit of an opening the shadows left. His eyes went wide when I stopped in front of him. The sun's energy pricked at my fingertips in hot, painful jabs. I grabbed the shadows from the man's mouth and ripped them away. The fiery touch of my fingers controlled the darkness.

I didn't have time to think about how I was able to command Sander's shadows. "Who are you?"

"I am Derik. A Solis guard."

"Emberlynn." This time, Sander's voice was much softer.

I glared at him. "No. You decided to keep another secret from me."

"No, there's no secret. I promise."

I raised a brow. "Oh, so then what can't I try?"

"Gabriel had a thought, that's all. He wonders if you can pull the ghosts to you and command them." He swallowed hard. "And if you can separate and burn out Helios from their spirits." He gestured to the guard. "Much like you just did with the shadows. I wasn't sure it was a plausible idea until you did that."

The sun was angrily thrumming under the surface, and I knew I wouldn't be able to hold it all in much longer. "Then drop the restraint."

"No. I can't." Sander winced. "I'm trying to protect you. Trust me."

The air sizzled around us. I could feel it tingling on my bare arms. "If you want to protect me, then help me learn. Stop forcing me behind you. Teach me how to help; how to do what I need to do!"

"Not here. Please." His expression turned almost desperate. "Try with Perseus first."

My head of guard's name snapped me back into focus. He was somewhere in the castle waiting to be judged. Waiting for us to find a way to declare him free of Helios.

Perseus was the only guard aside from Gabriel I trusted. Maybe if I could do what Sander and Gabriel suggested, Perseus could help train me. He knew the Solis world. He knew my parents. He should be down here now, interrogating his guard. If there was anything I could do or even try to do, I would do it.

I nodded. "Fine."

Sander relaxed, but his eyes remained sad.

The shadows quickly recovered the Solis guard's mouth. Gabriel gathered his men and took him away before I could continue my own investigation.

With them gone, it felt like the weight of the kingdom fell on me. I was so weak. The back and forth, highs and lows of emotions were exhausting. The intense vexation I had moments before dropped, and my knees buckled. I fell, but Sander caught me before I hit the cobbled road. The sky spun overhead, making me nauseous. I squeezed my eyes shut and clung to Sander's shirt.

"Emberlynn," Sander said. His voice was full of concern.

I didn't dare open my mouth, afraid lunch would resurface.

I hated feeling everything so intensely. The switch in emotions was so fast I couldn't keep them straight. One moment I was happy, then sad, then angry. It made me sick.

I hated this world and just wanted to go home. Who wanted to feel everything all the time with no reprieve?

Sander picked me up and carried me. He barked an order for the remaining guards to stay back. I hated being so weak, but I was grateful he was there to rescue me again with no complaints. No anger. No annoyance. Once more, my mind tried to persuade me that I wasn't worthy of him as a soulmate.

"I can walk," I tried.

"No." He shook his head. "You might be able to walk, but right now, I'm incapable of putting you down."

"I thought you were going to interrogate the guard?"

"Neither of us are going right now." His words were final.

I curled up against his chest. "I don't know why I'm acting this way. Maybe Lara can help me?" Maybe she had some fruity water to help reduce the excessive emotions. She did it once when Helios captured Andi, and I freaked out. Surely, she had something to help this too.

"As immortals, we are used to the elevated extremes to what we feel. It is normal, and without it, we feel as though we are hollow and missing a part of ourselves. But you have been gone for so long that our normal is not yours. It will take time." We passed the square where people were still making out. But instead of heading to the castle, Sander turned toward the sea.

He kept walking until the houses were far behind us. Neither of us talked. We didn't have to. Part of me wondered if the reason for my outburst was because I wasn't whole. I had a constant demand to join with Sander. Each second of every day, I was pulled toward him. My soul pleaded with me to be with him. If we stopped fighting ourselves, maybe I could focus more on everything else.

The cliffs below the castle stuck out in jagged, sharp ledges. The soothing sound of the waves lapping over the black sand echoed against the rock facing.

A path crept around the water's edge, up a shale trail to a small cave entrance. It was worn down but looked as if it hadn't been used for a while. Sander took each step expertly, knowing where to place his feet to get us both to the cave without falling into the water. A light spray of the water coated my bare skin.

He had to duck to get us both inside. The tiny glowing insects walked along the ceiling like radiant green stars. The opening of the cave could never reveal the size of the space. A few things were scattered around but abandoned. A pile of blankets, a few candles, and other things I couldn't make out in the lack of light.

"This is a place I used to go to many times during the first hundred years of life." He set me down but held on to me, keeping me to him. "I would come here and watch the tide after the sunset. In a way, I guess it was you with me."

"Sander," I started.

He held a finger to my lips. "I know this isn't easy for you. The last six months have been more than I could have ever hoped for. I have tried to be patient. I was willing to die for you, letting you choose our bond. I would still die for you." He sat down on the makeshift bed against the far wall and pulled me down to straddle him. "But right now, I need you."

My heart sped. It was too much to hope he meant it.

"Emberlynn Dawn Cyrus, marry me, be my mate, join with me. Without you, I cannot lead this kingdom. Without you, I cannot breathe anymore. I saw that guard's spirit reach for you, and I snapped. I felt everything you felt through our bond. Then you fell, and my heart stopped. I can't...." He buried his head on my chest. "I can't do this without you."

I ran my fingers through his hair. "Sander Lux, if you don't join with me tonight, then I will die." Even as I said the words, I worried they were true.

He looked up with tears in his eyes. "I promised you a wedding."

I leaned back and cocked my head. "Night Fall, I haven't forgotten. I aim to hold you to it. Besides, Jen would be devastated if she had to stop planning the wedding."

I lowered my mouth to his, claiming his next words, stopping him from cautioning me over what I wanted–what I needed.

The waves crashed outside, rising to the entrance, trapping us inside. There was now no way in or out. We were separated from the rest of the Night Kingdom. It was only us. No interruptions this time.

His hands gently ran down my arms, sending a blissful shiver through me. He gripped the bottom of my shirt and pulled it up. I reluctantly released his kiss to raise my arms and let him remove the garment. His mouth closed the distance between us, leaving a trail of soft kisses over my collar bone and lower neck. I arched into his touch. His lips held the heat of the sun, burning through to my soul.

He stopped abruptly and picked me up, turning to lay me upon the blankets, and then settled over me. His hand came to rest on my lower abdomen. "I am taking your wedding night from you, but I refuse to take it fast."

The desire to be with him ached low. I stared up at him, locking my gaze with his. "You're not taking anything I'm not freely giving."

"I love you. I could thank the gods on every star in the sky for you, and it would never be enough." Lowering himself down, his mouth found mine.

Sander was slow and gentle, making every moment a memory. While he admired and memorized every inch of my body as he removed each article of clothing. His hands trailed and caressed all of me. I was on fire under his touch. I'd never known such a pleasurable pain as to writhe under the man I loved, my soulmate, with a need so deep tears slipped from my eyes.

He kissed the tears away and lifted to look at me. The familiar tendrils of Sander's soul searched through our bond to make sure I was okay. He raised my wrist to kiss the tender flesh where his mark sealed us together.

I didn't know how to respond. I had no words to how I felt. I only knew I needed him. Whatever longing I had, whatever craving my soul desired... he could satiate it. He stood and removed his clothes.

I had imagined this moment many times. Sander wasn't a stranger, and I knew his body. I knew his soul. But seeing him like this captured my focus. Had there ever been a doubt that he was from the gods, it was doused and buried right then.

I licked my lips, trying to wet them as I watched him lower himself over me. I gripped his shoulders and gasped as we joined. The cave became a euphoria of colors. The rapture of our souls sought a climax of pleasure as we became one.

When he moved, I moved. The excitement of being with him mounted, bursting inside of me like fireworks. My soul left to meet his. I wasn't sure if I had died or just suspended in life as I watched Sander's spirit take mine against the cave wall. This was the first time I'd gotten to see his silver ghost truly take form.

Everything slowed as if time stopped entirely for us. The back of his fingers grazed my cheek. "For eternity, I am yours."

A flood of emotions filled me, but they weren't all mine. My skin heated then cooled, the colors faded then returned, Sander's voice came and went from my mind. Every nerve was on fire. It was heaven and hell. Our colors were woven together so tightly they were as one.

My body erupted in spasms of ecstasy, and I cried out. Sander's name was the only thing on my lips. Flames licked the walls, growing as my soul surged with each new ripple of pleasure. A blast of light filled the cave as the sun returned, colliding with the moon. The eclipse shook the kingdom.

Out of breath but completely satisfied, I grinned at my soulmate. "I always knew I would darken the sun for you."

His body trembled as he wrapped his arms around me and pulled me to him. I curled up with him, fitting perfectly against his frame. He kissed the top of my head. "Little sun, I don't think there isn't an immortal who won't know you are mine now."

I smiled but was worn out. The heat from his body comforted me like a blanket, and I let my eyes close.

ELEVEN

Kade

FORCING MY EYES TO OPEN was useless. I had no control over my body. A voice yelled at me from beyond, but it couldn't reach me.

Where was I?

Where was Emberlynn? I had to get to her. I had to save her.

I am Trejan. I will not fail.

My eyes flickered open to a dark room.

I am Trejan. I will not fail.

There was no sun. No light aside from the fire licking the walls on sconces. The cell was small but well-guarded.

I am Trejan. I will not fail.

My body was so weak I wasn't sure I could move. My side ached, but it wasn't as bad as before. If only I could remember what happened. The last thing I retained in my memory was Emberlynn's hand burning me. How did I get to her? Was she safe?

I tried to sit, crying out in pain as I did. I needed to get to her.

I am Trejan. I will not fail.

"Hey, tell the captain he's awake." The tallest guard watched me but made no move to come near me.

The other man hesitated before leaving his companion.

If only they knew I wasn't the enemy. It wasn't me they should fear.

"Helios," was all I could manage to say. Breathing hurt, but it was worse sitting up.

I am Trejan. I will not fail.

The guard stiffened and grabbed the hilt of his dagger.

It was too much too fast, and I fell back to the hard cot.

I am Trejan. I will not fail.

I am Trejan. I will not fail.

I am Trejan. I will not...

My eyes closed before I could finish.

TWELVE

Emberlynn

FOR THE FIRST TIME IN FOREVER, I was at peace. There was no pull demanding me to join with my soulmate. There was no energy fighting for control over my body. Except for the water outside the cave entrance and Sander's steady breathing, there was no sound.

Last night had been more than I ever knew I needed. As much as I thought I knew or felt Sander before, it was a thousand times stronger now. I raised my arm to inspect the mark on my wrist. His gold lips shined under the strange hue of the sky.

Sander stirred against me, his arms still holding me to him. Neither of us had bothered with clothes. "Good morning, little sun." He kissed along the back of my neck, causing a thrill of a shiver down my spine.

Even after last night, sharing the cave with him, I blushed. We'd slept next to each other before, but now we'd joined our souls. We were one. I knew without a doubt that anything I had was his. My mind, my body, my soul.

"Good morning," I whispered back.

Our bond felt different now too. It wasn't a cord between us. It was completely there, inside of me. No more stretching to reach him with my mind. He was, in every sense, a part of me. I felt him throughout my body, his essence embedded in me like DNA.

While I was on fire, he was the ice, soothing the ache my power left in me. Still keeping my hand up, I tried to call the fire to me. White flames sprang forth, hovering over my palm, waiting for an order. Strange. It didn't burn me or try to escape me this time. There was no struggle to control it.

"Do you plan on burning down the cave?" He continued to kiss me, trailing down to my bare shoulder. "As I recall, we nearly did that last night."

The flame disappeared. I lowered my hand and rolled over. "Everything is different now."

"Yes." He kissed my forehead. "I should have waited. I'm sorry."

"I'm not." I placed my hand over his heart. "I can feel you. I'm sure that means you can feel me, so do it. See if I regret it. See how happy I am. Feel how content my soul is for the first time in months." Looking up into his eyes, they looked dark and stormy. "We did what we did not because we were impatient, but because we were literally dying without each other. Our souls were trying to save us. I need you, Sander. We should never deny each other again. It's no wonder I couldn't concentrate or focus. I was starving."

"You are so wise." He propped himself up on an elbow. "And now? Are you starving now?"

I let my hand trail over his body. "I'm hungry but not starving."

"Then my queen should feast." He picked me up and rolled until I was over him. His hand cupped my head and pulled me down to kiss him. It was too quick, leaving me wanting more.

It felt so natural to be with him. Just like throughout the night, my body responded to his. The way he loved me filled my soul. I felt complete.

Laying in his arms, I watched the dim light dance with the water's reflection on the cave wall. It was a burnt orange hue.

At some point, I knew we would have to leave.

Being alone with Sander, cut off from all the worlds, meant so much to me. But a soft voice told me it wouldn't last. We needed to return to the world.

Regretfully, I got up.

Sander watched as I pulled on my clothes. I was sure I blushed all over. I wanted to turn away when it was his turn, but I was truly enthralled. He was everything to me, and I couldn't contain a prideful smile knowing he was mine.

"We should get back to the castle," he said. Standing near the entrance, he looked up at the sky. "That is beautiful."

I joined him to see the sun hiding behind the moon. Its rays were bright, giving the moon a fiery glow around the edges. "Wow."

"You did that." He took my hand and kissed my wrist. "You are amazing."

"I didn't do that." My voice squeaked.

He chuckled. "Last night."

"Oh," I whispered. "How do I fix it?"

He paused. "The moon is happy. The kingdom is thrumming with new energy. Everything is as it should be."

"How do you know?"

He placed his hand over my heart. "Listen. This realm, this world, this kingdom... it is me. Just as the Solis is you." He moved my hand to touch the cave wall. "Feel it."

My palm felt hot against the cool stone. A low, anxious frequency hummed through the wall. It felt like Sander, but it wasn't. I felt myself in it as well. "I don't understand."

He looked out at the sky again. "I am the night. You are the day. Our kingdoms are merging."

I frowned. "So much for keeping it on the down-low."

"Come on, little sun." He stepped to the edge of the water. The waves pulled back, revealing a slippery wet trail back to the city. He reached out for my hand. "I could carry you again?"

I took his hand and grinned. "Just catch me if I fall."

"Always."

Sander was right. The energy around town was different. A new ripple of power danced along with the breeze, teasing me. Each step as we climbed the hillside surged with renewed spirit.

Finally, we made it to the castle. An angry essence assaulted me before we got to the doors. I stopped, afraid of what I felt.

Sander laughed. "It's just Gabriel."

"What?" That was new.

"You feel him through me. He's a bit upset with me right now."

I couldn't imagine Gabriel being that angry. "But why?"

The front doors burst open, and Gabriel stomped outside. Jen quietly followed. "Because he closed me off! You did not return to the castle. I had no idea where you or Emberlynn was. No mention of your plans. Nothing. I had guards out looking for you. And then," he gestured to the sky, "that happened! Do you know how many questions I had to endure on your behalf last night?"

"I'm sure you handled it exactly as needed." Sander looked up at the eclipsed sun and moon. "It is beautiful, is it not?"

Gabriel's eyes narrowed on the Night King. "Sander, this is not the time to brush me off. There are still other Solis guards unaccounted for in the city. I was ready to go to war to find you."

Sander whirled to face his head of the guard. "Then why didn't you?"

"Because of the sun crashing into the moon. I knew then that you two, well... you two were together."

He clapped a hand on Gabriel's shoulder. "So then rest, my friend. We are safe."

The guard grumbled. "You make it impossible to protect you."

Sander did not remove his hand. "Had I not been with Emberlynn, you would have been told. It is only when I am not with her that I worry for her safety. I trust you with it and know in my stead she will be taken care of, but listen to me, Gabriel, it is because of my friendship with you that I let you talk to me the way you do, but I will not tolerate you insulting my ability to protect my soulmate."

"Understood, my king." Gabriel stood tall and sure, but the anger slowly vanished. The air softened, and the tension left.

Jen rushed to me. "I think now is the perfect time to let the men talk, and we plan for Night Fall."

"Agreed." It seemed Sander and Gabriel had more things to discuss. Especially if there were more guards in the city.

I only hoped they weren't planning on ruining my wedding.

Arms looped together, Jen and I left our soulmates on the steps of the castle. For the first time since meeting him, I wasn't pulled back. A stirring in the depths of my body pooled in excitement over seeing him again. I knew it would only last so long before I'd burn the castle down to find him, but at least I wasn't stretched thin.

"Oh, girl, you have got to tell me!" Jen rushed us through to the second level. "You should have seen Jamie this morning at breakfast. He was all sorts of shook."

I groaned. "I can imagine. It's not fair, you know?"

She pushed open my bedroom door. "What? That the entire kingdom now knows you're the king's soulmate?"

I kicked my sandals off and flopped on the bed. "No, that our joining is on display for the entire kingdom to see. It's not like you have a banner over your head saying that you and Gabriel did it."

She laughed and joined me on the bed. "No, but we aren't royalty. Our blood doesn't control an entire kingdom. The gods created the worlds, split the worlds, and now... they are bringing them back together."

Eww. I hated thinking Sander and I were only pawns for the gods to play with. "Ugh, thanks, but that's not helping."

She propped up on her side. "I wonder what the other kingdoms are going to think about it."

I scrunched my face. "Why would it matter to them?"

She sighed. "Because it might change their kingdoms too. If we were all one kingdom again, there wouldn't be Somnium or Verum."

I hadn't thought of that. But then again, I hadn't thought about all four kingdoms merging either. "Do you think they'll be mad?"

She sat up and shrugged. "I don't know, we'll see. They should be arriving tomorrow."

"What!" I jumped up. "What do you mean, they'll be arriving tomorrow?"

"Um, well, I sent them invites to your wedding. It's kind of a big deal to have a royal get married. If we didn't invite them, they could look at this as even more of an insult. We really don't need that."

I couldn't stand still. My feet needed to move. Pacing in front of the vanity, I gawked at Jen. "Why didn't anyone tell me?"

She stood and came to me, grabbing my hands. "Ember, slow down. Even in the mortal world you invite people to a wedding. Especially neighboring royals. It's not only strategic but well mannered."

I wasn't ready to meet a king or queen. Sander was different. He wasn't a king in my mind. He was just Sander. I slipped my hands from hers and wrung them out. "I'd love some of Lara's lavender water right about now."

Jen twitched her mouth to the side and tapped a finger over her lips. "That can be arranged. I'm sure she's still in the kitchens directing the staff. She kinda took over. I think she likes it."

Seeing Lara was precisely what I needed. Family. Home.

Home.

I missed the feeling of comfort that I hadn't yet found in the Night Kingdom. A part of me wondered if the Solis Kingdom would welcome me. Would I find the solace I desperately missed? I'd give just about anything to sit at Lara's counter right now and talk to her about everything over a cup of herbal concoctions she brewed up.

"Come on," Jen tugged on my arm. "I'm sure Lara will be excited to see you."

"But she knows... about last night." I pointed to the window. The brighter than normal sky was still illuminated by the eclipsed sun.

Jen waved me off. "Psh. Everyone knows. There's not a city in the kingdom that doesn't know."

Mortified wasn't exactly how I felt, but close. So very close.

At least in the mortal realm, the sun doesn't hide behind the moon the first time you are intimate with a partner. This world could suck it.

I buried my face in my hands and groaned.

"Emberlynn Cyrus, look outside." Jen marched to the balcony and swung the doors open.

I followed, but only because I was afraid of her stern tone. I hadn't heard her tongue so sharp before.

"Do you see them?" She pointed at the city. More so at the residents.

Laughter carried up the hill. Joyous music filled the streets, and it was so busy compared to yesterday. "Yeah, I see them."

"And?"

I shrugged. "I don't know what I'm supposed to see."

"They are celebrating!"

"I thought that was the point of Night Fall?"

Jen pinched the bridge of her nose and grumbled. "No. Night Fall is still a few days away. This... this is pure happiness. Their king has finally found his soulmate. You have given them a reason to cheer. And once the kingdoms merge, we can be one people again. This means so much more than you understand."

Agh! I flung my arms up and retraced my steps back into the room. "You're right. I don't understand. I wasn't raised here."

Jen followed me and pulled out the vanity bench. "Sit."

Obediently, I sat, staring up at her with wide eyes. Her color emerged and stood over me like a sentinel. It was no wonder Gabriel, the head of the Night Guard, was her soulmate.

"I had wanted to find you a teacher, but it seems queen lessons are starting now." She walked to the bookshelf by the closet. Running her fingers over the spines, she touched each one until pulling off a red leatherbound book. Gold chains wrapped around it like a belt. "Here," she handed the book out to me, "start with this."

I took the book but continued to stare at her, afraid of missing anything.

She sat down next to me and sighed. "I wasn't alive when the worlds split. But I've heard stories. Most of us have our own family narratives passed down from the gods."

"I wish I knew mine." Another fabulous part of never knowing my parents. Somehow, I was certain this history was important to me.

"Yours," Jen snickered. "Yours is the easiest and most notable. You know how the worlds were split. The mortals were envious of our magic and immortality. Separating them to a mortal realm caused the kingdoms to split. Trials were held to find the strongest blood link to the creators to rule a kingdom. You are a direct descendant of the creators. Your bloodline is pure."

She touched the cover of the book gently and continued, "Before the split, we were all one people. Now, the slightest change unbalances us. Soulmates are hard to find, probably in a different kingdom unable to touch. We're dying out. Because..." She stood and walked to the balcony doors and looked up. "Because what is the sun without the moon? I can't be the only one who craves balance. Who desires to feel the sun on my face, the moon outside my window while I dream, or the reality that soulmates are not threatened into extinction."

She turned to me. "So, yes, Emberlynn, they are celebrating. They have hope." Pointing to the eclipse, she raised her voice. "That gives them hope."

"What if I fail? What if I can't bring the kingdoms together again?" I placed the book on the vanity and joined her on the balcony. "I mean, how do I even join them? The gods or creators split them for a reason. I don't think they would make it easy to glue back together."

"The creation papers might have something on them. That's if they are still in your vault. Helios might have them by now."

I nodded. "I remember Lara saying something about those when we found the crown on my bed. There was a piece of paper that talked about how the kingdoms or worlds were split, but half of it was missing."

Jen leaned on the railing and watched the city. "I know Sander would disapprove, but I think after Night Fall, we should go to Solis. We need to get in your vault and find out if those papers are there. Among other items."

It was my turn to scoff. "I doubt Sander will let me step foot in Solis right now." At least not without an entire army with me. My mind went to Perseus and my promise to try to help him. "Sander told me that Gabriel thinks I can manipulate an aura to show itself. He thinks I can command it." I shrugged. "I don't know, but if I can, do you think I can sever Helios from a spirit?"

Jen took a moment, watching people in the streets. "I do."

"Help me, then. Help me get back to Solis. You know he won't entertain the thought while we have no way of knowing who is attached to Helios."

Leaning her hip into the railing, she folded her arms and considered me. "Fine. Command my spirit. If you can do that, then I think we can move on to others."

Nothing like being put on the spot. I had no clue how to do this. "How?"

She began strolling around me. "The same way you call the sun. You must command the spirit as well. Every piece of you is laced with deep magic from the gods. Use it."

That wasn't helping. Calling the sun wasn't something I controlled yet. So far, I only forced it down. And what would I make her ghost do if I could manage it?

Gifts from the gods. Psh.

So far, nothing good has come from my gifts.

Jen stopped. Her toe tapped the floor. "Go on. Try it."

I much-preferred battle training with Jen compared to this... this mind training. Ugh. Dodging a flaming bolt seemed easier than demanding a spirit listen to me. Some might say impossible.

I did a little jump like I saw athletes do to get pumped up. I could do this. I could do this. Rolling my head side to side, I made eye contact with her ghost. It cocked its head, watching me. Maybe I already had a connection to it? "Come to me."

Nothing.

I concentrated harder, filling my mind with only her colors. "Come to me."

My fingers tingled, and I remembered I had to use the same magic as the sun. Reaching out to her spirit, I tried again. "Come to me."

A spear of white, hot light shot from me, going straight through the belly of her ghost. It exploded against the wall in a spectacular eruption of sparks.

Jen and I both ran to make sure I hadn't caught anything on fire. She stamped on a few embers and laughed. "I think this will require more practice."

I laughed with her. "Maybe don't tell anyone I launched a firebolt at your ghost."

Making sure all embers and sparks were out, Jen slung an arm over my shoulders. "It's gonna be the only thing I talk about at dinner."

I groaned. "Great."

THIRTEEN

Emberlynn

BY THE AFTERNOON, I was ready to tear the kingdom apart to find Sander. Not being stretched thin was a nice break, but the new intensity of my attraction and craving for him was on a whole new level. Each hour that passed had me focused more on him and not around me. All I could do was imagine his fingers touching my skin, his lips on mine, his hand at the small of my back.

Lara swept by but quickly retracted her last step to stop beside me. "Oh, honey, you need to find Sander before I have to give you something more than lavender water."

Down in the heart of the castle was the kitchen. It was darker down here with no windows. Dark aged wood trimmed the massive room with black cabinets. Glass bottles and dried herbs lined the wall like an apothecary. It was where I found Lara busy ordering the staff around. Apparently, the room wasn't organized as efficiently as it could be, and she was rectifying the problem.

I shook my head. "No. We have to learn to be apart. Look at you and Jamie. You guys are doing just fine."

Lara laughed. It wasn't her typical, quiet chirp but rather loud and squeaky. "Emberlynn, there is more than one reason why I am keeping myself completely occupied down here." She took a seat next to me at the island that reached the length of the kitchen. It was the only place that halfway felt like home. "Soulmates aren't meant to be apart. We can get away with it in the mortal realm because we aren't tapped into our full powers. We are cut off from the immortal magic of the kingdoms. Here..." She fidgeted with the white rag in her hand. "Here, it is extremely hard to be separated."

I frowned. "Then why isn't Jamie here?"

"We both agreed he was needed in the talks with Sander and his men. Not only is his family arriving today, but you are our daughter." She stood and began wiping the black marbled top of the counter. "Besides, Sander asked him to sit in his council. That is an honor he can't just pass on."

"I imagine so." My heart warmed even more, knowing Sander included my dad. "How long will they be away from us?"

"I don't know for sure, but I know it can't be much longer." She shook her head. "Sander has more endurance than anyone I've ever met. That man could hold a line in a war and not blink. When it comes to you, he's stronger than the gods."

My mind went to last night and how strong he really is. He was determined to make me believe he wasn't strong enough to wait, but I knew better.

Phantom fingers brushed across my skin, caressing my cheek.

"That's it. If they don't break up their meeting soon, I'm going to break down the door and drag Sander out of there for you. He might be able to withstand being apart, but you can't."

I blushed.

She took my hand. "Honey, it is nothing to be embarrassed about. I'm not even worried about that part. It's the sizzling effect. Being separated is different for everyone, but one thing is the same, after too long, we die. There are two reasons why. One, the one you know, is because we are bound to each other, tied for eternity. Our souls are literally the other halves of each other. If one dies, the other dies. But two..." She continued to wipe at invisible dust on the counter. "Your own energy, your magic, it kills you. It builds in anticipation, sizzling under the surface. Think of it like a bomb. Every time you are apart, it sets a new detonation timer. If you aren't pulled back together by the time the timer ends...." She froze, her face ashen. "So, that feeling you have right now, the one where you want to burn the castle down to get to him? Well, that's your soul going into panic mode because you both are going to die if you don't."

I jumped up from the chair. "Seriously, these are things you guys should have told me! How long do I have? How do I know when the timer is up?"

An icy draft rushed through the kitchen while warm arms wrapped around me. "You will never have to find out."

Sander.

He nuzzled my neck before planting tiny kisses along the sensitive spot.

His body calmed the fevered need inside of me. Turning in his arms, I wound mine around his neck. "I hope not."

The blue in his eyes darkened. "Nothing could keep me from you."

"I heard you tried to kill Jen's aura?" Jamie chuckled from the other side of the island. He held Lara tightly to his side.

I groaned. "I didn't try to kill it." Moving to Sander's side, I shrugged. "I was trying to command it. The flames just kind of happened."

Sander's body shook as he stifled a laugh. "Well, you should have seen Gabriel's face when it happened."

Lara tsked, "I assume you got more work done than watching poor Gabriel fret over his soulmate."

The shift in the room was noticeable–even to me. I could only imagine how much it affected Lara.

Sander cleared his throat. "We did. With the upcoming Night Fall, wedding, and visitors, we have tripled the guards in the city and all the portals. I have sent out scouts to monitor the dormant Fores as well. After what happened in the mortal realm, I won't take any chances." He tensed. "Jamie, you know I won't let that happen again."

Jamie frowned. "I know, but I can't help but think about what almost happened. And now we're here, and we have no idea where Helios is. It's a concern."

Pursing his lips in thought, Sander nodded. "I understand. However, there is nothing I won't do to protect Emberlynn. I have sent men to every closed, abandoned Fores in the kingdom. No one is getting in or out without my knowledge."

"What about the Solis guards already here? Did you find them?" I asked.

"We think they have left Astraios for now. Though, with the portals guarded, the only way in or out is by ship. So, they should be easy to spot."

That made me pause. "How many cities are in the Night Kingdom? Are the other kingdoms connected to us? Geographically, how are the kingdoms set up?" It's not like Immortal Kingdoms 101 was a class in high school. At least not for me.

"That is an excellent question." Jamie rushed around the island and grabbed glasses, pots, herb bottles... He went into full teacher mode. "Okay," he said, centering a pot in the middle. "This is the mortal realm. And these bottles surrounding it are the kingdoms." He placed a spoon between each bottle. "These are the barriers."

"So, there are walls between us?"

Jamie pondered my question for a moment. "Okay, so you've been raised with knowledge of being open. The world, space, planets. We can go anywhere as mortals. Or so they think."

I tried to follow his teaching but wasn't sure I caught onto the point yet. "Yeah, I'm trying to wrap my brain around how this works."

He scratched his chin. "Without going into the depths of creation, which is an entirely different lesson, just think of space as a reflection from the kingdoms. The sun, the moon, all the stars. While Verum gave the reality to what is out there to us, Somnium hid the truth. It's all an illusion for the mortals."

"What about the walls?" I pointed to the spoons.

"It's darkness. They are the ripped seams from when the realm was divided." He began placing small cups between the bottles and the pot. "This is the sun. It can move through the kingdoms, giving the mortals a daily rotation. And the moon..." he picked up another tiny cup and moved it with the sun cup. "The moon follows suit."

"Then why was the sun only here for an hour?" I didn't want to draw too much attention to the fact that it was in the sky right now, hiding behind the moon.

Sander stood behind me and rubbed my arms. "Because, little sun, the energy you have is pulled and stretched thin while leaving the Solis Kingdom. It acts almost like a slingshot, slipping through the realms on its way back to Solis."

I knew all about being pulled and stretched. I'd spent the last six months denying the joining of our souls. "But the sun is here now."

Sander nuzzled my neck before whispering, "A slingshot. If I remember correctly, the sun crashed into the moon before taking its place behind it."

My cheeks warmed. There was no need to repeat what he said to the others. I'd work on understanding that part later. Alone.

Jamie placed the sun cup on one side of the pot and the moon on the opposite side. "The Solis Kingdom is here, Verum, then Night. And here is Somnium." His finger landed on the last bottle between Solis and Night. Then drew an invisible circle around the entire setup. "This is our world. But the barriers prevent us from being one. Our magic cannot seep through. It cannot merge. Just like the sun slips through quickly, so is the same for the others. Visiting other kingdoms can disrupt the realm."

"How? And I thought others from Verum and Somnium were arriving tomorrow? Is that safe?"

"Certainly, they can visit. They just can't stay. Without a soulmate, they would wither away. Their source of energy isn't here."

I looked at Jamie and Lara. "That means you guys won't be here forever?"

Lara placed a hand on mine. "Oh, honey, don't worry. As long as Sander gives us permission to stay, we will."

"But is that hard on you?" I worried about my parents. I'd already lost one set. I refused to lose another.

Her aura slipped from her to dance with Jamie's. "A little. It is easier for me to draw from any energy, but Jamie has a harder time in the darkness. He will draw from me until we visit Somnium or our home in the mortal realm."

I thought about how he and Jen were both from Somnium. Each had their own way of bringing a lighter mood than the rest, but also how drastically they could change. They took everything to heart. "I don't want you to hurt because of me. If you're only here because I'm here...."

"No." Lara shook her head. "I told you we left because I couldn't fight. Being in Verum makes it harder. We are a people of truth. Reality. Nothing is hidden from us. While not all have the healing powers like I do, most can absorb emotions from around them. I have it a bit stronger than others with the ability to feel pain and other maladies. I think it comes from my healing magic. But staying there isn't an option for me right now. It's too overwhelming. Until the worlds are one again, I can't say as I'd ever go home."

"What will bringing the kingdoms together do to help ease that for you?"

"It would create a balance. It would offer a reprieve of emotions and create a stable space to breathe without pain. It wouldn't be entirely the truth. It would be leveled by illusion, dreams, day, and night. Much like the mortal realm." She sighed. "It is why we left for so long."

Jamie took his wife's hand. "I hated knowing you were in agony." He looked at me. "Leaving was the only way to keep her safe from her own world. It was killing her."

"But if we can join the kingdoms, it would be okay?" I now feared Lara being in the kingdoms. I didn't want her to be in pain.

"Yes." She gazed up at Jamie. "We never thought it would be possible. But I have hope."

He kissed her forehead. "Me too, love. Me too."

Sure. No pressure or anything. What if I wasn't the person they thought? What if I couldn't do what they needed?

Sander's hand slipped down my arm and took my hand. The gentle reassurance calmed my nerves.

"So, the barriers. What happens when we get to them? Is it like a wall? Are we just unable to walk through?" While I couldn't fathom how to combine the worlds, I still had questions. Questions that couldn't all get answered in one night, but maybe if I understood the kingdoms more, I could find a way to help.

"No," Jamie said. He heaved a long breath. "The darkness is simply that. A void. A rip in the universe. There is no going through it, only becoming lost to it."

In some weird way, I think I was beginning to understand. "So, the dark abyss of space is actually a reflection of the seams?"

Jamie's brow rose. "I've been teaching astronomy for years, wanting to tell someone that very thing." He splayed a hand over his heart. "I didn't know how good it feels to finally have someone know the truth."

Lara smirked. "Trust me, the truth is the hardest thing to learn."

"Speaking of hard things," Sander cut in. "Jamie, how do you feel about tomorrow?"

Jamie blew out a long breath. "It's been a while since I've seen my family, but I think it will go well. They weren't exactly pleased with my decision to live in the mortal realm but understood my need to protect my mate."

I had almost forgotten Jamie's parents were the king and queen of Somnium. His older brother being the heir, left him out of the throne. I was a bit scared to meet his mother. She was trained in hand-to-hand combat. Jamie had passed down one of her daggers to me before Helios trapped me. It made it out of the building with me, but I hadn't felt confident enough to carry it since.

Sander gave a curt nod. "They will be guests in the castle. I've had Clearie make up suites for both kingdoms on the third floor. Night Fall is only three days away. I know Clearie will do her best to make sure they are cared for. She probably has on white gloves inspecting the rooms now."

I smiled, thinking of the woman. She was a bit brash but highly efficient. I still had no idea how she had everything prepared for me before I even knew what I needed. Clothes magically appeared on my bed before every outing. I had no doubts the woman would make the attending royals comfortable.

Lara cleaned up Jamie's teaching mess. Putting all the pots away under the island. "Has Jen completed her checklist for the wedding?"

I leaned against the counter and sighed. "She hasn't told me much. I'll be just as surprised as you the day of. I just told her I wanted sunflowers."

Lara's head popped up from under the counter. "Sunflowers? In the Night Kingdom?"

I shrugged. "She seemed to think it was doable. She said she'd handle it."

She grabbed the last of the bottles and gave them a shake, inspecting the contents before placing them on the back shelves. "If anyone can pull it off, it's Jen."

Somehow, I didn't think bringing sunflowers to the Night Kingdom would be the most challenging part of this week.

"Where is Jen?" I asked. "We were supposed to train more."

Lara twitched her mouth to the side and thought about it. "She's either in the gardens or the grand hall. She was in ball planning mode earlier."

"How about we train?" Sander asked. "Just you and me."

Without our souls begging for a release, training with him might be different this time. "Okay. I need to change first."

I hoped I could handle it this time and not lose control. Last time I nearly burned down the weapons room.

"See you at dinner?" Lara asked.

"Of course. Assuming I don't burn down the castle." I laughed and pulled Sander with me.

I was almost sure I knew how to find my room, but every hall looked the same. "I need a map for this place."

He chuckled. "Every hall has a guard. If you look, everything to the east of the staircase has wings. Everything to the west has claws. Here," he pointed to a statue standing against the wall, "see? He has claws. The grand staircase is in the middle. The side stairs are usually used by the council, staff, and other guests. There are even a few hidden stairs I'll show you later." He winked.

"So, follow the claws. Got it."

He held his hands behind his back as he leisurely strolled down the hall, watching me inspect the statue. "This is the lowest level of the castle. It has the kitchen, pantry, cellar, and storage. The main level has the grand hall, sometimes called the throne room, the dining room, weapons room, and the council room. The second floor is our suites on the east and another guest apartment on the west, a washroom, and my office. The third floor is mainly bed chambers. The other floors are hardly used. And then outside, there are guardrooms, servant quarters, and a gatehouse. Along with the gardens, of course."

"Yeah, that doesn't help me at all. Seriously, how will I ever figure this out?" My fingers trailed over the black iron statue as I left it behind to find the next one. "What if I go too far and get lost?"

"Wouldn't it be great if you had some secret link to the king who's lived here his entire life and could find you?" He stopped and tapped his chin. "Oh, wait, you do."

I playfully swatted at his shoulder. "Stop it. I'm serious."

"So am I." He gripped my arms and held my gaze. "There isn't a place in this world that you could be lost to me. I will always find you."

I groaned. "For my sanity, let's pretend something happens to you, and you can't get to me. Then what?"

He contemplated my request, knowing he would only answer to satisfy my strange need to know. He was against anything that remotely made him feel as if he couldn't help me. I knew it. "Then you follow the claws to the stairs. Each floor is marked by a dragon. Count his talons. Every talon is a floor, except for the lower level. He has none."

"Why not have a 'you are here' map?" If the Solis castle was this confusing, then that was the first thing I would do as queen. Count dragon talons. Ugh. I felt like I stepped into a fantasy book.

He laughed again. "Come on, little sun. Let's go change so you can train."

Sander let me lead the way back to our suites. Surprisingly, I found them. I wasn't about to tell him I counted the talons, but I did it. Just like before, a training outfit was folded on my bed. I wasn't sure how Clearie knew but was grateful for her help. It was another tight-fitting one-piece. I supposed it was perfect for training. It allowed me to move freely without anything cutting into my skin.

I grabbed a hair tie from the vanity and pulled my hair up. The red book Jen handed me earlier caught my attention. I'd left it there but never opened it. Carefully, I unwrapped the gold chain around it and lifted the cover. There was a slight cracking sound from the spine, and I cringed. It had to have been forever since it'd been opened.

Night History
Volume One

I wondered how many volumes the Night Kingdom had to thoroughly document its history.

Flipping the page, I found almost unreadable handwriting. Archival cursive was hard to read at best and indecipherable at worst. How did Jen expect me to read this? I'd be lucky if it was still English.

I skimmed the words looking for any I might be able to recognize, hoping to pin some of the sentences together. Lux. Trials. Blood. Royal. Death.

Not enough to understand, but enough to know this was about Sander's family line and possibly how they faired in the trials. The death part didn't settle well with me, though. Whose death?

My stomach dropped and rolled around, twisting until it was tight. Maybe trying to read this right now was a bad idea. I needed more time to study the words before I jumped to conclusions.

The door between our rooms burst open. Sander looked panicked. He held a dagger ready and posed.

I scooted back on the vanity bench. "Sander?"

"You were thinking about death, and then I felt your stomach drop." He lowered the weapon. "What are you doing? Woman, you are going to give me a heart attack."

"I was doing some light reading." I held up the book and gave it a little shake.

"Light reading?" He bent over and released a long breath. "We need to come up with a code word or something. Being your protector is a lot harder here than in the mortal world."

I set the book down and went to him. "How about, if I'm truly in trouble, I say... popcorn."

He looked up at me and raised a brow. "Popcorn?"

I shrugged. "Yeah. I hate the stuff, so I would never want it. No one would guess it, and you will know I am truly in need of your assistance."

He stood up straight. "I was thinking more along the lines of help, but popcorn works."

Hands on my hips, I shifted my weight. "Oh, come on, if I yell popcorn, my attacker won't even know what I'm doing. It's perfect."

Rubbing his forehead, he tipped his head. "You've got a point."

"Now that we have a code word, how about we go train?"

Sander looked me up and down, a slow smile spread across his face. "Remind me to thank Clearie for these outfits."

Turning from him, I put a little more sway in my step, knowing he watched my every move. I opened the door and led the way to the weapons room. Not having the strain between us left lots of room for teasing.

"Little sun, you don't play fair." I heard him call out in the hall.

I turned to walk backward, giving him a playful smile. "Hum... maybe you need a code word?"

He darted toward me. I squealed and ran toward the stairs. But he was faster. His arms wound around me, catching me. Laughing hysterically, I fell into his embrace.

"I love hearing you laugh." He moved the stray strands of hair off my face that had fallen from my messy bun.

Still feeling giddy, I rose up on my tiptoes and kissed him quickly.

"What have I told you about that?"

I shrugged, knowing good and well what he'd said about my quick pecks. But I was betting on that very thing.

"That's not a kiss." His mouth moved to mine.

My soul awakened and sprang forward, and I felt his do the same.

The familiar bergamot and chamomile scent filled my senses. It was like breathing him in.

He broke the kiss but kept his hand at the back of my head, holding me to him. His forehead rested on mine. "Little sun, you're learning to play with fire."

I grasped his wrist, tipping my head back to look up into his eyes. "I'd burn the world down for you."

The storm in his eyes raged. "I have no doubts."

FOURTEEN

Emberlynn

THE SUN WAS STILL HIDING OUT behind the moon when dinner came. I'd trained all day with Sander. He added a dagger to my training, adamant that I needed to learn. Hand-to-hand combat wasn't my strong suit. To be fair, he was patient with me, but I sucked. He'd had hundreds of years of battles and more training than I'd ever be able to fit in.

Everywhere ached. I was exhausted. Hungry. But above all, I just wanted to sleep.

Sander proved to be a worthy teacher and didn't go easy on me. I trudged back to my room, debating on a hot bath or falling into bed. Each step up hurt. Drowning out the world, I focused on the stairs. One at a time. One more. Another.

A chill swept over me, and I stopped. Nothing looked right. There were more doors than I remembered. I retraced my steps back to the staircase. The dragon guarding the banister stared at me. I shivered. Creepy things. I knew they were iron but couldn't help but think there was some energy inside of them.

Count his talons.

Four.

Ugh. That meant I walked up two unneeded flights of stairs. I had been too tired to pay attention and kept trekking up. Whining was a probability at that moment. I didn't want to move to go back down.

A door down the hall opened and closed.

Peering down the dim passageway, I watched as a woman briskly carried a tray of empty dishes to one of the smaller stairwells.

Curiosity always got me into trouble, but that didn't stop me from heading toward the room she came from. I stopped a foot from the door and listened intently.

Nothing.

Disappointed, I turned to leave.

"Emberlynn, I know you're close."

I froze.

It was Perseus. My heart skipped a beat. I was conflicted. I wanted to open the door and give him a hug. I hadn't seen him since arriving. But I was also worried Helios could be with him.

I went to the door. "I don't know how to see the truth."

"I know." He sounded tired.

"I'm open to ideas," I whispered.

"I can't be the one to help. But I am willing to be whatever you need to figure it out." He was on the other side of the door now.

I slumped against the door and slid down to sit against it. "I shot a firebolt at Jen's ghost trying to figure it out. I nearly burned down the castle. I don't know what I'm doing."

He chuckled. "I know. They've had to add extra guards while you practice because I broke the door down trying to get to you."

I pictured Perseus storming the castle to put out my fires and laughed. "I'm sorry I haven't figured it out." I wondered where his guard was now.

"Today was hard for both of us. As your Trejan, the simple act of your training puts us in overprotective mode."

Leaning my head against the door, I sighed. We sat like that in silence until my eyelids drooped.

Orange fog grabbed at my ankles as I ran through the gardens. There were people everywhere, but no one saw me. No one saw the mist. My heart thundered as I tried to escape it. I knew who it belonged to, and I refused to slow down. The sun was still behind the moon, but it was fading. I was fading.

"Sander!" I yelled for my soulmate.

Where was he?

I picked up the skirt of the dress I wore and ran faster. Auras burst from everyone I passed. Their actual forms shifted as I moved through them. They each reached out for me, trying to touch me. Black shadows rushed around me. I knew it was Sander. His shadows blocked the auras from getting too close, allowing me to run.

I made it to the edge of the gardens to the steps leading to the city. If I went down there, I'd be bringing Helios to the people. I couldn't do that. Winding my way through the gardens, I found the tunnel entrance to the underground Fores. Maybe I could lead Helios away from here... away from the Night Kingdom.

It hurt to breathe now. My lungs burned. The tunnel was dark, but I kept running. Sconces lit along the cavern, revealing the portal. I turned to see the fog following me. Clutching my pendant, I took a step back.

Helios's ghost emerged from the orange coloring. He looked the same as I remembered. He was on the older end of an immortal, looking closer to thirty. He had a boney structure with high cheekbones, a wide nose, and thin lips. His jaw came to a square point and jutted out.

"Did you think I forgot about you?" His voice warbled. I had to remind myself it was his aura and not truly him. "I actually learned a great deal about you the last time we were together. It has helped me plan accordingly."

"Whatever you think you learned, you're wrong." I took another step back. If I could just make it through the Fores with him, everyone would be safe.

He closed the distance between us. "Say hello to Sander for me." Then, he pushed me back and disappeared through the portal without me.

I gasped as I woke with a painful crick in my neck. Absently, I reached up to rub it.

It was just a dream.

I tried to slow my breathing, but it had been so lifelike. A nightmare. Nothing more.

I wasn't sure how much time had passed since I'd fallen asleep in the hall. A shadow of movement startled me. A guard stood across the hall from me, watching Perseus's door. I supposed I arrived during a change. Although Gabriel would be furious to know there was a lapse in time when he wasn't guarded.

Though I knew Perseus wasn't one to run. He would stay there and prove he was the head of my Trejan.

Standing up, I stretched and groaned with each new pain. Between training and sleeping on the floor, my muscles were mad.

"How long was I asleep?" I asked the guard.

Nothing. He made eye contact once but then returned his watch.

Of course. No talking to the soulmate.

I really hated that rule.

"Emberlynn?"

Perseus was still there. "Yeah. Sorry, I didn't mean to wake you."

"No. I can't sleep. I didn't know you were still there."

I smiled. "I should get going. But..." I got closer to the door to whisper. "I'd like to come back later. Maybe we can practice together?"

"I am here for you, my queen."

I hated leaving him there under a guard like some criminal. I needed to focus and work harder to help him.

The staircase loomed ahead. I cringed. My legs wobbled as I began my descent. Between the dream and the extensive exercise earlier, I was spent.

"Emberlynn?" Sander's concerned voice echoed through me.

Shadows encased me, lifting me from the ground. A squeal of surprise escaped my throat. My heart picked up the pace, and I reached out to grasp something tangible, but they wouldn't allow it. They swathed me in a cloud of support. Sander's essence embraced me, and I sank into his comfort. The shadows carried me to the second level, where they set me carefully on the floor.

Sander was there. "I thought you were sleeping. But then I felt you in pain. You were scared."

I wasn't sure I was ready to tell him about the dream. Applying my best smile, I sauntered closer to him. "I never said popcorn."

He carved a hand through his hair. "I almost didn't care." He looked me over. "But you're okay?"

I nodded and folded my arms. "I'm just sore. Training really kicked my butt."

"That's my fault. I shouldn't have pushed you so much. I'm sorry."

"Don't be. I need it. There will be a day when I will need everything you teach me. Would you want me to be lacking because you didn't push me?" The dream haunted me. I wanted to learn more now than ever. There was no way I wanted to be caught unable to defend myself with Helios ever again.

He grumbled. "I really don't want to think of you ever needing to protect yourself."

I waved him off. "I know. You're always going to be there. I have my Trejan and Gabriel... but it's important. We both know it's possible we could be separated again. I don't want to be without at least a general knowledge on how to protect myself."

"No." His jaw clenched. "I will not allow that again. It almost killed both of us."

I touched his arm. "Sander, I think there is more to it than that. You said yourself we are still at war. In war, things are unpredictable. The only thing we can do is prepare. Train."

He winced.

There wasn't a lot I could say to help him through this. He would need to find a way to let me train. "Come on, let's go to bed. Assuming I haven't slept the entire night in a hall."

He cocked his head. "Why were you sleeping in the hall?"

I relayed to him how I found Perseus and fell asleep. I didn't tell him about the dream or the missing guard, though. He was already upset enough. I'd let Gabriel know first thing tomorrow about the guard. Not because I didn't trust Perseus, but because the guard should be reliable. What if they were that negligent while guarding Kade? My stomach turned. I had mixed thoughts about him.

Sander sighed. "I understand you want to practice, but I'd feel better if Gabriel and myself were there to help. Maybe even Lara in case things go wrong?"

He meant in case I hurt one of them. In case I couldn't control whatever energy surfaced, and I burned them all to a crisp. Yeah, those were my fears too. I nodded. "Deal. I need to do this. I need him as my guard."

He kissed the top of my head and led me to my room. "Then I suppose we should try first thing in the morning. We have guests arriving in the evening."

With the sun and moon still taking up residence in the sky, I lost track of time. It could be midnight or noon, and I'd not know the difference.

Tomorrow something more than just Night Fall festivities would start. I could feel it. The energy thrummed through the air. The shift slid over me, warning me. Sleep didn't come easily. But with Sander curled around me, I let myself relax.

IT WAS MUCH LATER the next day than what I wanted to start, but Sander let me sleep until I woke. Clearly, I was exhausted as it was already noon. At first, I was infuriated with him. He should have woken me, but then as usual, his words made sense. He told me I wouldn't be any good depleted. Perseus deserved me at my fullest. It still bothered me that I slept in, but now there was nothing I could do to fix it. What was done, was done.

Gabriel almost exploded when I told him about the missing guard. I would not want to be the guards on duty for Perseus after hearing him rant about their incompetence.

"Mortal high school students have more reliability!"

I tried to contain the laugh bubbling in my chest. "If I recall, you said the mortal teens didn't have enough focus and wouldn't last a day in your guard."

He grumbled, "And they wouldn't."

Sander was already waiting for us outside of Perseus's door. He smiled at me but then watched Gabriel closely. "Everything okay?"

"He's contemplating conscripting mortal high schoolers for the guard," I teased.

Sander's laugh was rich. "One of those days."

Gabriel pointed at us. "You two keep laughing, but I do not take my job lightly. Protecting the king and now his mate is not something anyone should ever take lightly."

"I agree," Perseus said through the door.

Gabriel frowned. "Why is it that the only one who understands the importance of this is the one being guarded?"

Lara padded down the hall. "Oh, Gabriel, I can assure you he is not the only one."

I ran to her and gave her a quick hug. "Mom. I'm glad you're here."

"I'm not sure what good I will be, but if I can help you, then you know I wouldn't stay away." She linked arms with me, and we walked back to the others.

"You might be needed if I end up catching everyone on fire."

Sander quirked a smile. "I think you have more control than when you first arrived."

Almost as if on cue, the energy inside of me sizzled. "Let's hope so."

Gabriel opened the door. "Do you know how you're going to do this?"

I shook my head. "No. But I'll never know if I don't try."

Perseus's room was simple. Few decorations and furniture filled the tiny space. A few books were stacked on a table by the window. His bed was neatly made, and I wondered if he did that or if he had someone come in daily to tidy up.

Gabriel guarded the door. Sander stood with Lara off to the side. His arms were folded. Confidence rippled off him.

Perseus bowed his head as I approached. "My queen."

"I've thought a lot about this," I started. "Before, when I was younger, auras would only show around objects. Things like the moon, shadows, objects that I now know are attached to the kingdoms. Some items were tangible, like the note my parents left with me. But others weren't. Jamie and Lara were the first people I'd ever seen the colors emerge from. Even then, it took a while before I saw them take shape. It seems that the longer I was around others connected to the kingdoms, the more my gift showed me. Here, everything is intensified." The auras from last night's dream interrupted my thoughts. I shook off the intrusion and continued, "I think I can control them."

Perseus stood tall, his head high. "I trust you."

I gave him a sad smile. "I know. But I want you to know that I have no way of knowing if it will hurt you. Kade taught me what to look for. Helios hides well in the colors. If I find him..." I swallowed the guilt of keeping him here, or worse, the dungeon. "If I find Helios in your colors, I'll try to separate him, but there's no guarantee. If I fail, you'll have to stay here until we can figure it out."

He looked unfazed. "I already told you, I am here for you to do what is needed. You are my queen, and I am your Trejan. I am not scared."

Yeah, well, I was. No one knew if this was even possible, let alone any way of teaching me how to do it. I had to wing it and go with my gut. It was a process of trusting myself. Something I needed practice in. The last time I tried, I thought I'd already had a connection to the aura since I saw it but was wrong. When I grabbed Sander's shadows and ripped them from the Solis guard, I imagined them as tangible. I didn't recognize them as anything but in my way.

So far, no one's aura had greeted me in the room.

It was too quiet. I could hear everyone breathing. Whispers of thoughts muddled together in my ear. How did Sander shut that part off? Sander's heart thumped steadily next to mine. It was so loud compared to the whispers, so I focused on that, making it the only thing I heard.

The ambiance of our souls combined crashed like waves between us. His heart continued to pulse strong while mine sped up. His calm constant support pulled me back and kept me from diving off the edge.

Taking a deep breath, I concentrated on Perseus. Using Sander as my ground, I was able to push myself out and feel with my energy. My ghost launched from me as if I called it.

It was strange seeing my own aura. I'd only seen mine when I touched Sander and then again when we bonded. She was a beautiful gold that illuminated more than others. It was like an outline of me filled in by translucent gold paint. A ghost. It walked with its head high to Perseus. I felt her move away.

I gasped.

No. Not a ghost... my soul. I had been wrong about what I'd seen this entire time. It wasn't auras I saw but souls. I had it all wrong. I was so focused on the colors and shapes I missed the whole point. I had thought about it once, at Scurradiem. I had wondered if that's what I saw but brushed it off. It was all so new to me I barely had time to expound on any new theories.

But now... I felt it. I'd never felt a color like that before. It was me. It was an actual feeling. Like when I felt Sander when he wasn't around.

Sander's heart picked up a bit. Surely, he was reading my thoughts and understood too.

"It's your soul," I whispered.

Perseus cocked his head slightly. "I'm sorry, my queen. I don't understand."

"It's not just a color or aura. It's not a ghost. It's your soul."

"Emberlynn," Sander spoke softly.

I turned to him. "It's our souls."

He nodded. "I think you're right."

Spinning back to Perseus, I watched my soul stand before him. "I want to see him." I mentally projected to my spirit.

My body felt disconnected. I was draining. But I had to keep trying. I was finally on to something.

A flicker of gold pulled from Perseus, but it didn't fully emerge.

Sander stepped closer, but I stopped him. "No. Wait."

The world darkened, and my limbs grew heavy. I pushed out more of myself. "I need to see him," I tried again.

Again, a flicker of gold slipped from Perseus but not his full form.

My soul was the last thing I saw before hitting the ground.

VOICES SURROUNDED ME but were too far away. But I locked on the one I would know anywhere. Sander.

I blinked and found Lara hovering over me with Sander cradling me in his lap. "What happened?"

Lara sat back on her heels. A hand splayed over her heart. "You scared me."

I tried to sit, but Sander wasn't having it. "Just relax for a moment, little sun. No need to rush and pass out again."

I frowned. Why was I so weak? "What happened?"

Lara touched my forehead and grimaced. "You didn't draw from the sun. You have a deep well of magic, probably deeper than any of ours, but you took the surface and used it up."

"Picture it like the ocean." Sander helped me sit. Carefully keeping his hands at my back for support. "You can dive deep into your reserves. How much you have and what is waiting for you there, we still don't know. But you only used what was washed up on shore, ignoring the vast sea of power behind it. Once it was gone, you fell."

"That is so embarrassing." My head hurt, and everything felt like I was run over by a train.

"Do not be embarrassed, my queen." Perseus was there too. He sat on his heels, watching me. "You have more power than expected. No one else has ever tried to command a soul. Aside from the gods."

I shrugged. "Well, figuring out this power is exhausting. There should be an instruction manual or something. I have no idea what I'm doing."

Perseus shrugged. "I think it is hard because we all use ours differently. There are no two same energies. Growing up, we learned them like we learned to walk and talk. It is second nature to us. Teaching you would be difficult."

I stared him down. "That's not helping."

If anything, that made me feel worse. There was no way to be taught.

"I should try again." I went to stand, but my legs were still too weak to do so without support. Sander caught me and held me to him.

"I think you are done for today."

Perseus held his hands out as if to catch me as well. "I have to agree, my queen. You are not strong enough to attempt it again."

"I am strong enough." Even as I said the words, I knew they were a lie. But I hated everyone telling me what I was or wasn't.

"Ember," Lara said. "It might be for the best to give yourself some time to build your reserves again. Besides, you have guests coming soon."

"Fine." I pushed off Sander. "But I want to try again as soon as I am able." I had to. There was too much at stake.

Maybe it was the dream from last night, but I felt like the air around me was trying to warn me. Something was going to happen.

I turned to Perseus. "I hate leaving you here."

"I don't think it will be much longer." His faith in me made my guilt burrow in even deeper.

I should have been able to do it. I should be able to see his soul and know. Tears filled my eyes, and I blinked, trying to clear them before they fell.

Sander placed a hand at the small of my back, leading me from the small room. I passed the guard and ducked my head. I didn't need anyone else seeing my disappointment.

Back in my room, Sander shut the door and watched me. He made no move to come closer. "You're quiet."

"I only passed out in front of everyone because I'm stupid. I don't know how to handle these powers, myself, the colors, any of it. At times I want it to all go away. To be normal. But I've never been normal. It has followed me my entire life. But now it's stronger. I don't know how to control it." My breath quickened as I let it all out. "What if I can't do this? What if the people are wrong and I'm not the one to bring the worlds together? What if I shouldn't be here at all? My own mother placed me in the mortal realm. Maybe I should have stayed there."

In two strides, Sander was with me. His strong arms held me close. "No, Emberlynn, you are supposed to be here. With me. I know this is hard on you, but this is where you belong."

I curled my hands into his shirt and clung to him. "I feel the sun calling me. It's strange but beautiful. I can't help but wonder if I will be able to fully wield it. I don't feel strong enough."

"Look at me," he said. Tipping my chin up, so I had to meet his gaze. "You are more than enough. I know the feeling, though. When my parents died, I wondered if I'd be able to harness the night. The moon pulled at me, testing my strength. The sun will do the same with you. Use me. Use my strength. I have more than enough to give you."

"I'm sorry you lost your parents."

"So did you."

"But you were there. You have that memory. I can't imagine."

"You may not remember, but you were there too. Our history has been intertwined since the beginning. Even then. I was so caught in my own grief… But now, I see why it happened. I would never have found you. I wouldn't have even thought to look at the Solis princess as a potential soulmate." He wiped at the single tear that fell down my cheek. "I was a warrior. I wanted to serve my kingdom. Never thinking I'd actually have to rule it one day. I didn't see other royals as equals. I was less than. I was just me."

"And I am just me." Up on my toes, I leaned in to capture his mouth. "Titles aside, you are mine. The kingdom can fall, the worlds disappear, and I will still be here with you. The gods might have written our history, but I refuse to give them our future. We decide. Together."

"Together."

FIFTEEN

Emberlynn

THE HOT WATER FELT HEAVENLY as I sank into the deep tub. The smell of berries and flowers filled my nose. The oils Sander had poured into the water were made in the Night Kingdom. He said a shop in the city carried all kinds of bath oils and soaps and promised to take me soon.

I replayed earlier with Perseus over in my mind. The way my soul felt as it left. The way it was still a part of me but stretched painfully thin the farther it got. I wondered about the deep reserve of magic Lara said I had. Could using that help my soul go farther? Could it be used to coerce other souls to submit to my commands? How much power was hidden in the depths of that reserve?

Sinking lower, I fully submerged under the water, blowing out bubbles with the last of the air in my lungs. I laid there, suspended in the tub. The water had a gentle hum of energy that blocked out the world.

A dark shadow fell over me, but I didn't move. My body warmed, knowing Sander was there. Slowly, I rose to the surface and took a breath.

He sat on a bench not far from the tub. A mischievous grin lifted his lips.

"Mr. Lux, I am bathing."

"Ms. Cyrus, I am well aware." He leaned forward and laced his fingers together, resting on his knees.

I rolled my eyes and stretched out a hand. "Since you're here, will you hand me that towel?" As much as I loved the bath, I needed to get ready. The visiting royals would be arriving at any time.

He stood and grabbed the towel, holding it open for me. I went to take it, but he shook his head. "Let me."

Fine. Two could play that game. Boldly, I stood giving him a full view and stepped from the tub, dripping water on the floor before moving into the waiting towel. He wrapped it around me.

Keeping the towel secured around me, I slipped past him into my room. Clearie had already set out an outfit on my bed. I held it up to inspect it. "I think Clearie has forgotten to bring the rest of it."

Sander chuckled and leaned against the frame of the hall, joining our two rooms. "You are meeting the kings and queens of neighboring kingdoms. Our kingdoms come from the gods. Not only are you the descendant from the creators, but you are the rightful Solis Queen. You are my soulmate and soon-to-be Night Queen. You have an impression to make."

I tossed the flimsy material to the bed. "That I'm a whore?"

He nearly choked. "No. Absolutely not. The dress will show them your confidence, your position with the gods, your title. A meeting like this is not the same as a court dinner. It is a power play. Think of it as a costume."

"This," I picked the sheer napkin up and held it out to him, "is not a costume. I'm not wearing it."

"Put it on." It was a challenge. "For me."

I felt it. A shiver coursed through me.

Dropping the towel, I didn't take my eyes off him. He held my stare, but his eyes darkened in desire. I slid the dress over my head and let it fall over my body. It barely covered my breast and had slits all the way to my hips. If I moved just right, everyone would see all of me.

Sander's heart raced. Its phantom pulse echoed in my ears. "You're right. You're not wearing that."

I quirked a smile but followed quickly with a fake pout. "But I thought you said I needed to exude confidence. They need to see I have descended from the gods."

He licked his lips and swallowed hard. "Yes. But not in that. You wear that, and I'll be killing every man who looks at you."

I enjoyed toying with him. "I thought immortals didn't get jealous. I thought you were proud to show off your mate. Would this not be a grand way to show me off?"

"Little sun, you are different." A hunger deepened his voice to a growl. "But to be honest, I had Clearie bring that dress in for me. I actually picked out something else I'd like you to wear tonight."

I raised a brow and lifted the dress, flinging it to the bed. "If you want to see me in lingerie, you just had to say so." However, I was relieved this wasn't what I had to wear. A part of me was excited by how he looked at me and would have to remember to wear it sometime for him—only him.

The gravel in his voice deepened. "Perhaps you can put it back on later. For now, however, let me go get your actual dress before I am unable to leave the room." He left, but the way his soul shook at leaving me quaked through our connection, rippling throughout my body.

It didn't take him long to return with a new outfit. "I don't know how I will survive this night without murdering anyone who looks at you for more than a glance."

"But isn't that what they are supposed to do? To see me?" I laughed. "But you will spare them because you know the only man who has permission to touch me is you. It is your bed I am sleeping in tonight."

"I'll hold you to that."

"I hope so." I took the new dress and held it up. "Well, it's got a little more coverage." I didn't want to admit that this one I found to be gorgeous. I wasn't sure I was woman enough to pull it off, but I hoped so.

"I'll let you dress while I change." He gave me one last lingering look before departing to his room.

I touched the new dress with care. It meant even more because Sander picked it out for me.

I slipped on the form-fitting material and gasped. This was more than just a dress. The high collar revealed bare shoulders. It dropped down across my chest in a diamond shape, covering my breast with a deep, plunging neckline. The top was beaded in moonstones and diamonds. The sides were open, revealing my trim waist and a black mermaid silhouette skirt that billowed out towards the floor. The back was completely open as well, with a diamond cutout.

He returned, and my breathing hitched. He wore all black, but his shirt was open, showing off his hard abdomen. His crown sat a bit crooked but gave him a sultry charisma. My body tingled and warmed as I admired the man in front of me.

But his eyes were on me. Making my core even hotter.

I twirled once for him slowly, letting him take it in.

The way Sander looked at me told me he approved. "You are exquisite."

Turning to the vanity mirror, I gasped. I couldn't believe it was me in the reflection. I filled out the dress like it was made for me.

My hair was already drying in soft waves. I pulled the brush through it and let it cascade over my shoulders and back. The soft glow only illuminated the beauty staring back at me. I'd never felt so confident before.

Sander came up behind me and picked up my crown. He set it on my head and watched me in the mirror. I looked like a woman. A queen. A goddess.

A slight flicker of his silver coloring escaped looking as well. Shadows swirled up around me as if they, too, needed to approve.

A knock on the door broke the spell.

"It's Gabriel." Sander opened the door, but I still felt him inside of me. He was completely lost in my appearance.

Gabriel and Jen waited in the hall. "They've arrived."

"We'll be right down." Sander dismissed them and turned to me.

Jen lingered in the hall to give me two thumbs up. Her jaw dropped when I stood, and she mouthed a few words of praise.

I tried not to laugh.

Slipping on the strappy heels from the first dinner, I felt as ready as I could be. Sander held an arm out to me. I linked mine with his and let him escort me from the room. This was it. No turning back now.

Walking through the castle, I played with the sun's energy letting it rise under the surface, and then pushed it back down. Keeping it close but under control. The more I did it, the stronger it felt. I shouldn't need it, but the caution in the air still had me worried.

Sander led me to the grand hall. It was the room Jen was prepping for the ball in two days. It also had two thrones set up on a dais to overlook the room, where there was previously only one. That was where Sander headed. People I hadn't met and a few I had from my first night here filled the room. My heart raced, but I kept my head high.

Whatever confidence I felt in my room was long gone. Whispers filled the air, and souls emerged as we passed. Colors filled my peripheral vision, but I didn't dare look. There were too many of them, just like in my dream.

"You're doing great." Sander's thick voice engulfed my thoughts.

He guided me to the throne on the right. He rubbed a small circle over his mark on my wrist. "Show it off." He winked before taking his seat.

Butterflies erupted throughout my stomach.

Gabriel and Jen stood off to Sander's right below the dais. Guards were stationed throughout the room. I wondered how many were given a speech from Gabriel before tonight. Knowing my own Trejan was not here actually bothered me. I wanted to run up to Perseus and free him from the room. I needed him. I needed them. I couldn't explain it, but I was nearing panic. The energy around me shifted, and I knew it was too late. Whatever was in motion had already begun. The warning I'd been feeling exploded, and I had to focus on slowing my breathing.

"What's wrong?" Sander took my hand, scanning the crowd. Shadows slowly rolled up the dais.

"I don't know." I didn't. "Can you feel it?"

A commotion with the guards caught my attention. A few of them went running from the room, and I froze.

Gabriel casually walked up to whisper to Sander. "It's Perseus. He's trying to leave his room. Something about Emberlynn not being safe. I have my men checking it out and sent more to his room."

"No." I went to stand, but Sander held me down. "Sander, it's me. He feels me. If I could talk to him and let him know I'm okay."

"Not now." He turned to Gabriel. "Make sure there are no threats before we depart this room. I'll be with her at all times tonight."

"Sander, please." I couldn't explain it, but I knew I needed Perseus with me. "Let him out."

"We haven't been able to rule out any involvement with Helios. I can't do that."

"What if I could?" The room began to spin. I needed to calm down. If not for me, then for Perseus.

"We tried earlier. Now is not the time, Emberlynn."

I gripped his hand. "Then have the guards surround him but let him come down. Please. I need him here."

He sighed and turned to Gabriel, giving him a nod. "Make sure he is secure but let him attend. Make sure he knows he is not to confront anyone. He is to keep his distance of Emberlynn."

"You make it impossible to protect you." It was only his thoughts, but I heard Gabriel clear as if he'd just said it. He nodded and stepped off the platform.

"Thank you."

Sander traced his mark on my wrist. Conflicting emotions raged inside of him. He was worried but also upset that I didn't think he could defend me. He warred against himself. An overwhelming protectiveness stirred deep inside of him.

He continued to rub my wrist while scanning the crowd. "There is something off."

"So, you feel it too?"

He gave me a lopsided grin. "No, but that part of me that would murder a man for looking at you is elevated."

Several minutes later, a group of guards surrounded Perseus in the back corner of the room. His eyes locked on me. He was physically shaking as if he'd been fighting every one of them to get to me. Blood dripped down his hands, and I was confident that was precisely what had happened.

I mouthed, "I'm okay." Hoping it would help him.

Alred made his entrance known by opening the back double doors. Since the first dinner, I hadn't seen him, but he looked the same in an outdated suit and neatly trimmed beard. He stepped off to the side and cleared his throat. "Your Majesty and his Favored, may I introduce their majesties, the king and queen of Somnium."

A man who looked a lot like Jamie entered the hall, a woman I could only assume was his wife on his arm. The way he carried himself was regal.

In reality, or at least mortal reality, these would be my grandparents. Adopted or not, I felt a kinship to them. These were Jamie's parents.

The queen had long black hair woven into an intricate braid with diamonds making her hair look like the night sky. Her dress dipped low in the front and back, but the entire thing glistened with diamonds. The skirt trailed behind her.

The king wore a fitted suit with a jacket. His lapels matched his wife's dress. He, too, had his button-down shirt open and revealing.

They walked to the dais. The king quickly looked me over and smiled, turning his attention to Sander. "King Lux."

"King Knight. I'm glad you could make it." Sander's fingers intertwined with mine. "I'd like to introduce my soulmate, Emberlynn Cyrus." He paused. "And since we are soon to be family, you have permission to speak to her. With respect, of course."

The king grinned wider. "Granddaughter, I suppose. We heard of our son's great fortune at finding you and taking you in. The Solis Queen, the soulmate of the Night King. Our kingdoms seem to be in great hands." There was no malice in his words. He seemed genuinely happy about the situation.

Some of the tension released from my shoulders. "Thank you."

The king took his wife's hand and led her toward the small platform off to the side set up for our visiting royals.

Sander leaned in. "See, that wasn't so bad."

"It's not done." The buzz of energy grew, and I held my breath. "Seriously, you don't feel that?" I knew that feeling. I'd felt it before. But when?

"I feel you."

Alred introduced the Verum king and queen.

As soon as they entered the hall, I felt another shift. The queen locked eyes with me. It was her. I didn't know how I knew, but I knew.

She wore a deep red but an entirely sheer dress. It was hard not to look. She left nothing to the imagination. I didn't care how much confidence she wanted to project; she made me want to grow claws and rip her to shreds for being so brazen in front of my soulmate.

The king of Verum had a little more covered, but barely. He wore a red, long, open robe. I'd never been so grateful to know he wore a pair of tight black pants under it. While they wore simple, unembellished attire, they held the attention of everyone they passed. Perhaps that was the point.

The queen broke eye contact with me to greet Sander. "King Lux. Thank you for the invite. It has been a long time since we've all come to celebrate Night Fall."

"Queen Triggs." Sander kept his calm demeanor, but I could feel the tension building through our bond. "The queen of Solis and I are excited you could attend our wedding."

Interesting. It wasn't just me who felt her abrasiveness. I wondered how many others knew something was off as well.

Catching a glimpse of Perseus told me we weren't the only ones. He was having a hard time staying put.

Queen Triggs grinned and returned her stare, looking me up and down. "It will be a great event for sure. We wouldn't miss it." She didn't necessarily talk to me, but she was breaking the rules in a roundabout way, but I wondered if Sander caught it. Surely he wouldn't let it go so easily, even with a visiting royal.

"King Triggs, I'm sure you and your lovely wife will enjoy your time in the Night Kingdom."

The king made a noise that was half-annoyed and half-agreeance.

After they left the dais, I tried to look away but couldn't. "What was that?"

"I don't know." He followed my gaze to watch the Verum royals. "But I don't think we should ignore it."

Alred cleared his throat again and introduced Jamie's brother. "Prince Kai of Somnium." He paused for an identical version of Jamie to step through. Only a slight birthmark that went up his neck to his chin showed the difference between the two men.

"Prince Jamie and his Favored of Somnium."

My breath quickened as my parents were introduced. I didn't think about them having a royal entrance. Lara looked stunning in a black dress with a high collared top. The only skin shown off was her shoulders, but the dress fit so snug against her she exuded her own appeal. A diamond belt loosely hung on her hips.

But Jamie... He wore a black suit with a half-sun, half-moon crest pinned to his lapel. He looked like he belonged in the Night Kingdom. They both did. They were representing well, and I was secretly proud.

They each came to the dais to greet us. Sander did not give permission to Kai to speak to me, but he formally had to announce approval to Jamie and Lara.

After the introductions were done, I nearly flung myself off the throne. "Is that it? Are we done?"

Sander chuckled. "For now. There will be people here until the early morning. We can stay as long as you'd like."

I grimaced. "Or not like. This is way out of my element."

He took my hand and kissed it. "You handled it well."

The Verum royals were sitting in their seats. The queen was still staring at me. "I noticed you didn't give everyone permission to speak to me."

I knew he noticed her too but didn't pay her any attention. "Do you oppose?"

"No!" I said almost too loud. I looked around to make sure no one noticed my outburst. "No. I was kinda glad. Especially with Maleficent over there. She gives me the creeps."

Jen approached us with a wide smile. "Okay, you two, go mingle. Show off your bride to be."

I hesitated. "Jen, I don't think that's a good idea."

"I do." She gave a side glance at the queen of Verum. "Trust me on this."

Trusting Jen and following through were two different things.

"She is right," Sander whispered. "Remember what I said about a power play?" He looked at the red queen. "There can only be one queen in my court."

Sander returned his gaze, giving me a slow provocative smile. Images of how he'd like to rip my dress off flittered through my head. I gripped his hand and tried not to moan out loud. The visual he projected was detailed, making me feel every thought as if we were alone in his room.

Jen cleared her throat and grinned.

The room and all our guests came back into focus. The blush creeping up my face deepened.

She locked her stare with mine. "Hold your head high and show them all you are the queen. Got it?" I couldn't help but hear a small plea in her tone.

I nodded. "Got it."

Sander stood and held his hand out for me to take. "My queen."

Accepting his hand, the sun's energy roared to life, making my soul burn with a need to be with him. "My mate."

A low rumble sounded from him as I stood. A deep protective growl that warmed every inch of my body. His hand slipped to the small of my back, then to my side, where he gripped me gently. "Little sun, show them why you are the queen and burn them all down if they forget to bow."

SIXTEEN

Kade

"EMBERLYNN!" I SCREAMED her name as her call woke me from the unconscious void I'd been drowning in.

The ominous warning flooded our connection. She was in danger. Pain in my side shot through me as I sat up. Gripping the wound, I felt her handprint. She had burned my flesh to save my life. A debt I didn't deserve and would never be able to repay.

I am Trejan, I will not fail.

My queen's panic rolled through me so violently it made me sick. I had to get to her. I had to save her.

"Let me out." My words came out less than forceful. Still winded from pain and lying here for an unknown amount of time, I was weak. There was no sun to renew my strength. "The queen needs me. Let me out!"

I stood, and my guard scoffed. "You are not going anywhere."

"She's in danger. Help her! Let me go." No amount of yelling made the guard listen to me.

I rushed the bars of my cell and struggled to pry them open. Emberlynn's enemy was close, and that knowledge ripped at my mind. I couldn't stop myself from attempting to break the cell door down. The iron sliced my skin as I tried to force my way through.

The guard used the hilt of his dagger and hit me over the nose. I stumbled backward. The pain was intense, splitting through my skull, but it didn't stop the urge to rip myself through the bars or die trying. I had to get to her.

I am Trejan, I will not fail.

Again, I rushed the door and steeled myself against the beating of the guard through the bars. Another guard... and another. Each one attempting to force me away from the door. A dagger pierced my upper arm, digging all the way to the bone.

"Somebody get the captain! We need help down here!"

"Get back!" Guards yelled and threatened me, but they wouldn't listen. Emberlynn was in danger.

The iron creaked and slowly began to pull apart. I was losing all my strength, hardly able to breathe, but if I could free myself... If I could just get to her.

Blackness filled the space. Shadows owned by the king wrapped around the cell. The guards were no longer able to restrain me, but the shadows could. Their icy fingers clenched around my throat, cutting off any chance I had to alert the king of Emberlynn's demise. Helios was here. I didn't have to see him to know him.

The room went black, taking with it my opportunity to protect my queen.

SEVENTEEN

Emberlynn

THE VERUM QUEEN openly stared at me. Her gaze followed me around the room.

Sander proudly introduced me to nearly everyone gathered for the event. Thankfully, I didn't have to speak because he didn't grant anyone permission. I hated the rule before, but now it was working in my favor. It was finally making sense to me, and I appreciated the protective bubble it offered me. I had always been socially awkward, but this was a new level of social I wasn't prepared for.

I felt Perseus's eyes on me as well. His presence, while still guarded, helped ease the discomfort of the night. I knew without a doubt Sander could protect me, but this was different. I hated thinking it had to do with some ancient blood link but was beginning to think the Trejan were more than a simple guard. Being the only direct descendant from the creation gods, I suppose there was a reason.

More now than before, I wanted to find a way to clear him. To prove to Sander and myself that he was not connected to Helios.

I ran a hand across Sander's back as I slipped behind him to talk with Perseus. The guards blocked me.

"I'd like to speak with my guard."

"Move aside," Sander commanded, moving to stand behind me.

The guards moved to let me see Perseus.

"My queen," Perseus said. His voice strained. "I'm sorry. I couldn't fight it. I had to be here."

"I know." I felt the red queen shooting daggers at the back of my head as I spoke to my Trejan. "I didn't mean to scare you. I was just worried. I felt this strange shift in the air and... well... I think I know what or who caused it now, but I never meant to cause you that kind of pain."

Perseus shook his head. "No, my queen, it was not your fault. As your Trejan, it is my job to protect you, and when you feel threatened, we have no choice but to follow the command. It is a blood oath."

I flinched at the words. "One you were forced into, not one you made."

His entire countenance hardened. "It does not matter. I would gladly swear my life to you even if I weren't born into it. Do not think I am ever regretful. I am honored to be your Trejan."

"I didn't mean that. I just hate that none of you seem to have any choice. Our lives are all planned out without any opinion from us." It made Sander's dedication to give me a choice, at least as much of one as he could, mean so much more. He understood. Even if the gods hadn't put us together, I think I would have searched the world for him. He was my choice.

"Not everything is planned, my queen. There would be no contention, no war, no peace, without choice. You need a vice to understand virtue. Without a choice, neither would exist."

I hoped he was right.

Gabriel cleared his throat gently. "My king, Keira Knight is approaching."

The queen of Somnium made her way through the lesser crowd. She was graceful in every movement. I remembered how Jamie said she was skilled in hand-to-hand combat. I wondered if she'd ever had to fight in a battle. "King Lux." Her voice was soft but steady.

"Please, call me Sander. We've had too many years of family between us to remain so formal. My parents thought highly of you."

"Your parents were good people. They led the Night Kingdom with mercy." She turned to me. "And your parents..." Her eyes watered. "Your mother was one of my greatest friends. Seeing you tonight brought back many memories. You look just like her except with your father's hair."

That was the first time anyone had ever compared me to my parents. I'd not met anyone who knew them well enough to do so. "Thank you."

She smiled. "And now, it seems right that Jamie brought you into our family. I'm sure Selene would approve. Although," she gave Sander a quick smirk, "I'm not sure any of us saw this match."

Everyone laughed.

She looked past us to Perseus. "I haven't seen you in a very long time."

Perseus dipped his head slightly. "I have been searching for my queen."

She cocked her head and narrowed her eyes on him. "And now you've found her, but you're... guarded?"

"It's complicated," I interjected. There was no need to place doubt in any other mind unnecessarily. "But he is the head of my guard." I was careful not to say Trejan. The fewer people who knew the truth about my guard, the better. I didn't need that being used against me—or them.

That seemed to appease her curiosity. "As he should be. He was with your parents for many years before the last battle. I wondered where he went but should have known he wouldn't do anything less than look for you." She looked over her shoulder at her husband. He was with Jamie and Lara. Kai was off chatting with a group of women. Presumably single unmated women. "It is getting late, and with so many festivities in the next few days, I would like to wish you both a good evening."

"I'm glad you made it. We look forward to celebrating with you." Hum. Not too bad. Maybe I was getting the hang of this formal speaking thing after all.

She left to say goodnight to the others and then left with her mate. It was then I noticed the escort outside the double doors. I had wondered how they knew where to go.

I wasn't sure if my first impression was enough to prove to anyone I was a queen, but I was exhausted and ready for bed as well. "I think she has the right idea."

"It is late. Perhaps we should get you some rest."

"And first thing tomorrow, I want to try again." I looked at Perseus. "If you're up to it?"

He looked hopeful. I hated giving him any kind of hope when all I'd been able to do so far was pass out. "Tomorrow then."

Looping my arm through Sander's, I leaned against his shoulder.

Sander kissed the top of my head then began to lead me from the room. "Gabriel, we are going to turn in for the night. Make sure all the guests are accounted for at the end of the night. And... perhaps think about extra guards for the third floor. For their protection, of course."

Gabriel quirked a brow. "Of course."

Sander used the shadows to conceal us from the guests, hiding us from sight as we made our way through the hall. At the staircase, he dropped the shadows. The blue in his eyes swirled. Nothing but love shown through them. "I could carry you."

Heat rose to my cheeks. I was reminded of the cave and our first night. "Just don't let me fall."

"Never." In one swoop, I was in his arms. The shadows swarmed around us, carrying us up the stairs. "I think I remember a promise you made me earlier."

"Which one? I made quite a few."

He pushed the door to his room open. "Let me remind you."

OPENING MY EYES, I blinked and tried to stretch, but Sander's arms and legs were wrapped around mine. I smiled and snuggled in closer. Outside the windows, the sun was still hiding behind the moon. I wondered how the people of the kingdom were adjusting to so much light. It wasn't bright by any means but gave a glow to the kingdom, like dawn light.

Slipping from the bed, I wrapped a blanket around me to walk out on the balcony. The city was still asleep. The crashing waves in the distance lulled the kingdom into a mock sense of comfort. Something was wrong. I could still feel it. Maybe it was the Verum Queen, but maybe it wasn't. Last night was supposed to be a show. We were supposed to exude power and confidence. Perhaps I was wrong about her. But if I was, then what, or who was causing such ill energy in the kingdom?

"You're up early." Sander met me on the balcony. He had already donned pants, but his upper body was bare, revealing a sculpted chest.

"I couldn't sleep. There's something in the air. Something that isn't right. I can't explain it." Turning into his arms, I opened the blanket to encase us both. Leaning against his chest, I relaxed.

"I feel it too. Not like you, but the unbalance. I thought maybe it was because every royal from the Immortal Kingdoms is here, but now... I'm not sure." He kissed my head. "We should get ready."

I nodded, but I wasn't ready to leave his arms yet. Here the world stopped. I could breathe and not worry.

"Emberlynn, you know I will never let anything happen to you. Right?"

"I know." And I did. I knew he would die protecting me. But that scared me too. The idea that the war wasn't over created a dire need to control my powers. All of them. I needed to see how far I could dive into that well. It scared me to dip my toes in, but if it meant saving just one life...

Leaning back, I did my best to smile for him. "I suppose I should go see if I can coerce a soul to listen to me. No better way to start a day than to be a demanding soul queen."

He chuckled. "Little sun, I pity anyone who ever goes against you."

Inside his room, I dropped the blanket and strolled to my room naked. "Remember that."

Shadows met me across the threshold and swirled up around me. I shivered as they caressed every surface of my body. Sander approached slowly. "And it would do you good to remember that I take every tease as a promise."

"Noted." I was breathless and close to falling from reality.

The shadows tried to slip away, but I called to them, grasping them with my magic. They listened. Sander watched with a new desire crashing through his eyes. I pulled them to me, letting them settle over me.

Outside, the light grew brighter in flares. It was euphoric. Blissfully letting my soulmate's shadows touch me while he watched. And then I found it... the well. My soul dove deep as I reveled in Sander's touch.

The deeper I dove, the lighter I felt. There was no bottom. No end. Limitless power to bask in.

I locked my heated gaze with Sander's. A heartbeat of a moment passed, and then he was there, his lips crashing down on mine. The shadows continued to embrace me, but now their master claimed me.

The light of the sun burst through the room. For a moment, the kingdom was filled with its brightness. I felt it search for me, seeking its source of magic. Once it found me, it went back to its hiding place behind the moon. Except now I knew... it wasn't hiding. It was waiting.

"Emberlynn," Sander whispered. His thick, husky voice dripped with a request.

I'd never get tired of this between us. "My king."

THE CASTLE WAS WIDE AWAKE, buzzing about how the sun woke them all early this morning. I tried to pretend I heard nothing, but everyone I passed had something to whisper about. Sander was proud, telling me it was an honor to show off such power, but I disagreed. It was embarrassing.

Climbing the stairs to the fourth floor, I tried to push all the staff's thoughts from my mind. If they would all stop projecting so loudly, I might be able to pass without hearing them. Sander's gifts were in full effect today.

Jamie was with Lara already in Perseus's room. They were all lost in conversation. Thankfully not about the sun—or me.

"Good morning, kiddo." Jamie stood to greet me with a hug. "I miss being able to do that over breakfast."

I hugged him back. "Me too. Nothing has been the same since arriving here. I miss the kitchen."

Lara cooed, "Oh, honey, we can go back whenever you want. The house is still there."

"Thanks, but that won't fix things here. I don't see how that will be possible for a while." I gave her a quick hug too.

Gabriel and Jen joined us. "Sorry I am late. There was a thing I had to take care of."

"A thing?" I questioned.

He frowned at Sander, who nodded for him to answer. "It was Kade. He's awake. The guards are having a hard time containing him. Apparently, last night there was an incident, and he nearly escaped."

I gasped. "What happened?"

"So that was where the shadows went." Sander rubbed my shoulders. "I had some slip from the room last night. They were compelled to keep Kade in his cell. If he should escape his guards, they were ordered to stop him. He must have been close."

Gabriel looked at my guard. "He was. Except, he kept going on about how Emberlynn was in danger. The same way Perseus was."

I hated that I was beginning to feel bad for Kade. I was so confused over him. "He was trying to get to me, to save me?"

"It makes sense," Perseus said. "I told you, as a Trejan, we cannot deny your call."

I grimaced. "Blood oath."

He nodded. "Blood oath."

Gabriel sighed deep. "He has calmed down for now, but Lara, he could use to see a healer after this. I guess he took a dagger to his arm last night."

"He's hurt?" The last time he took a dagger was to come save me, and he nearly died. My stomach rolled, thinking history was repeating itself.

"Emberlynn," Perseus spoke. "Maybe you can help him too? I can't imagine him not being able to be with you last night. As a Trejan, he would have died trying to save you. Perhaps not all is lost with him."

"Maybe not." One step at a time, though. I couldn't help Kade if I couldn't compel one soul out in the open. The only way this would work was if I could force souls out to see them. I had to be able to see Helios coming. "How about we do this. I don't know about you, but I'm ready to have my Trejan back."

Perseus's lip curled into a grin.

The energy inside me flowed back and forth as I let the well open, flooding the reserves and then some. I didn't need flames or fire. I needed my soul. She was the source of my magic. At least that's how I found my well–through her. I felt her dive deep.

It didn't take much before the room exploded in light. It radiated from me like a sun flare. I controlled the power that flowed from me. It emanated authority and commanded truth. Sander might control the shadows, but I ruled the light. And in the light, all things shall be seen.

Every soul in the room emerged. Even Sander's silver apparition manifested beside me.

I gasped as I watched them all bow low.

One by one, they stood and waited. Each respected my presence, and I almost felt guilty. Perseus's soul kneeled. I went to it first. There was nothing dark in his coloring. "Stand," I ordered it.

It obeyed.

My fingers slipped through his presence. A shiver raced through me. I'd never experienced a substantial touch with a soul other than Sander's before. I felt everything he was bound to, including myself. He was not attached to Helios. As a matter of fact, I could tell that if given a chance, he'd kill anyone associated with him to keep me safe. The way he felt when around me, the emotional connection he had with me, and the Trejan oath running through him flowed through me. I felt it all. Who he was, who he wanted to be, what he wanted… all of it was there.

"Emberlynn," Sander spoke.

Everything I felt and saw, I pushed to him. But I wasn't done yet. Sander's soul held me in a gaze of respect. It reached out to me. It was the only one I'd ever let touch me, after knowing what a simple touch could reveal. I learned more about Perseus in those seconds than any words could ever convey. Information like that could destroy a person. But there was nothing about me he didn't already know.

"What is happening?" Gabriel asked.

I'd forgotten no one besides Sander and myself could see the souls. I stared at my soulmate. "It worked."

"So, he is good?" Gabriel almost sighed in relief.

I laughed. "He's good." I'm not sure who was more relieved, Perseus or Gabriel. I knew they had formed a close friendship back in the mortal realm. This had to be a test of loyalty for both of them.

"Now what?" Jamie asked.

"Now we help Kade." The pool of power was still overflowing inside of me. If Sander wanted a confident queen, then that's what he was about to get. I was sick of playing the game of the gods. If Perseus was right, then I was about to make a choice to change the way the game was played.

For a moment, the dream of being chased by Helios haunted me. But I refused to let him win.

"We only have today." I wasn't sure how I knew that, but I think the dream had told me more than I wanted to admit. "We will need everyone tomorrow."

Sander's soul had already disappeared. But I would cherish the moment I saw it. He stood watching the others and nodded. "He is not here. He's on the island in a cell."

"Then we go to him."

Jamie held a hand up. "Wait just a minute. This is not a good idea."

"Dad, you'd have me living in a bubble if you could."

He pulled his face into a hopeful frown with brows raised. "So that's an option?"

I rolled my eyes and smirked. "We're going to the dungeons. If you'd like to stay here...."

"No," he cut in. "We're a family. We do this together. I think we've already proven that we do much better when we're together versus when we separate."

"Agreed," I said. I never thought I'd have a family, especially one this strong. Lara wiped a tear from her cheek. I could only imagine all she felt in that room. But I worried about her in the dungeon. "Mom, I don't know what will happen down there."

Lara held her head high. "I am aware of what we are heading into. But like your father said, we do this together. I have been around more than I hope you ever have to know. I will be fine."

Gabriel hesitated. "I have to ask you both to stay here. There seems to be a new guest arriving that was unannounced."

Perseus remained calm. "It is not a threat."

"I cannot be sure." Gabriel had Jen stay with us and left.

Perseus shook his head. "It is not a threat. I have no resounding need to kill anyone."

Sander chuckled. "I agree. I have had the most intense desire to murder anyone who comes close to her. And right now, there is nothing."

Perseus cocked his head. "Are you sure you are not a descendant from the Trejan?"

Sander stiffened. "My bloodline can be traced back to the first gods. If there was a Trejan secretly mixed in there, I think I'd know."

Perseus continued to scrutinize Sander. "You seem to have more of a protectiveness than other soulmates I've encountered."

Jamie scoffed. "You have no idea. A bit obsessive even."

"Dad," I chastised.

He shrugged. "What? He is. You are. You both are crazy about each other, more than normal."

"Yeah, and you and mom aren't?"

He pointed a finger at me. "That's different."

Just because Sander and I had an intense relationship didn't mean it was wrong. I mean, the sun did crash into the moon, but still....

A commotion came up the stairs. Perseus darted to the door, grasping for his dagger that wasn't there. I'd left it in my room.

Sander pushed me back behind him.

Gabriel roared, and another man yelled. A rough sound of fists and a thud of bodies plowed down the stairs. "My queen!"

I didn't recognize the voice, but the desperate need in the tone had me running. "Wait!"

Gabriel captured a man in a chokehold on the stairs. He looked up at me. "Emberlynn, do not tell me to let him go."

"Release him."

Gabriel grumbled under his breath but continued to detain him.

Sander joined me. "Gabriel, her words are the same as if I spoke. I believe she said release him."

"You two make it impossible," he started.

"To protect us, yes, we know," Sander finished for him. "Now release him."

Gabriel let go, and the man gasped for air. He fell to all fours and crawled up the stairs. "My queen." He collapsed on the top landing, passing out from the fight.

Lara immediately went to him. "Flip him over."

Jamie and Perseus carried him to the hall and laid him on his back. Lara began analyzing him. She sighed and sat back on her heels. "He'll be okay. Gabriel had a strong hold on him."

"He was trying to get my king's Favored." It was the first time Gabriel had used my formal title. A small amount of irritation rent the air, and I knew he was probably ranting to Sander silently.

Perseus still kneeled next to the man and chuckled. "That's because he is Trejan." He ripped open the man's shirt to reveal his tattoo.

Another Trejan.

"I don't understand." I inspected the tattoo, making sure it was like the others.

"I might have put out a call, but it was a silent whisper compared to what you did last night. I think any Trejan around felt the need to protect you. My guess is most don't even know they are Trejan. He might not have known until you called him."

"I didn't call anyone," I squealed.

"But you did." He sighed. "And whatever had cause to hurt you called us. I wonder how many others are on their way now."

"Can you see his soul even though he's passed out?" Jamie asked.

I shrugged. "I don't know. I don't see why not."

Using the well to fill myself with power, control pulsed throughout me. His soul seeped from his unconscious body. It was slow at first, but then recognized my spirit and bowed. I touched the warm green and gold colors. Everything about him came to me. Perseus was right. He was Trejan, but he didn't know until last night. He traveled through the night to get here. He was in Fairos, a city across the sea in the Night Kingdom. He wasn't Solis.

I furrowed my brow as I tried to understand. "I thought my Trejan was made from Solis guards only?"

"Yes." Perseus lifted the man and carried him to his bed.

I followed him. "But he's not."

Sander filled the doorway. "What do you mean?"

"He's from the Night Kingdom. He's from Fairos."

Perseus pondered over the man. "That is strange."

Jen raised her hand. "I have a theory."

Sander chuckled. "Of course, you do."

She smirked at him. "What if the Trejan was Solis because that was the kingdom where Cyrus' blood ruled. But now, you two are joining your kingdoms. What if the call of the Trejan can now be answered by Night guards too? And therefore, if the other worlds merge, the Somnium and Verum guards as well."

"A Trejan made from every Immortal Kingdom?" Sander questioned.

Jen shrugged. "It's possible. This might be the proof you need to know that it's working. The kingdoms are merging. Can you imagine a Trejan with all four magics?"

He looked at me. "I think I am beginning to understand."

"Was he attached to Helios?" Gabriel asked.

"No." I shook my head. "His name is Knox, and he hasn't ever been away from Fairos. He's young. He is the same age as me."

"How is that possible?" Gabriel went to the foot of the bed. "Our guards aren't even chosen to start training until they are at least twenty."

He was still learning life. But I took it away from him. He didn't have a choice. "I don't know." But I did know what I needed to do now. "Perseus, you stay with him. He's going to need you when he wakes. I'm going to Kade."

He looked torn. I knew he wanted to stay with me but also knew the new Trejan would need his guidance. Especially since he had no idea what was happening to him. He was the first Night Kingdom immortal to become a Solis Trejan. He wasn't even a guard yet.

I didn't wait for a response. Whatever was in the air warning me was now spreading to my Trejan.

EIGHTEEN

Emberlynn

SANDER HELD MY HAND as we stepped through the Fores. "Are you sure about this?"

The wind whipped around us as waves crashed into the island. The salt air assaulted my nose. Even with the sun giving the realm a glow, it was dark here. Shadows moved along the jagged edges and rocks of the mountain. We were high up, overlooking the sea.

I wrapped my arms around my middle. "I'm sure." Kade and I had a turbulent history, but no one deserved to be controlled by Helios. If I could help him, I would.

The entrance was more of a cave. Cool, damp air trickled through the corridor. Fire licked the stone walls illuminating the tight passage. Narrow steps led us into the heart of the island. I followed Sander as he went deeper.

Whispers floated around us. Some were heard, and some were thoughts that seeped through Sander's gift. Water dripping echoed through the hollow cavern. The first room we came to was more of a platform. A flat blanket of dark rock made the floor and walls. A large pit in the middle roared with fire. It helped to warm the air and dry out the humid moisture. It was much brighter in here than in the stairwell.

"My king." A guard bowed his head and waited for orders.

Sander retook my hand and pulled me close. "We are here to see the Solis prisoner."

The word prisoner dripped with distrust.

"Certainly," the guard said. He hesitated a moment looking at me. "Forgive me, my king, but perhaps your Favored would be safer out here?"

The flames on the wall and in the pit roared. Shadows climbed the walls. "My mate is safer with me."

For months Sander told me about being king. About the Night Kingdom. He was patient, kind, calm. But here... here I saw a new side to him that exuded power. In the mortal realm, he was a man. Here he was a god. He was everything the night offered. A thread of pride slipped through our connection as I watched him.

Mine. He was mine.

My heart skipped a beat.

The man I loved and would marry was the king.

The guard cast his gaze down. "I'm sorry, my king. Forgive me."

We followed the guard to another set of stairs. Sander leaned down to whisper, "You sure pick the oddest moments to have revelations, little sun. How am I supposed to control my kingdom with those thoughts distracting me?"

I shrugged, keeping the pace behind the guard. "I can't help that I'm equally proud and extremely turned on by my soulmate."

A low growl was his only response. It vibrated through our connection and warmed my soul.

Again, we descended the mountainous island through a winding passageway barely large enough for Sander to fit. The walls were so close I could feel them closing in on me. Breathe. Just breathe. I wasn't claustrophobic, but I'd never been spelunking either. This made me realize I never wanted to.

The mouth of the stairwell widened, and I nearly ran to the open room. More guards lined the walls. Bar doors led to multiple cells. It didn't look like any of them were occupied, but I assumed the one Solis guard who found us in the city was there, yet I wasn't about to go looking. I was only here for Kade.

I imagined Helios rotting behind one of the bars and grinned. A fitting place for such a terrible excuse of a man. I'd gladly place him in the mountain for eternity.

"One day, little sun. One day." Sander continued past the guards to another hall.

I groaned inwardly. Another passageway?

"I assume he is down one more level?" Sander asked.

"Yes, my king. There are always two guards with him. We change shifts multiple times to keep alert."

"Gabriel will be here soon. It will just be us down there, no other guards."

The man looked confused but dipped his head. "Understood." Slowly, he cast his gaze up at me.

A flicker of his soul erupted around him in color. Dark blue hues that mimicked an early night sky made his spirit blend in with the shadows.

Already skimming the surface of my well, I felt myself dip lower as he emerged. The sun demanded respect, forcing his soul to notice my reign. To respect my power. A bit of madness crept up through the well wanting to consume me. Giddy feelings of excitement replaced the uncertainty. For years I'd been closed off, afraid, insecure. But here, in the Night Kingdom, I was beginning to feel confident. Losing myself in the magic helped me find the woman standing beside my soulmate.

"Back," I commanded the soul.

It returned to the guard. No flicker of light, no trailing essence lingered around him.

A swell of emotions warmed around Sander's phantom heart in my chest. Pride and love engulfed our connection. Images filled my head of how he saw me standing there, directing souls with shadows begging to touch me.

I tsked, "Now look who is distracting who."

"I can't help if I am proud of my mate." Desire lingered in each word.

A new presence of authority broke through our playful banter. Gabriel emerged from the tunnel. "Perseus is with Knox. He is awake and taking things rather well. A bit too excited and young, but we can train him."

"We are just waiting for you," Sander said, giving me a wink.

"That is a first. I half expected you to be down there attempting to do this without me."

Sander clapped a hand on his friend's shoulder. "Gabriel, my friend, I was half a breath away from doing just that."

"You are impossible to guard."

"Where is Lara?" I asked.

Gabriel hitched a thumb over his shoulder. The whites of his eyes looked brighter in the cave, with his skin blending in with the darkness. As the head of the guard, he looked every bit the part. "We decided she would wait in Astraios until needed. I didn't want unnecessary bodies here." He looked at the guards. "It isn't exactly a place to visit."

Sander stepped between the guards and me. "Shall we?"

Gabriel led the way down to the next hall. Left, right, right, left... we traveled through the maze of cells. At the end of the hall was a door unlike the others. This one was iron and had a powerful current that called to me. The energy marking it was strong. Stepping closer, I placed my hand on the door.

A zing of pain shot up my arm. "Ouch."

Sander pulled me back. "It is protected. Only the guards are permitted to travel through."

"Like a spell? A ward of magic?" I reached out but didn't touch the metal. I just wanted to feel the tingle of power. It resonated with mine like lightning crashing over the sea. I captured part of it and held it, refusing to let go even though it hurt. Minor cuts appeared on my palms, dripping blood. Using it against itself, I tried again, this time pushing the door open, but I had to let it go. It wasn't mine and keeping it would be painful.

"How?" Gabriel's jaw slackened.

"Emberlynn," Sander said, taking my hands in his. "You're hurt."

I pulled back. "No. It wasn't mine to possess. But it was pretty cool, though, right?"

"I'm impressed." He ripped his shirt and wrapped my hands. "But I wish you wouldn't do that again. It's not worth you getting injured."

"I didn't even know I could do that. Did you?"

"No." He shook his head as he tied the last of the shirt around my hand. "Gabriel leaves a loophole in his wards to allow me access, but I've never seen anyone use magic not their own like that."

"She is going to continue to surprise us, I think." Gabriel heaved a long breath. "I only hope this does not end badly." He left us to descend into the darkest tunnel yet.

I turned my hands over to inspect Sander's quick wound treatment. "I didn't know it would do this."

"I think there is a lot we don't know. Once we arrive in Solis, there could be all kinds of things that revive in you. We have no way of knowing all your gifts from the gods." He paused to lift my face to look into my eyes. "We do know that your power is growing, and you are stronger than anyone thought. I don't want you to get hurt."

"I know."

Two guards surfaced from the stairwell. Each bowed as they passed Sander. They retreated down the hall without speaking.

This was it.

I kept a grip on the tail of what was left of Sander's shirt. I couldn't see two feet in front of me. Finally, the darkness began to lighten as we neared the bottom.

Flickering of flames dancing on sconces illuminated the space. It was one large room with a single cell in the middle. Kade clung to the bars as I approached. Relief flooded his bruised face. He was bare from the waist up, and it was hard not to notice my handprint burned into his side. Dried blood caked his left arm. One eye was almost swollen shut.

Knowing he had fought hard enough to endure that kind of beating just to get to me–to save me–made my heart twinge.

He bowed his head but winced. "My queen," he whispered. His voice cracked.

It was the first time he'd called me his queen to my face. Memories of high school marred any emotion I had for him. Being here confused me more. I couldn't deny there was a connection to him. An oath unspoken between us. "Kade."

He looked up. Hopeful remorse clouded his good eye. "I'm sorry."

I held my hand up. "Don't."

Pushing my soul out, I pulled his to me. His gold apparition bowed reverently. I walked closer to it needing to know everything.

"What are you doing?" Kade asked.

Sander stepped closer to Kade. "Be quiet until you are asked to speak."

Kade's soul watched me but made no attempt to move. My fingers warmed as they slid through his presence.

His life flashed before my eyes. Images of before the war. Memories of the last battle. His fear of losing those he guarded warped the picture. Pushing my magic into his thoughts, I slowed them down to watch as he recalled the last moments of my parents.

Tears fell down my cheeks as I dropped into the memory.

I was there, observing, unable to do anything but watch it unfold. Kade fought. He tried. Perseus was there too. The scream from my mother haunted Kade, and now it would me too. My father had fallen. I spun to see Helios grinning as he pulled out the dagger. For a split second, I thought he could see me, and I panicked.

A ball of fire filled my palm as I readied to defend myself. But he walked away. The fire died, and I ran to my parents, but the scene flickered as a new image flipped the world around me. They were gone, and I was in a cave.

A tiered black and white marbled fountain ran thick with blood. My blood. My life pooled with the red lineage of the gods in the quatrefoil base. I felt myself in the fountain as strongly as I breathed.

A scuffle of footsteps at the entrance startled me. It was Kade. He was detached from reality, focused only on the fountain. He crawled to the base, where he collapsed. Tears fell as he cried out my name.

Again, the world shifted, and I was in the dark. I couldn't see anything. I felt Kade's presence but couldn't see him. He screamed, and the image shuddered. This was it. This was the memory I needed. He had blocked it out, and it would be painful to relive, but it was the truth.

Off in the distance, I heard Kade crying. He yelled at me to stop. But I couldn't. "I'm sorry," I whispered.

I refused for the memory to shift. I controlled it now. Light began to fill my vision. We were in a small room filled with herbs and crystals. Kade was strapped to a slab of quartz. I gasped and took a step back. Helios was there with a woman who looked up. She smiled at me. She knew I was there.

Her eyes looked at me but through me. She was blind.

Her wicked grin widened as I watched. She was beautiful, but her essence was evil, ugly, and haunted. She hunched over Kade and pulled something from him.

My stomach rolled and twisted when I saw what she had in her hands. It was Kade's soul. And Helios's. She was burning them together with her hands. She had sun energy. She was using my magic, my power, to bind them together. I was sick.

The smell of charred soul was worse than flesh. Kade screamed again, this time in both the memory and in reality.

Helios laughed as a sheen of sweat broke out over his forehead. The sick demon was enjoying this. His soul stretched thin as tendrils now piggybacked Kade's.

I coughed and gagged.

The woman snickered and looked up one last time before searing the remaining strand of Helios's soul to Kade's.

I stumbled back, falling into Sander's arms. The room disappeared, and the cell came back to me. I turned to bury my face in his chest. His scent replaced the horrid burnt soul.

"Shhh, it's okay. I've got you." He rubbed up and down my back. "It's okay."

I shook my head. "No. That was definitely not okay."

"Emberlynn," Gabriel spoke softly. "What did you see?"

Kade silently wept on the floor of his cell.

"I saw everything." I wasn't the one who lived through it, and I didn't want to talk about it. But now I knew… I knew what I had to do. And I hated myself for knowing.

Wiping at my eyes, I turned to Kade and knelt next to him. I gripped the bars to steady myself. "Kade."

He shook his head. "Just kill me. Please. Don't do it."

"I can't do that. I need you." Being there with him, seeing it happen, I couldn't help but protect him now. He was my Trejan. Tears continued to run down my face. "I need you, Kade."

"I can't… I can't do that again. I didn't even remember…" His breathing quickened. "Please."

"I refuse to let you die attached to that demon." I sucked in a long shaky breath and straightened. I would pull the queen card if I had to. "You will not die. You are my Trejan, and you will fight him."

"I am Trejan, I will not fail." His whisper was weak but still held conviction. I believed him. He wouldn't fail.

"That's right." Sniffing back more tears, I moved back from the cell. "Okay, um, he's gonna need Lara after I'm done. I'm glad you made the decision to keep her in Astraios because there is no way she could be here for this." I wasn't sure I wanted to be here for this.

"Emberlynn," Sander started.

I looked at him. He was my grounding. He knew what I knew. "I don't know if I can do this."

"You just got him talked into it. Don't go talking yourself out of it." His confidence in me helped level me.

Gabriel looked between Sander and me. "Would either of you like to tell me what is going on? What do you have to do?"

"I have to burn Helios out. I'm not sure how to do it without carving pieces of his soul off."

"Can he survive that? Can anyone survive that?" Gabriel turned to Kade. "He's already weak."

"He'll die if I don't. He is my Trejan. If he can't be with me, he'll die trying." The cool rush of shadows swirled around my arms. The comfort they provided healed the ache in my chest. Kade wasn't alone. I was here. If I failed, he wouldn't die alone.

I looked at Gabriel. "Remember, get Lara. But do not bring her to the island until after I am done." I gripped Sander's hand as if my entire existence depended on it. "Don't leave me."

He squeezed back. "Never."

Kade attempted to sit.

"Don't." I sat on the ground next to him, leaning against the cold metal bars. "I'm sorry."

I didn't give him time to respond. I pulled his soul to me. Its haunted stare broke my heart. It knew.

The fiery heat of my magic glowed at my fingertips. The sun created a tangible essence between us. I was able to grasp his spirit instead of slipping through it. He winced. The memory of being held before rushed to the surface.

"Shhh," I cooed. "I'm trying to help."

It felt like silk, sliding under my touch. Gently, I ran my hands over his body, looking for the parts connected to Helios. Black, wilted sections defiled the smooth gold coloring. There had to be ten of them.

My stomach rolled. Bile rose to my throat.

I hovered over the well of my power, afraid of diving too deep and hurting Kade more, but there was no way to do this on the surface. I couldn't even imagine doing this without using all my energy.

I took a slow, steady breath and then slipped into the light of the sun. I fell deeper than I'd ever been before. It burned. My body shook as I slowed my descent into the power.

I was on fire. My soul, my body, all of me. It wasn't red like a small flame, but white, hot, and searing. I carved through his soul using my hand, cutting Helios out and sealing Kade from the dark magic.

Screams of agony tore through my head. I wasn't sure if it was me or Kade.

The blackness of Helios's soul turned to ash and crumbled to nothing. It blew away from the cell floor with nothing to cling to.

It was so hot.

"Stop! Please..." Kade pleaded with me.

My heart shattered for him. I hated being the one to cause the pain. I hated Helios even more for making me do it.

I found another piece and removed it. The smell of charred soul assailed my senses. I gagged, hardly able to breathe.

Kade's body shook violently. I had to hurry.

"Kade," I whispered. "Don't you dare die. You are my Trejan."

"I am Trejan..." His voice faded.

"And you will not fail," I finished for him.

I scoured his soul, looking for more sections. Each one was harder than the last to remove. I hadn't found the bottom of my well, but I was close. I felt it draining as I weakened.

One more. It was the biggest of them all, and I worried I wouldn't get it all. I carved through his essence. The stench violated my nose as a new deathly odor mixed with it. I vomited on the floor of the cell.

Kade's body jerked and writhed on the ground. His scream echoed in the belly of the mountain. I pushed the last of my magic to seal his soul and fell beside him.

I was too weak. My chest barely rose as I took a ragged breath. I couldn't stop shivering as the heat of the sun left me.

Sander picked me up and rushed from the room. I wanted to argue that Kade still needed me, but he didn't. He was free. I'd burned the damned devil out of him.

Sander swept me up through the caverns, the small tunnels, and out into the open ocean air. The Fores gleamed like a beacon. It promised an escape.

"Stay with me," Sander pleaded. He stepped through the portal and ran through the tunnel under the gardens. The world sped by as the shadows picked us up and carried us to the castle. "Lara!" Sander's yell echoed throughout the halls. There wasn't a soul immortal or mortal who wouldn't have heard him. The kingdom rattled as he cried out.

He carried me to our joining bathroom and placed me in the tub. He let the hot water run until I stopped shaking. His touch was gentle but demanding.

My eyes closed, but he yelled at me to stay awake. I tried. Desperately, I tried. I didn't want to disappoint him.

"Ember!" Lara was there. "What happened?"

Sander explained the events with Kade. A tear slipped down his cheek. "I should have pulled her back sooner. I shouldn't have let it go that far."

Her hands hovered over me. I felt the draw of her energy as she searched for wounds, both visible and invisible. "She is just depleted. The fire in her is barely alive. Keep her warm. Take her into the sun. She needs whatever it can give her. Don't let her move much. She needs to rest." Lara's voice faded. "I'll be back to check on her later."

Sander picked me up and carried me to the bed. He removed my clothes and wrapped me in a heavy blanket. He climbed out onto the balcony and cradled me in his lap. The heat from his body enveloped me, and I sank into him.

A tiny flicker of energy sparked to life in the well. But I was too tired to do anything with it. But the heat from it grew and began to warm me from the inside. Going from searing hot to no flame at all was an extreme I'd like to never repeat.

I worried about Kade. Was he okay? Did he survive? His screams would haunt me forever. His soul now carried my mark. Many of them. He and I had a history, yes, but now we had a future. Knowing what he went through gave me a new version of him. I knew the truth. I saw it. I was there.

But now he was free. He could heal and come back to the Trejan. We could start over.

I was glad I didn't have to do that with Perseus. It scared me to think I would have to do that with anyone else ever again. Bile rose to my throat, and I tried to swallow it. It burned. I sputtered and coughed.

Sander held me up, rubbing my back.

I blinked, trying to focus on the sky, but it was darker than it had been. "The sun." I tried to talk, but it was too hard.

"Shhh. It's still there." I didn't believe him, but I didn't have the energy to argue.

I sank back against his chest. His heart thumped steady but fast. I couldn't keep my eyes open any longer. I let the thump of his heart lull me into sleep.

NINETEEN

Emberlynn

WAKING, I WAS STILL WRAPPED in Sander's arms. The slight glow of the sun returned to the sky, and I sighed in relief. Last night felt like a dream. I still wasn't sure what was real. Reality felt disconnected. My limbs were heavy and ached.

"What happened? Is Kade okay?" My throat was parched, making my voice rough.

Sander stirred. "You scared me." He yawned. "And I don't believe I like you asking about another man while still in my arms."

I sat up. Every muscle in my body protesting the movement. "Did he make it?"

Dark circles under Sander's eyes attested to his sleepless night. "Yes, little sun. He's awake, and Lara is with him. I will take you to see him later if you wish. Right now he needs rest. Lara's orders. As well as you… if she asks, I held you down and forced you to sleep all morning."

I laughed. "Somehow, I doubt she will believe that." I sighed. "But you're sure Kade is okay?"

"Yes," he said. "I imagine he will be in Astraios by tonight."

"Tonight?"

He shifted the blankets and stretched. "Night Fall. Our wedding. I don't see why he can't come now. If he's feeling up to it."

I couldn't believe the day had finally come. I was going to marry my soulmate. There were so many things to do today. Jen had gone over the day's events over and over. She wouldn't let me hide today. No matter how exhausted I was.

But, first, I wanted to see Kade for myself. The memory of what I did was burned into my head. I could never forget. Slipping from the blankets, I realized I was still naked. I'd forgotten how Sander rushed me to the tub last night. His protector role took over, but the way he looked at me as if I'd died would always be something I remembered.

"I guess clothes would be a good idea if I want to leave the room." A stack of freshly pressed clothes sat folded on the vanity. "I see Clearie has already been here. I don't know how she does it."

Sander chuckled. "She was careful to be quiet. The entire castle has been restricted for sound while you rested."

"Even our guests?" I slipped on the short, silky dress. Jen had already prepared me to change clothes at least three times today. This morning I would be in a simple, black satin dress. It had thin straps and a straight neckline. The back was open, and it had a darted bodice. A high waist and a simple slit up the thigh in the knee-length skirt.

"Especially our guests." He chuckled. "The king and queen of Somnium were quite worried about you, but the Verum royals were less than concerned. They have been ordered away from the castle until you awakened as they couldn't seem to grasp the idea of silence."

I gasped. "I can't believe you did that."

He chuckled. "Oh, that wasn't me. That was Jamie."

"Of course, it was." I piled my hair up on top of my head and pinned it into place. Rogue strands fell and tickled my neck. Jen had plans for my hair later today for the wedding and ball. She has been a bit secretive about the ball, saying she was using the wedding to her advantage to create a night to remember. Although, I didn't need a ball to remember the night I would marry my mate.

Sander came up behind me and snuck in a quick kiss on my neck. "Hey," I said. "That's not a kiss."

Turning me to face him, he gripped my shoulders and leaned in. "I wasn't finished."

His lips met mine, and the world exploded. The warmth of the sun's energy flared to life. Sander was everything I would ever need.

He pressed against me. His hands roamed my bare back, sending shivers over my flesh.

Pulling back, he grumbled, "Gabriel is always interrupting us."

A knock on the door told me all I needed. Sander's perceptive ability to hear Gabriel's thoughts gave a heads-up at least.

Sander begrudgingly opened the door. "I'm going to have to set out time frames when we are not to be disturbed."

Gabriel ignored him and entered the room. He saw me and grinned. "You look lovely, Emberlynn."

"Thanks, I feel so strange constantly dressing up. Jen has a strict dress code for this week."

Gabriel laughed. "It is not just for the week."

I groaned, "Thanks for the warning."

Sander rubbed my arm. "Maybe I should come with you?"

"To walk around the castle?" I raised a brow.

"With everything like it is, I worry. Maybe I could assign more guards..."

I cut him off. "No. No more guards. I'm sure Perseus will have things smoothed out with my Trejan soon. But really, no more guards. I need some space."

"We could always have her join our council meeting?" Gabriel countered.

"And that, is my cue to leave." I slipped on my sandals and made my way to the door.

Sander folded his arms and leaned against the doorframe. "Asking about other men, fleeing my arms, and now the room...."

I laughed and gave him a quick peck on his cheek.

"That's not a kiss."

Images of exactly how he'd like to kiss me–and where– flooded my mind. He was getting entirely too good at projecting his thoughts to me.

"That's a kiss," he whispered.

"I might need a reminder later."

Remembering Gabriel was still in the room, I blushed. He chuckled, and I wanted to slam the door. Sander stifled his own laugh and watched from the door as I made my way to the staircase.

Maybe I could find Jen and see if she needed any help. She had promised to be everywhere, but no clear destination. The castle buzzed in excitement. Guards walked the halls talking and laughing. Everyone I passed had genuine happiness to them. Each one had a smile for me.

Absently, I played with my pendant as I strolled through the halls. Like home called to me, I found my way to the kitchen. Jamie sat at the counter drinking a cup of something hot. His face lit up when he saw me. "Hey, kiddo. I didn't think I'd see you until tonight."

"Mind if I join you?"

He tapped the stool next to him. "I wouldn't mind at all." He got up and poured a cup of what looked like coffee for me and sat back down. "It's not the same as home, but not too different."

"Thanks." I picked up the mug and inhaled the rich aroma. He was right, it didn't smell like coffee, but strangely the smokey, bitter scent hit the spot. There was something oddly familiar about it. "Where's Lara?" I looked around the kitchen, but she wasn't there.

"She's still with Kade."

Kade. The stench of his soul burning under my fingers clung to me, and it was all I could smell. I set the mug down and pushed it away. He had endured so much, and I hated him for it. I hadn't known it was Helios the whole time, but now I felt horrible. I wondered if I could have helped him sooner. Instead, I yelled at him. I pushed him away. My gut twisted.

Jamie mulled over his drink for a moment, swirling it around before taking a swallow. "Emberlynn, I haven't thanked you."

My mind was still on Kade. I couldn't imagine anyone thanking me right now. "For what?"

"Your life has not been easy. Not even before you left Solis as an infant. You had great parents. You had a family. But..." He set the cup down and looked at me. "But you chose to accept us. I think being chosen as a dad means more than if you were my own blood. Tonight is a big night for you, and I get to be there to share it with you. I can't think of anywhere in any world I'd rather be than to be here supporting you. Thank you."

This was a much deeper conversation than I was prepared for. I knew Jamie gained energy from emotions and could easily fall into an illusion of depression. Somnium souls faded fast. The somber mood Jamie was slipping into worried me. I took a sip of my drink and shrugged. "Dad, I hate to tell you, but you chose me. So now, you're stuck with me."

His smile returned. "My survival instincts are telling me not to argue with you."

I clapped a hand on his shoulder. "I'm sure you haven't become an old man by ignoring those instincts."

His laughter filled the kitchen. "No."

"Alright. I was looking for Jen to see if she needs help. I might keep looking." Maybe I could sneak off to see Kade too. I knew Sander said he'd take me later, but I needed to know he was okay. Guilt made it impossible to forget what he'd lived through.

"Good idea." Jamie swallowed the last of his drink. "I think we will be in town later today before the festivities tonight." He winked.

"Bye, dad." Hopping off the stool, I gave him a quick hug and went to search for Jen.

Following the claws to the staircase, I found myself wanting to keep going. Up. Another flight. The fourth floor. I swallowed the lump in my throat. I hadn't been back up here since yesterday. Since before Kade.

Stepping quietly, I found myself at Perseus's open door. I knocked softly on the doorframe.

Perseus straightened and came right to me. "My queen."

"Hey." I wasn't sure what to say. I didn't know why I was there. "How's Knox?"

The boy from yesterday stepped into view. He was tall and burly. I was impressed that Gabriel took him down. Red curly hair fell down his forehead. His eyes went wide when he saw me. "You're her."

Perseus grumbled. "We are working on protocol and etiquette." His nostrils flared when he spoke to him. "It is always my queen when addressing your queen. Never her."

Knox rubbed his palms on his pants. "Oh, yeah, sorry."

Perseus massaged his temples. "The lingo is quite modern for the Night Kingdom, even for someone so young."

I laughed. "You remind me of Gabriel when he was in high school. He couldn't handle the teenagers in the mortal realm."

Perseus gestured to Knox. "But he is not mortal. I'm not sure what I did to deserve this."

Peering around Perseus, Knox watched with rapt attention. His entire future had already been decided for him, and now we were discussing it as if he were invisible. It had to be weird for him. I was sure he didn't even know what a Trejan was. "I'm sure he will have the best guidance with you, Perseus. I trust you. Besides, it's an oath, isn't it? He didn't choose this. Who better to train him than you?"

My head of Trejan scoffed. "You are only trying to flatter me."

I leaned in close. "Is it working?"

"I have a question," Knox said.

Perseus pinched the bridge of his nose. "What?"

Knox looked hopeful. "Do we get to go to the ball tonight? As her guard?"

My Trejan shook his head. "No. You are not guarding anyone until you are trained."

"Well, it appears you have things under control here. I will see you tonight, though, correct?" My heart skipped. I wanted Perseus to be at my wedding. It wouldn't be right without him. He was a part of my life too.

"Of course, my queen." Perseus gave a slight bow.

"Tonight then." I waved at them both and left.

"Sander," I whispered through our bond, afraid I might be interrupting.

"My love?"

I grinned as took a step down the stairs. "When you are finished, would you be so kind as to return Perseus's dagger?"

"Of course. Did you find something to do?"

I sighed. "I'm on my way to find Jen. I think she's downstairs."

"Be safe."

I made my way back to the main level. A commotion came from the grand hall. If I was to bet, it was there that I'd find Jen. Sneaking through the double doors, I kept to the shadows and watched.

Jen was directing everyone. Vines of greenery swooped low overhead, and glass spheres filled with candles hung from twine. "Ember!" Jen spotted me and jumped. "You look beautiful. I'm glad the dress fit."

I smoothed the front of the dress. "Yeah. It was a hard choice between this and the yoga pants."

"Ugh, those are not allowed. Not today." She snapped her fingers at one of the men hanging the orbs. "I don't want them far apart. It's supposed to be an illusion of the night sky. Like stars." She groaned. "I am trying to create a balance between day and night in here."

I grinned. "I think it's perfect."

"Well, it will be." She picked up another string of twine and held it up to a man on a ladder.

Looking around, there were so many people doing a plethora of things. I had no idea where to start. "What can I do to help?"

"Help? Oh no." She looked offended. Her hand splayed across her chest. "This is your day. I will not have you working. What I want you to do is go with Sander into the city and enjoy Night Fall. It's your first one. You should be there."

I gasped and looked down at my outfit, tugging at the end of the skirt. "You had me wear this short little dress to go into the city?"

"Appearance is everything. We have visiting royals, and you cannot be seen in yoga pants." She shooed me off. "Now go. Your mate is waiting for you."

"How do you know...."

"As usual, Jen is correct." Sander's voice filled the grand hall.

I spun to see the king of night staring at me. My heart skipped a beat. He was decked out all in black. A silk top to match my dress. He left the top half of his buttons undone. The collar was popped up, framing his thick neck.

I couldn't believe this was the man I was going to marry in a few hours. My soulmate. My king. A man descended from gods. He ruled the night and my heart.

There was no thought, just magnetic attraction that pulled me to him. He winked and slid an arm around my middle. "I'd like to show off my bride."

"Just have her back here an hour before the ceremony." Jen waved us both off.

Sander led me from the castle and down the road into the city. There was so much going on. Music poured from almost every courtyard, every house, every shop. The smell of baked goods wafted up through the streets. Bottles of every size were passed around between people.

A man with rosy cheeks handed Sander a vase-like jug. "My personal bottle of Slava for my king and his Favored."

Sander took the bottle and nodded. "Thank you. We shall enjoy it. Please take this and enjoy Night Fall." He handed the man a silver coin. It wasn't an ordinary coin but rather a piece of metal that had a moon stamped on one side.

"Thank you, my king." He bowed and then bowed toward me.

"This is a strong drink made by the Night immortals." He handed it out for me and chuckled. "Too much of this, and you may not remember the evening."

I took a sip, not trusting a full swallow. I'd tried other drinks and wasn't too fond of any of them. The cold liquid burned but had a sweet, creamy taste. Like caramel and berries. "Wow." It was finally a drink from the Immortal Kingdoms I liked. I took few more swallows before handing it back.

Sander took a full swig. "This is a good batch. I might not have paid the man enough. I think we can take this back to the castle and drink it later."

It was an exciting notion.... Already my fingers tingled as the drink warmed me. My limbs felt heavy, but my mind floated. I'd have to be careful with how much I drank, just as he said.

The middle of the city was alive with soulmates. Drinking, dancing... kissing. I remembered the last time we were here and how Sander promised me he'd kiss me in the square. I blushed but pulled him with me to the center of the city. The fire of the sun ignited under my skin, lulling me into a fake bravado.

Between the drink and the intoxicating look my soulmate gave me, I was warmed thoroughly. I wrapped my arms around his neck and let the music lead my body.

His lips swept over my neck, slowly grazing over my skin. His breath was hot as he trailed up to my lips. I pressed against him and let myself brazenly return the kiss. Swaying with the music, our hands were everywhere.

The thumping pulsed with my energy. I was lightheaded but didn't care. If Sander continued to kiss me, then I wouldn't stop him. It all felt so good. I was drunk on his love. And possibly the Slava.

It obviously was much stronger than anything I'd ever drunk before. Not that I was well versed in alcoholic beverages. I hadn't ever wanted to get drunk. I'd been in a few homes where they were alcoholics, and it scared me. I never wanted to be that person.

"Come on," Sander's voice dripped with desire. "I'd like to show you more before we head back."

I swayed, but Sander kept me upright. "Where?"

"The edge of the city. The docks to be exact." Slipping his hand around mine, he tugged me with him away from the square.

The people of Astraios were everywhere. Sander had at least five more bottles of Slava offered to him, but he refused each one. Too bad. It was good stuff. But he gave each resident a coin for their offerings. It wasn't like the one he paid with for our bottle, but I was still impressed by his kindness. I could see the respect given back to him by each passerby. There was also a level of trust. I wasn't sure how, but I could feel it. Like an energy wave their emotions spoke to me. The trusted he would keep them safe. He would protect them.

I had to say I felt the same way.

Waves crashed into the docks creating a spray. It was now later in the afternoon, but the glow of the sun still kept the sky as if it were early dawn. Tents lined the pier as merchants set up their shops. Silky materials, oils, soaps, baked goods, jewelry, blankets… all sorts of colors and smells filled the space.

Whispers floated past me as we walked.

"It's the king's Favored."

"The Solis Queen."

"The king's soulmate."

Everyone seemed to know who I was, but I knew nothing of them.

Sander strolled through each shop giving individual peddlers attention. Each time he introduced me but left out any consent to talk to me. I remembered the first time he'd explained the rule to me. We were at Moonstone during Scurradiem and Helios arrived. We had to leave, and he had a man bring us a get-away car. The man didn't even look at me, ignoring me the entire time. Sander said, "He showed you respect by not speaking until proper approval. He acknowledges his lower place of rank."

I supposed each merchant here accepted their rank as well. Night customs were still so new and strange to me.

We made it to a tent filled with potion bottles and herbs. I picked up a crystal pitcher that had the symbol of Solis blown into the sides. "I thought everything here would be with the moon for Night."

"We come from Solis. Many of our cultures and customs come from there."

It was so beautiful. "It reminds me of Lara."

"You should get it for her."

I laughed. "I don't have any of those coins you keep passing out. I have human money, and hardly any of that."

"Emberlynn, you are never without wealth. Here, in Solis, or even in the mortal world."

"Well, I can tell you that I have none."

Sander tapped the merchant's table. "Excuse me, should the Solis Queen wish to purchase a pitcher from you, how would she pay?"

The man had a thin mustache and beady eyes. He looked confused at first but answered, "My king, your Favored would only have to ask. Currency is exchanged through the castle. But I would be honored to gift any item to your soulmate."

Sander grinned and then turned to me. "See?"

I rolled my eyes but got dizzy. The effects of the Slava were still very much in control. "I'm not sure I will remember any of this later."

"This pitcher, if you please." Sander gestured to the Solis crystal. "Have it sent to the castle, and we will make sure you are compensated for your efforts as well."

The man's eyes lit up. "Thank you, my king. And all the blessings of the sun for your Favored."

"What did you do?"

"Well, you, bought the pitcher for Lara." He wrapped an arm around my shoulders and squeezed. "Although, I think we should head back. It will take at least an hour to make it back to the castle with these crowds."

Yes, back to the castle. Back to our rooms. And back to bed.

Wait. No.

Jen would be mad. She wanted to do my hair for the wedding.

I gasped. "We're getting married!"

Sander laughed and brushed the stray strands of hair off my face. "Yes, little sun. We are."

I giggled. "I love it when you call me that."

He picked up the bottle of Slava and laughed harder. "I do believe two swallows is your limit."

I waved him off. "Psh, I'm fine."

He took my hand and led us away from the square. "Jen is gonna kill me if we're late."

"Yeah, yeah. It's our wedding. It's not like she can start without us." I stumbled once and stifled another giggle. Okay, so Slava was way more robust than I thought.

Sander caught me in his arms. "I could carry you."

I thought about declining, but the steps ahead looked fuzzy. "That might be a good idea."

He lifted me effortlessly. "My queen is drunk."

I cringed. "No, don't say that. Say... my mate." I shivered as I thought about it. "Yes. My mate."

A deep growl emanated from his chest. "My mate is drunk."

His words pooled heat in my abdomen.

It didn't take long for him to ascend the stairs. Shadows assisted him, making it faster. On the castle grounds, he set me down. People were everywhere in the gardens, and I nearly tripped over my feet again, stepping out of the way. "What are they doing?"

"I believe they are here for a wedding." He winked at me. "I'm going to go find Lara. I'm sure she'll have something for you. Stay here. I'll be right back."

He walked to a guard and ordered him to stand with me. I almost laughed at the horrified look of the man's spirit when Sander threatened him within an inch of immortal death in the dungeons if anything happened to me.

An empty bench overlooking the city called to me. It looked like a safe place to wait. I wouldn't have to mingle, trip, talk or otherwise embarrass myself. The guard, ever so quietly, stepped with me. He kept his space of about three feet, but never farther.

The moon was brighter tonight. Its light filled me with energy, almost as if Sander were there touching me. I closed my eyes and basked in the moonlight.

"If we were in the Solis Kingdom, I could speak with the king's Favored." The Verum Queen walked behind me. Her voice trailed like a phantom whisper. She was purposely talking to me without actually breaking the rules. She sighed. "I've never liked that rule." She leaned against a small retaining rock wall. Her gaze still never met mine. "The truth is, neither has she."

I froze. I didn't want to draw more attention to myself than needed, but she was calling me out. I knew it. She knew it. Whatever game she was playing, I wasn't focused enough to compete.

The guard looked equally confused. I assumed he knew she shouldn't be speaking to me either, but yet she hadn't. His eyes followed her as she left us to return to the gathering on the lawn.

"Ember." Lara's voice startled me.

She carried a bottle and gave me a sly grin.

The Verum Queen was gone now. She disappeared into the crowd, and I wondered what the purpose of her coming over to me was. Aside from trying to upset me. What did it matter if she could talk to me or not? Her disregard for the rules and the disrespect she carelessly showed Sander by speaking to me was infuriating. The truth.... Ugh. She didn't know the truth about me.

"I heard you drank a bit too much Slava." Lara laughed and held out the bottle. "Drink this before Jen finds out. She's in full Night Fall wedding mode, and I fear for the immortal who tries to ruin it. Including you."

The guard choked back a laugh and I wondered how much Salva he'd drank in his days... or years. Well, bottoms up. I took the drink and tipped it back. Sputtering, I coughed half of it back out. "What is this? It's horrible."

"Sander said a quick fix, not a sweet one." She sat on the bench with me. "It shouldn't take long before you feel the effects of the Slava wear off."

The warm fuzzy feeling vanished. My mind began to focus and clear up my thoughts. But that part sucked. I wished I'd paid more attention to the Verum Queen. Did she say anything else? I couldn't remember. "Thanks."

"Slava is tricky. It's more potent than mortal drinks because immortals can't die from alcohol poisoning."

"Yeah, I found that out pretty quick. I swear I only had like three swallows." I couldn't imagine drinking any more than what I did.

She gave my leg a pat. "I think it's time to get dressed. Are you ready?"

The stars twinkled in rhythm to the sun's rays glowing softly behind the moon. Everywhere I looked, I saw Sander. I couldn't imagine life without him. "Yes."

TWENTY

Emberlynn

THE VERUM QUEEN'S VISIT bothered me more than I wanted to admit. If I hadn't been intoxicated, I might have been smart enough to pull her soul, but I didn't. Thoughts of confronting her overwhelmed me. I forced myself to continue trudging up the stairs instead of finding her. Who did she think she was anyway? Ugh... she just met me. Kind of. She basically showed up naked to the greeting and wasn't allowed to talk to me, but still....

I was glad Sander hadn't given her consent to speak to me. I could only imagine what more she would have said in the gardens.

Everything about her bothered me. Her dress—or lack of—her tone, her staring eyes, her harsh energy that poured from her every pore. The more I thought about her, the more she disturbed me. It was like those first months with Kade all over again.

My stomach rolled. Bile rose in my throat. I had to stop on the stairs, afraid of moving.

No. No, no, no. It wasn't Kade. She wasn't Kade.

Kade was controlled by Helios. I saw it. I was there. He was tortured and held against his will while the woman burned his soul. Again, the bile rose, burning the back of my throat.

The Verum Queen was a royal. There was no way Helios could have her. Could he? I had to find her. I had to see for myself. I turned to run back down to the gardens.

"Ember, are you okay? What's wrong?" Lara's hand went to her stomach.

"Sorry, nothing. It must be the after affect from drinking." I knew she would know I lied, but I had no proof that Queen Triggs was evil.

"There you are!" Jen rushed to the stairs and pulled me the rest of the way up. "I can't believe Sander got you drunk."

A squeal escaped as I landed on the top stair. "He didn't. I only had three swallows." Talking about how much Slava I drank was the last of my worries right now. But I supposed the queen could wait. I was probably overthinking it all anyway. There was no way to let it go, but I pushed it to the back of my mind for later.

Jen was already dressed in a flowing dark red dress. Her hair was piled on her head with tiny braids accenting the curls. She looked perfect as usual. The flawless immortal woman.

Lara joined us and laughed. "She might have learned to stop at one swallow."

"Gee, thanks, mom." I gave her a faux frown.

The door to my room was wide open. Clearie held up a dress that belonged to a queen. My jaw dropped, and I touched the material carefully. "Is this mine?"

"Obviously. No one else is getting married in thirty minutes!" Jen busied herself gathering items from around the room. "You're late, so we have to hurry."

Clearie gestured to another woman I didn't see earlier to close the door. "We don't need an audience for the king's Favored."

Stripping down to nothing would have made me uncomfortable in another time. Another place. But that was another girl. One I hardly remembered. She was mortal, and nearly all of her had died. Like a phoenix, I rose from the temporal ashes into a queen.

Lara took the dress from Clearie and helped slip the fabric over my head and buttoned up the side.

"I can't believe this is my wedding dress." It wasn't the traditional dress most mortal girls dreamed about.

The black figure-hugging bodice had a plunging V-neck, leaving the chest open between the lace in the front. The long-sleeved arms were sheer with delicate accents. The back was sheer with an ebony moon accent in the middle. The satin mermaid skirt flowed out to the ground like a pool of shadows. A sweeping train of black translucent material drifted behind me from my waist like a cape.

Clearie held out a pair of black lace sandals. I slipped them on and laced them up my calves. The delicate moons swirled around my legs.

Jen rushed me to the vanity, where she went to work on my hair. "Sander likes it down. But... I can do it up if you want."

"No, leave it down." Once, a long time ago, I only wore it up. Before Sander... before I knew who I was. What I was. It seemed symbolic to leave it down.

Jen's smile widened. "I was hoping you'd say that." She knew already. She'd seen our wedding long before me.

Lara began applying a layer of makeup. It was something I rarely did beyond mascara and lip gloss, and since arriving in the Night Kingdom, I'd only done that once.

Jen went to work, and in minutes I had soft curls cascading down my back. The glowing strands held an energy to them that I hadn't noticed before. An aura of gold radiated from me. It pulsed with the sun's energy.

Lara applied a tint of smokey shadow around my eyes and two coats of mascara. A light rouge of blush gave me a bit of coloring in my cheeks. It wasn't much, very natural, but was dramatic nonetheless. Nude lip gloss, my favorite, was last.

Jen held up my crown. She paused behind me. Her voice dropped to a near whisper. "For my queen."

Lara sucked back a whimper and a tear slid down her cheek. She quickly wiped it away and gave me a smile.

The moment was significant to both of us. She placed it on my head and then bowed. Watching in the mirror, everyone in the room followed her lead.

I swallowed hard.

Clearie wiped a single tear from her eyes. "The gods have chosen well for our king. He deserves this happiness."

The other lady in the room looked at Clearie. "Our king's Favored looks absolutely perfect."

Her words were for me. Just like someone else tonight who tried to speak, but unlike the Verum Queen, I was happy to have the woman's praise. I touched my pendant, and for a moment, my parents were with me. I wondered if they'd have approved of this moment. Of Sander and our joining. But mostly if they would approve of me.

Clearie clasped her hands together and took a step back to approve of my appearance. "That she does, Bree."

"And with only minutes to spare." Jen swept around and gathered a bouquet of flowers. Black sprigs of a feathery blossom, bunches of eclipse berries, golden leaves, the violet blooms I saw in the gardens, and a single giant sunflower in the middle completed the spray.

"You found a sunflower," I said, taking the large bouquet from her. Sweet floral scents wafted up from it.

She planted her hands on her hips. "Next time, give me a real challenge."

Someone knocked on the door. My heart skipped a beat wanting it to be Sander. Already my soul searched for his.

Bree opened it, and Jamie stood waiting in a sharp suit. He looked every bit the part of a prince. His eyes widened when he saw me. "Wow, kiddo, you look.... You look like a queen." He cleared his throat and shifted his weight. Rubbing his neck, he stuttered, "I know it's a mortal tradition to give the bride away, but I'd like to at least walk with you."

I smiled. "I like the idea of you giving me away. If you don't mind acting human for a moment."

He coughed and looked away but not before I saw his eyes fill. "Emberlynn, I would be honored."

Holding out his arm, I linked mine with his. Jen brushed past me into the hall and ran to Gabriel, who waited near the top of the stairs. He wore a dark suit with a red button-down shirt that matched Jen's dress. His jacket looked more like something out of a history book but had embroidered stars on it.

He bowed his head when I approached. "My queen."

"Stop it. You guys are gonna make me cry and ruin all of Mom's work." It was already hard to hold back the tears. So many emotions in this world, and all of them are intense. Everyone cried at weddings. Why would this one be any different?

"We are going to head down first." Jen pointed a finger at Jamie's chest while passing a tissue to me, tucking it into my hand that held the bouquet. "You take her through the side door into the gardens."

"I won't lose her," Jamie teased.

Everyone, including Clearie and Bree, went downstairs, leaving Jamie and me alone. I wasn't nervous about marrying my soulmate, but I was worried about the crowd of people who came to watch. Their approval of me mattered a great deal. I was going to be their queen. My stomach tightened.

"Breathe," Sander's voice filled my head. "I won't let you fall. Promise."

A thundering of steps sounded heavy on the stairs below. I tensed. Everyone was supposed to be outside.

Kade came into view. He wore a simple black shirt and pants. More than what he'd been in last night. His breathing was labored, but he was alive.

He lifted his face to see me and stopped on the second to last step. "My queen."

"Kade," I whispered. Impulsively, I pulled his soul out to mine. Weak, tender spots trembled under my inspection, but he remained free of Helios.

He winced, almost afraid of what I might say or do. But he didn't move. He let me look. He had nothing to hide. "I couldn't stay away. I felt you. You... you were worried. I can't place it, but you were upset, and I just knew. I came as fast as I could."

I smirked, shrugging my shoulders to lighten the mood. "It was the Verum Queen."

Jamie furrowed his brow. "What happened with her?"

"Nothing really, she just rubs me wrong." A shiver coursed down my spine. There was no need to dive into theories yet. I wanted to see her soul for myself first. Calling out another queen without proof could be disastrous.

Jamie hummed in agreeance. I wondered what he knew about her and his opinion about the Verum royals. He probably had more insight than most being the son of Somnium royals. But then, Sander was the Night King, and he hadn't said anything. Maybe I was wrong about the queen.

Jamie bumped my shoulder with his. "We should get going before Jen sends a search party for you."

Kade looked up. Hopeful lines creased his forehead.

"Kade, I'd like it if you walked ahead of us." There was a deeper connection between us now. I felt it. I felt him. Not like I did with Sander, but I knew what we'd been through carried over a new bond. Two people couldn't go through that and not become more. I'd seared his soul. I saw his torture. My mark was on him, on his soul....

"Thank you." His shoulders visibly relaxed. With his head high, he kept about ten feet between us, leading us down the stairs, and held the door open for us.

Jamie stopped shy of the door. "Alright, kiddo. This is it. Are you ready?"

"I'm ready." I was. In every way, I was ready to marry my soulmate.

Nothing in my life ever led me to believe that I'd be here, in a kingdom made of shadows, marrying the king, and becoming queen. I had spent eighteen years alone, and now I was surrounded by family. At that moment, I felt much older than what my mortal years led me to believe. Sander was right. Age meant nothing. We couldn't count time by age and doing so would disparage our immortality.

I looked up at the man who helped me regain my life. He was the dad I chose. I traced my pendant and let the familiar shape bring me to another time. I was sure my father, the king of Solis, would be happy I had Jamie. To have someone not take his place but to fill a void. To love me as a daughter.

A short breeze blew into the castle. A soft floral scent mixed with the salt air. Outside, the air was brisk but not cold. Shadows swirled around the edge of the path. Wispy tendrils teased my feet before capturing the edge of my train and billowed out as if the night followed me.

Rounding the corner, my heart stopped. Candles filled the gardens. Black and white pillars of all sizes with tiny flames flickered, making the shadows dance. Rows of wooden chairs occupied the lawn. Smaller bunches of flowers that matched mine, minus the sunflower, draped over the aisle seating. Everyone stood, but they all disappeared when I saw Sander. He stood upon a raised dais overlooking the sea right above the cave. Our cave. His eyes locked on me, and the emotions that rushed through our connection could never be put into words.

He matched me all in black. He wore a long jacket embroidered with moons but pinned to his lapel was a gold sun. His button-down shirt had a high collar and silver latches across the chest. A deep red sash crossed his body. His crown finished the look.

But it wasn't his attire that held me. It was his eyes. The storm danced in the blues, darkening as a new craving took place. I wasn't moving fast enough for him. The need to touch me overwhelmed him. It was causing him pain to not come to me.

"Just breathe," I teased him. Our connection tensed in response.

"You are everything, little sun." His breathing hitched. "My mate." Even in my mind, I heard the growl in his words. A primal desire that pooled in the deepest part of my soul awakened.

Jamie stopped me at the foot of the platform. He held my hand up for Sander. "Take care of her, Sander." It was such a dad thing to say. I gave him a peck on the cheek and smiled.

The moment Sander's hand touched mine was like the first time all over again. Our souls emerged, joining each other in a burst of gold and silver. It sucked the air from my lungs, and I held onto him tightly, afraid of falling.

"I've got you," Sander whispered low enough for just me.

He pulled me the rest of the way onto the dais with him. It was then I noticed there was no one else up there but us. No minister or anyone to marry us. I hadn't thought about how much different a wedding would be in the Immortal Kingdoms. Jen told me it was a formal declaration of love between soulmates. We didn't need another's approval or anyone to bear witness for the kingdoms to know we were mates.

Sander held me in his gaze. "Emberlynn Dawn Cyrus, for years, I have been alone, waiting for my other half. I wondered if the gods had forgotten about me. But now I know they had set you aside for me, and I had to learn patience. I had to learn to be the best me because nothing less would be enough to give you. I promise to always love you, to care for and encourage you, to protect you. I vow to never let you fall. Today you become my wife, but we will be soulmates for eternity." Silently he added, "I also vow to cherish you in every way possible, to feed you, and to make sure every desire is fulfilled."

Images of how he'd fulfill the last of his vows pushed through our bond. It was a good thing Lara added rouge to my cheeks to keep everyone from seeing the blush creep up to my face. I focused on my breathing, trying to keep it steady. It wasn't fair. I still had to give him my promises, but now all I could think about were his. "Sander Lux, I'd been afraid of living for so long, for people to see me, the truth of who I was, but now, because of you, I dare to dream of a life I'd never imagined. You've been patient and kind. I already chose you to be my soulmate. But today, I am choosing you to be my husband. I promise to love you every day for eternity. I promise to stand by your side. I vow to always care for you, cherish you, to help you. I trust you. I honor you. I devote myself to you."

The shadows darkened around the gardens while the glow of the sun brightened the sky. They approved of the vows.

Although, something itched at the back of my mind. Still warning me. I looked past Sander to Perseus and Kade, who stood off to the side. Neither of them moved.

"Emberlynn," Sander whispered, bringing me back to him. "What's wrong?"

I smiled just for him. "Nothing. Absolutely nothing."

"I'm going to kiss you now," he warned with a lopsided grin.

A single breath away, his lips crashed onto mine. Cheers erupted beyond us. It was as if the city below celebrated. He pulled back but held me tightly against him.

"I think they approve," I laughed.

The back of his hand caressed my cheek. "Little sun, every kingdom will bow before you. And I will be there standing with you. It will be your name they chant. Tonight is only the beginning."

Time froze as his words fell like an oath bestowed on all immortals. My breath caught as I lost myself in his promise.

Jen raced up to us. "Inside the grand hall will be the Night Fall ball where we will celebrate the marriage and joining of our king and queen."

More cheering erupted from the gardens.

"To the king and queen of Night!"

"Praise to the king's Favored!"

Jen stepped off the platform and joined Gabriel. Jamie and Lara were with his parents and brother. Their happiness radiated from across the lawn.

A mix of praise echoed in the air. Sander held me to him while the guests departed for the castle. In the back, the Verum Queen watched us intently. Her glare focused on me. I shivered and turned away, not wanting to give her more attention than needed.

Kade moved closer. Perseus wasn't far behind him.

I held my hand up. "I'm fine."

Sander peered through the crowd watching for a threat as well. "The feeling to protect you is sometimes overwhelming. I am ready to fight, but there is no one to battle."

"I'll try to control my emotions a bit better. I can imagine it's not helping when I'm bothered by stupid people." I sucked in a long shaky breath and looked for the queen, but she was already gone.

"Perseus," Sander called him over. "Stay close to your queen. I'll have Gabriel add guards to watch for the Verum royals, but something is wrong. There shouldn't be a reason Emberlynn feels this way when they are around."

Perseus frowned. "Agreed. I've felt her distress when the queen is around, but I've also felt danger. Almost like a warning. Without knowing what I'm looking for, I am scouting every angle."

So, he felt the warning too. That bothered me, but it also made me feel better because it wasn't just me. "Do you think it's Helios?"

Sander lowered his gaze to me. "It's hard to say. But I think since we all are feeling this way, we shouldn't ignore it."

I wondered if I should tell him about the dream I had. If maybe there was a connection. Once he said to me that in our world, a dream might not be a dream. He mentioned possibly talking to a dream weaver. I wondered if perhaps I should seek one out before worrying him unnecessarily. Not that I wanted to venture into Verum to find one. Maybe Lara could help me?

Slowly, the crowd of people exited the gardens, leaving myself, my husband, and two of my Trejan. The city below clamored with noise. Celebrations erupted all over. They had no idea there was a dark cloud ready to still the entire world. Only we knew there was something wrong. Something threatening our world.

Kade winced and grabbed the back of a chair for support. His body shook, and a sheen of sweat broke out over his forehead.

"You are not well," Perseus said. He placed a hand on Kade's back. "You should be resting."

Kade swallowed hard and glared at Perseus. Ignoring the pain, he stood up straighter and let go of the chair. "No. I will be fine. Our queen needs us. She needs me."

"He is Trejan," I said.

Kade looked up at me. His jaw clenched as he fought the ache of his soul. But his eyes... his eyes held the agony untold. "I will not fail."

I nodded. I knew he wouldn't.

Knox briskly walked around the corner of the garden wall. His attire was less than the others, aside from maybe Kade. Spotting us on the dais, his steps slowed. He hesitated and froze, turning back to the castle, but then veered back to his first path.

"Knox," Perseus started. "I thought you were instructed to remain in the grand hall."

Knox grimaced. "I know. I'm sorry, but... I couldn't ignore the feeling to be here." He hitched a thumb over his shoulder. "And then these two showed up when I left. They were climbing the steps from the city."

Kade and Perseus sprinted to stand guard between me and whomever Knox pointed at.

"Who showed up?" Perseus asked.

Knox dragged out a groan. "I don't know. They were just behind me."

Sander roared. "What do you mean? You lost them?"

Taking a hard swallow, Knox looked at each of us. "No. I mean, yes. Maybe?"

"How much training has this kid had?" Kade grimaced and scoffed at Knox. "I wouldn't let you guard my dog, let alone our queen."

Knox lowered his gaze. "I didn't know what to do."

Perseus pinched the bridge of his nose. "He came from Fairos yesterday. He heard the call of our queen but is only eighteen. He hasn't even been accepted by a guard yet."

"No excuses." Kade's knuckles went white as he clenched his fists. I wasn't sure if it was from anger or pain. Maybe a mix of both.

"It doesn't negate the fact that we have two guests unaccounted for." Sander pulled me back, putting himself ahead of me. "Gabriel is on his way with my guard."

A whoop and a curse came from around the garden wall. The shadows rolled over the ground carrying two men. The darkness let go and dropped them onto the lawn. The inky tendrils retreated into the ground.

They stood up and looked around wide-eyed and freaked out. "What was that?"

Sander stood confidently in front of me. "Who are you?"

I touched his shoulder. "Maybe they are guests for the ball?"

The men looked at each other and shook their heads. "No, my queen."

"State your business. If not the Night Fall ball, then what brings you to the castle?" Perseus asked, his hand now resting on the hilt of his dagger.

The man on the right was thin but muscular. He had a slight rubble on his chin and eyes so dark they looked black. He was taller than the other man, but not by much.

The second man looked lost. He kept staring at me, but every now and then, his eyes flickered to Sander, then my Trejan. Kindness softened his eyes. A trimmed beard covered the lower half of his face. "Her."

"Excuse me?" Sander tensed. Shadows were already wrapping themselves up the man's leg.

"Wait! I didn't mean any harm." The man tried to move from the shadows but was unable to budge. "I'm sorry. Please, I am not here to hurt her. He asked why I'm here." He bowed his head quickly. "I meant no disrespect. She is the reason I'm here."

The shadows released their grip on him but remained close by.

"First," Perseus grumbled. "It is never her or she."

Knox flung a sorry look over his shoulder. "Yeah, it is always my queen."

Perseus glared at the kid. Kade stifled a chortle.

The head of my Trejan continued, "You are here for our queen. Why? What is your business with the queen?"

The man gulped. His attention flicked from the shadows to us. "I'm not sure. It's gonna sound strange, but I couldn't stop myself. I came from Somnium to visit family for Night Fall. I was in the city and felt compelled to... help her. And then... this appeared on my forearm." He pushed the sleeve of his shirt up, revealing a new tattoo of the sun on his flesh. The Solis mark.

The first man nodded. "The same for me. I mean, I'm not from Somnium. But I was in the city and was overcome by the strongest need to be here. It was as if I would have died fighting anyone who tried to stop me. It was strong."

I looked at Perseus. "Trejan?"

"I think so. But it is growing rapidly. And again, they aren't Solis." He stepped forward and asked their names.

The second man held his head high, but his voice had a slight quiver. "I am Sam Darke. Most just call me Darke." He shrugged. "I'll answer to either."

The other man gave a slight cough. "I'm Ezra."

"My queen."

We all spun to face Brayson emerging from the Fores tunnel. He looked worn and weak. He bowed his head. "I'm sorry. I tried to fight it. I stayed as long as I could, but even in a different world, I felt your call."

"What is going on?" Perseus bellowed.

I wondered the same thing. It wasn't a coincidence they all began showing up at the same time.

"Emberlynn, can you see them?" Sander asked.

I hadn't been ready to dive into my well of magic so soon after Kade, but I didn't have a choice. My soul shivered over my bones as I fell into the deep pool. I pulled their souls out. All three of them stood before me. Each one showed respect and waited with their heads lowered.

Kade waited with bated breath as I inspected each one. I knew he was worried, probably more than the rest of us. He had every reason to be. He'd been attached to Helios. He'd gone through the hell of it all and back again.

Each spirit was unblemished. I let out a sigh of relief. "They're good."

But it didn't explain why they were arriving in droves. And why tonight? Again, the warning sizzled on the air.

"That," Kade spoke up. His eyes were wide. "Did anyone else feel that?"

Sam shrugged. "I feel the same thing... to save her."

Brayson stood next to Ezra. "I'm afraid I didn't. I've been in the mortal realm, and my senses are just coming back fully."

I knew how that felt. The rush of emotions from entering the Night Kingdom was overwhelming.

Perseus's brow furrowed. "I have the same feeling to protect our queen, but nothing more pointed."

"I did," I said.

Sander nodded. "I felt it through our bond."

So just us three. What did that mean? Was it only those connected to me through some deeper bond that felt it? Why me?

"Does anyone know why we are here?" Ezra asked. He looked anxious, but I couldn't blame him. The shadows were still hovering around their ankles, waiting to restrain them if needed.

Perseus took his place as head of my guard and commanded the attention of his newly acquired men. "You are part of an ancient line of royal guards. You are Trejan."

"Trejan? I thought that was a myth for the Solis Kingdom?" Sam looked at Ezra as if they'd both been punked.

I felt terrible for them. They didn't choose this. Whatever choices they wanted to make in life were now ripped from them. Born to obey an oath forced on them by the gods. There was nothing I could do to break it for them either. Nothing aside from death. But I wouldn't let Kade die, so I wasn't about to go killing men unjustly to break their blood oaths to the gods.

Perseus moved between us, keeping the new guards pushed back from me. "Emberlynn is both the Solis and Night Queen. Her blood is descended from the creation gods. It is her you are bound to. We do not know why there are some of you from other kingdoms." He gathered them together. "But I can tell you that you will have to train long and hard to earn a place in the Trejan. It is not just a title you carry, but it is for our queen's safety. It is her and only her that you live for."

Sam and Ezra nodded. Brayson cast his gaze down. He'd barely been called as a Trejan before I left for the Night Kingdom and asked to stay behind. Now he was here. So much was being placed on these men in a short amount of time.

"Our queen is expected at the ball," Perseus grumbled and turned to Kade. "Are you up to guarding?"

Kade's brow rose. "Absolutely."

"It appears I am babysitting tonight. We can't have untrained Trejan guarding the queen." He let loose a heavy sigh. "Sander, would you please have Gabriel fill in?"

Sander pulled me to his side. "You already know I have a guard in place for my wife."

It was the first time he'd used the title of wife, and my heart flipped.

"It's settled then. Kade, stay with our queen. I'll take these guys and see what more I can learn." Perseus rubbed the back of his neck. "I hate splitting up like this when we all feel on edge but having untrained Trejan could be worse than none at all. When it comes to our queen, we can't afford to not be in sync, to follow a plan and execute it properly." He held his hand out for Kade.

"Once a long time ago, we worked as one. It was a different time, but I think we can regain it."

Kade took the offered hand. "Thank you."

Perseus herded the men to the castle. Basic training would begin tonight, I was certain.

Sander kissed the top of my head. "Well, little sun, we should get to the ball before Jen kills us both."

"We're immortal. She can wait a minute longer." I leaned on his shoulder and breathed in the moment. "I'm afraid everything is about to change."

He gave me a quick squeeze and helped me off the platform. "Because it is. The moon has been talking. I can feel it shifting, making room for something bigger."

"Do you think it's Helios?"

Sander stopped and tipped his head up to the sky. The moonlight embraced him. "I think the gods lost their grip on him, and you, my mate, are the only one strong enough to reign him in. I think he is behind many things. What he did to Kade... and possibly others is something unlike anything in our history. It makes me sick to think of what he could be doing to other immortals. I think him trapping you in the mortal realm was only a test. He didn't want to hurt you there. He wanted to see how strong you were. He wanted to know if he could.... I can't think about what he'd do if he caught you again." He choked up.

I turned his face to look at me. "You don't have to think about that. We now know what he's capable of, but we also know what I can do. I am here. If he wants me, he will have to come through my Trejan and my soulmate." The last part killed me. I knew deep down I could never let Sander take my place with Helios.

Sander's jaw clenched, and he nodded. "He won't get through me."

It was a promise, an oath, stronger and more profound than any bond.

"He won't get through either of us," Kade spoke up. "Trust me, I will in no way let him have my soul again. And he will never have hers."

TWENTY-ONE

Sander

JEN HAD OUTDONE HERSELF for the Night Fall ball. I found it puzzling that the Verum royals departed immediately after the wedding ceremony. It was odd they didn't stay for the ball. I knew Jen was perturbed by their dismissiveness over her event as well.

Decorations were never something I cared for, but they were important to Jen, though I had to say the room looked enchanting. But not near as stunning as the woman across the hall. I couldn't shake the need to watch my wife as she mingled with guests. A black lace mask covered half her face, but it didn't hide her beauty. My wife. My mate.

Knowing it was me she would be with tonight sent my pulse racing. For an eternity, I would desire and cherish every inch of her. I would be the one behind her, protecting her, supporting her. No one would get through me.

The gods had sent her to me for a reason, and I would do whatever needed to keep her safe. My soul ached to be with her, to touch her. I slipped through the crowd toward her. I would never restrain myself from her touch again. In every way, she was mine, just as I was hers.

My hand slid to the small of her back. It fit perfectly as if her body were shaped for me. I leaned in close to her ear. "My wife, I have a need to dance with you."

I loved the blush that darkened her cheeks. Her eyelashes batted against the mask. The champagne coloring in her eyes shimmered like gold flakes. It was the same hungry look she got when we were alone. "My husband, I believe I have the same need."

I would never tire of our playful banter.

The crowd split for us to enter the center of the room. Pulling her close, I refused to let any space between us. I needed her. The music drifted on around us, but I didn't hear it. I was focused on her thoughts, wanting to know them all.

I twirled her out and then spun her back into my arms. Her laughter echoed in the room, filling my heart with happiness. I loved her laugh.

Protect her.

The moon whispered to me. I couldn't ignore it. There was something wrong. As I twirled her again, Kade slipped through the crowd and stood only a few feet away. He had to have heard it too. For a moment, he and I were on the same page. We were together in this strange call.

Perseus and the others showed up at the door. My heart dropped. There was only one reason he would be here with the new Trejan. He said so himself that an untrained guard was worse than none at all. He would not risk Emberlynn's life unless he was unable to deny the call. A call I was quickly beginning to understand. After seeing the others show up without a Solis bloodline, the idea that perhaps I was not only her soulmate but part of her Trejan was beginning to make sense. He scanned the room, but like me, he wouldn't see anything. There was no enemy to fight.

Protect her.

I tried to shake the internal prompting.

The dance finished, and Emberlynn continued to laugh. "That was fun."

"Little sun, forgive me, but I have a need to speak with Perseus." I held her wrist and kissed my mark.

She tensed. "Is everything okay?"

"Yes," I lied. "Something about babysitting." I winked and led her to Kade. A silent agreement passed between us. Take care of her. Don't let her out of your sight. Protect her.

Handing my soulmate over to him made me sick. It wasn't Kade, but rather the thought that I wasn't with her that hurt. I hurried over to Perseus. "What's going on? I thought you said these guys needed to stay away tonight?"

Perseus looked pained. "Impossible. It's like I'm being forced here. She is calling us without calling us. I don't think she knows she's doing it."

"What if it's not her?" The moon continued to whisper to me, warning me to protect our mate.

"Then what? Who?"

I watched Emberlynn laugh at something Kade said. "The kingdom. I am the night. It is my blood that flows through the fountain. It makes sense that the Night wants to protect her as much as we do. What if it knows something we don't? What if it sees someone we can't?"

He pondered my theory for a moment. "It's possible. Do you think it is Helios?"

"Who else?" Even as I said the words, I felt the pull. I wanted to scream her name as my stomach twisted in pain. Whipping around to her, she was fleeing the room with Kade behind her. Her fear pulsed through me in violent waves. "Emberlynn!"

An orange fog rolled over the hall floor. No one saw it but me. Emberlynn's gift.

No!

Pushing through the guests, I ran through the hall. The doors to the garden were open. Where was she? Panic rushed through our bond. "Popcorn!"

"I'm coming!" Gods, please, save her.

In the gardens, a swarm of Verum guards closed in. Summoning the shadows, I grasped each guard with ethereal fingers and slid the darkness through them like a knife, ending them immediately. More guards came, and

I called the last of my shadows. Perseus and the others fought the new arrival of guards. They kept coming in waves.

Emberlynn screamed, and I dropped the shadows, commanding them to find her. "Go!" I yelled at them to save her. I would take my chances in hand-to-hand fighting to give her a part of me. A gust of cold air rushed with them as they left to help her.

I darted to the garden wall where I had a dagger hidden. Weapons were something Gabriel demanded to be placed around the castle.

Gabriel. "Gabriel!" I yelled at him through our link.

A second later, he was there, my guard with him. He dove into fighting the Verum army.

"Sander, help," Emberlynn's plea shattered my heart. I sliced through a guard and jumped over his falling body. "I'm coming. Just hang on."

As the orange fog rolled toward the Fores tunnel, the world froze. No. He was leading her away from here. We wouldn't survive being separated by realms again. I couldn't. She wouldn't.

"Emberlynn, stay with me. Please." I ran toward the tunnel. A hand caught my ankle, and I went down. Twisting, I was back up and had my attacker's head rolling before I could look him in the eye. His attempt to stop me could have been the second I needed to save my mate.

Kade's voice echoed through the tunnel. He was fighting. His grunts and heavy breathing held a sense of urgency. "Emberlynn, don't you dare!"

"No!" I ran to the entrance of the tunnel. Bodies were strewn all over the ground. Kade had done a decent job of stopping the guard from getting to Emberlynn.

Hands grabbed me from behind. I tried to pry them off, but there were too many. Shadows ignored my demand to stay with Emberlynn, splitting to help me. They gripped at my captors, wrapping icy fingers around their necks.

"You'll do nicely," a woman said, emerging from the shadows.

Emberlynn and Kade ran from the portal toward me. The fear on her face burned into my memory.

The woman cackled a hideous sound that echoed through the tunnel. She turned to my mate. "Too late." She reached out her hand and gripped the air. But it wasn't air, it was me. My soul was in her hands.

A hot, white, blinding pain seared through me. The world darkened as I fell. Emberlynn's name was the last thing on my lips.

TWENTY-TWO

Emberlynn

EVERYTHING WAS LIKE MY DREAM. I couldn't breathe. The orange fog rolled over the ground, pushing me farther into the tunnel. Kade was fighting off another Verum guard, but I didn't know how much strength he had left to continue if they kept coming. He was already weak.

"I'm coming. Just hang on." Sander yelled for me. But I was unable to cry back. I didn't want Helios to find him either. And right now, he had me.

"Kade," I whispered as the fog got closer, pushing me back into the wall. "Kade, I'm trapped."

The last guard dropped, and Kade ran to me. He stood between me and Helios's spirit. He wouldn't show himself, but I knew it was him. The orange fog was the same as before. The same as Moonstone and my dreams. It was the same as when he held me in the old church.

"What do we do?" The Fores beckoned me, but the only place I knew to go was in the mortal world. I wouldn't have the power I had here to be any good. I couldn't fight back there.

My heart thundered in my chest.

"We fight." Kade was weary. His arms shook as he held up his dagger.

A commotion at the entrance of the tunnel held my attention. It was Sander. The fog rolled away, disappearing from the cavern. It headed toward my soulmate.

No, Helios couldn't have Sander. I rushed after the fog, trying to think of a way to stop it.

My stomach rolled as I spotted the woman at the entrance. It was the same one who tortured Kade. Her evil grin spread wider when her blind gaze landed on me. Her hand was already out. "Too late."

Her hand closed, and I saw Sander's soul snapped from his body. White light burned through him. Everything froze around me. Time. The worlds. Life itself.

"No!" I heard the scream but couldn't place the voice as my own.

Fire burned over my body, and I used its power to attack the woman. Outside the tunnel, I charged her all while throwing everything I had at her. Verum guards tried to pick up Sander, but I placed a ball of fire around him. "You cannot have him!"

The woman had her own flames to throw. All my training with Jen and Sander helped me know how to dodge each one.

Kade fought off the other guards. He was trying to get to Sander.

The moon whispered to me, giving me guidance. The shadows would obey me. They swarmed my husband's body and held him for me, covering him in protection.

Kade was fading. His body slumped over, and his breathing labored.

I had to do something. Anything. I would not lose them this way. I would not let Helios have my soulmate. The fire inside of me raged. The deep well of magic erupted like a fountain of lava. Blinding light exploded out from me, completely lighting the Night Kingdom. Deadly fire burst from my hands as I gripped around the woman's neck. Her eyes widened as her life slipped away. My flame seared through her, cutting her through, sealing her fate.

"Emberlynn!"

The woman fell at my feet, and I turned to see Jamie and Lara rushing through the gardens toward me.

"No, go back!" I yelled. A guard caught Lara and held a dagger to her throat.

I pulled the shadows from Sander to save her. They rushed to her captor and dove down his mouth, suffocating him from the inside out. He let go of Lara and gripped at his neck. I felt his energy reach out, begging for life, but I wouldn't release the shadows. Not until they finished him.

Jamie grabbed the guard's dagger and swung it expertly at the next man.

As he took down another Verum guard, two more guards grabbed Sander. They rushed into the tunnel dragging him toward the portal. His soul had barely snapped back in place from the attack with the witch, causing him to be too weak to fight them off.

Scrambling to run after them, I was caught around the waist. I grunted and released another cry for help, about to call upon my powers. A burly guy gripped my attacker around the throat and picked him up, making him drop me onto the ground.

Knox's eyes were wide, and his nostrils flared. "You do not touch my queen."

I got up and ran. "Sander!"

I made it to the Fores just as they stepped through, my fingers just missing them before they disappeared. My soul tore in half, and I shrieked as tortuous pain ripped through me, dragging me to the ground. I grabbed at my chest and screamed for my soulmate.

Everything went silent around me as a burst of flames shot out from me, and every immortal soul in Astraios who belonged to Verum fell. My flames knew no friend as it searched for the enemy.

Kade's arms wrapped around me, preventing me from crawling to the portal. "I've got you. I've got you." He kept repeating the words, but I hated him for restraining me. I couldn't stop screaming.

Sander was gone. They took him through the portal, and I wasn't fast enough to get to him.

Kade pulled me in and cradled me in his lap. "Emberlynn, you'll get him back. You saved me. You can save him."

The pain intensified with every word. My soul felt like it was being shredded, demanding I go after him. I couldn't breathe around my screams. I couldn't think about anything other than getting to my soulmate.

But he was gone. And I had no idea where to find him.

GLOSSARY

The Four Kingdom aka Immortal Kingdomss
Solis Kingdom – sun/day (So-Liss)
Night Kingdom – night/moon
Somnium Kingdom – dreams/illusions (Som-Knee-Um)
Verum Kingdom – reality/tangible (Vair-Um)

Scurradiem – Holiday celebrated by the Somnium Kingdom during the mortal Christmas season. A night filled with illusions, pranks, and jokes. 'Nothing is as it seems' (Scur-A-Diem)

Moonstone – Resort for the immortals set in Wyoming.

Moonsliver – Silver drink with bubbles like champagne. A sweet bitter like lemon juice over blackberries. It is made from the Moonberry.

Eclipse Berries – A liquor filled berry found in the Night Kingdom.

Cardtail – An animal with the top half of a bird and the bottom of a fish tail. Lives in small ponds with low hanging trees. Found only in the Somnium Kingdom. A delicacy and eaten at many celebrations. 'Glazed Cardtail'

Fores – A hidden mortal entrance to the kingdoms. Guarded by generations of the same mortal family. (For-Es)

Night Fall – Seasonal holiday celebrated by the Immortal Kingdoms. It signifies the end of the Griatto Season.

Trejan – A bloodline of royal guards linked to the Solis Goddess. (Tree-Shen)

Slava – A very potent liquor made from Moonberries and Moondust.

ACKNOWLEDGMENTS

ALWAYS, first and foremost, I thank God, our Heavenly Father, for the gift, ability, and time to be able to write.

This book could not be what it is without my team of editors, betas, and proofreaders: It was not the ideal turn around this time, but you ladies plowed through! I will forever be grateful for you.

A special shoutout to Antoinette. I promise it's not always like this.

My Polish Witches... ladies, you keep me going. I can count on you to push me when I need it.

Booktok. WOW. What a difference you made for me. All my new readers that found me there... I love you all.

Oh boy... The buddy readers. You girls are AMAZING. I love you all so much. Thank you for taking the time to read my books and enjoy them. Thank you for the fun memes and encouragement. I swear... this book came to life in your discord! I can't wait to see book three through your eyes.

Colleen, for keeping me sane and willing to jump off the proverbial ledge with me. You share my crazy ideas and let me run my crazy stories past you. Everyone needs a bestie like you. Now to plan a writing retreat! We deserve it.

And always, my family. It's been a rough year. But you always push me to live my dreams. You have more faith in me than anyone else. Your support means more to me than you'll ever know. Thank you for not giving up on me and sharing my excitement.

Jym... I promise I'll make you something not from a can. Thanks for supporting me.

ABOUT THE AUTHOR

M.R. POLISH has been writing since she was a young girl. She would tell her stories to anyone who would listen until she discovered she could put them onto paper.

Out on the ocean is her favorite place to be and would live on a cruise ship if she could, traveling the world, but alas, adulting and responsibilities keep her grounded.

M.R. is happily married to someone who would gladly follow her onto a ship and sail away. They have four kids, who might be more adventurous jet-setters than their mother.

"*Life is too short to stand by and watch everyone else live your dreams. The bigger the dream, the bigger the adventure!*"

~ M.R. Polish

Made in the USA
Middletown, DE
03 July 2024